FROM THE HELICOPTER, THE SCIENTISTS LOOKED DOWN AT THE FUTURE OF THE WORLD

It was beautiful—terrifyingly beautiful as the fog began to lift. There, revealed, lay an entire continent of ice, a White Atlantis of rampant crystal towers, undulating hills, deep ravines, and a crazy profusion of iridescent crags blazing white fire and stretching away to the horizon.

Around it was the winter chill that it created to insure its survival as if it were a living thing with an intelligence and purpose of its own.

Its position seemed frozen to the unsuspecting eye, but the scientists viewing it knew all too well it was moving—heading with hideous directness straight toward New York...

...and nothing, not even atomic bombs, could stop it.

ICE

james follett

popular library • new york

ICE

Published by Popular Library, a unit of CBS Publications,
the Consumer Publishing Division of CBS Inc., by
arrangement with Stein and Day Incorporated

Copyright © 1978 by James Follett

All Rights Reserved

ISBN: 0-445-04484-5

Printed in the United States of America

First Popular Library printing: November 1979

10 9 8 7 6 5 4 3 2 1

For Joanna and Richard
and anyone prepared to Think Big

The definitions at the beginning of some chapters are from the *NATO Glossary of ABC* [American/British/Canadian] *Standardized Terminology*.

Quotations from the bulletins of the International Ice Patrol are reproduced by kind permission of the Commandant, United States Coast Guard, Washington, D.C.

All the characters are fictitious. The hardware they use and the dangers they face are not.

PROLOGUE

The ice moved.

It moved slowly.

One yard...Two yards...Twenty yards...

The long, lonely scream of the white wilderness lasted for one week as the twenty-thousand-square-mile delta lurched toward the sea. The stupendous roar of freedom circled the earth in thirty hours. Creatures grazing in the primeval coal forests on the far side of the planet raised inquiring nostrils to the reverberating thunder that echoed from the south against the sullen skies.

The ice moved.

And the ice stopped.

The mountains that reared into the ice cap, with their roots firmly embedded in the jaw of the earth's mantle, arrested the great slide to the ocean. Stresses heaved and pulsed through the attenuated rocks, probing the hidden valleys and undulating strata for weaknesses, and found none. The fractured ice cap tested its inexorable mass against the unyielding mountains, and the mountains held. They were far older than the life that stirred on the planet; they had been thrown up in the turmoil of the creation; they would not be moved.

The searching stresses simmered and weakened. The cycle of tremors that had dealt repeated hammer blows to the planet faded into tranquillity.

The ice fell silent.

The imprisoned mountains, deflected by the remorseless movement, settled to their eternal task of stemming the march of the ice to the sea.

The ice was patient.

The exposed peaks of the mountains, thrusting through the ice cap, were eventually buried by the unceasing blizzards.

After five million years, the ice was ready to challenge the mountains.

PART
ONE:

cold war

There was something in the room.

Julia Hammond woke and lay very still in the darkness, hardly daring to breathe. The strange noise and her imagination joined together to edge icicles of fear down her spine.

Her nerves screamed back at the insidious moaning of the Antarctic wind outside the steel shutters and the thick glass. But it wasn't the wind—there was something in the room. Something singing: a barely perceptible hum like the distant music of a tuning fork in an empty tomb.

She walked frightened fingers along the wall behind her bed until they gratefully found the light switch. The sudden explosion of brilliance chased away the nightmares.

There was nothing in the room.

She wanted to laugh but the strange noise hadn't been frightened away by the light. It continued. Soft and low.

Julia swung her feet onto the floor, keeping them away from the bed, and tracked down the strange sound to her cabinet, which contained several hundred plankton specimen slides. The top drawer was open. Two of the glass slivers were occupying the same groove. They were vibrating against each other. She touched them and the singing stopped. It started again when she took her finger away. She repositioned the slides, pushed the drawer shut and listened. The soft musical note had stopped, but her fingers, resting on the top of the cabinet, registered a mute vibration that seemed to reach up through the floor.

She chided herself for her overactive imagination and went back to bed. Such was her relief that it didn't occur to her to ponder the cause of the delicate vibration. She switched out the light and was soon asleep.

She didn't wake.

Even though the gentle music had returned.

2

SUBMISS
When a submarine has failed to report at a scheduled time.

There was a silence.

A silence that was noted by a Honeywell computer. It digested the silence for fifteen minutes to allow for human frailty, then flashed a terse message on the night duty officer's screen:

UNIT 7 / / IDENT SCHEDULED 23 + 00 NOT RECEIVED / / TIME NOW 23 + 15 / / MESSAGE ENDS +

Frank Knight remained engrossed in his paperback novel. The Honeywell patiently waited another two minutes then sounded a muted warning buzzer. Knight looked up at the screen in the center of the console. Somewhere in the world an embassy communications officer was late reporting. A common occurrence, especially around Christmastime when the embassy party season was in full swing. Knight returned to his book.

At 23:20 the buzzer sounded again. Knight swore softly to himself. The trouble with the computer was that it hadn't been programmed to accept wide deviations. His coffee was cold. He was about to cross the deserted communications room to the hot-drink vending machine when he noticed that the message on the screen had lengthened by three words:

REACTION STATUS URGENT

Knight forgot the coffee machine. He sat down and reached for the blue standing-orders manual. He flipped through the pages until he came to the instructions relating to Unit Seven. Unit Seven?

Knight frowned. He had never heard of Unit Seven. Yet the Honeywell had. According to the manual, Unit Seven, whatever it was, identified itself once every twenty hours. Until now.

The instructions were simple enough: all Knight had to do was call a London number by landline and tell them that their precious Unit Seven had lost its voice.

Knight picked up his phone and dialed the nine-digit number. It was answered immediately. "Yes?"

Feeling slightly foolish, Knight said: "This is the night duty officer at the Government Communications Headquarters, Cheltenham. Unit Seven is nearly twenty-five minutes late reporting."

"What's Unit Seven?" asked the London voice.

Knight felt aggrieved. "How should I know? It says here that I've got to tell you."

Knight checked with the voice that he had the right number.

"Okay," said the voice, "I'll check this end."

The line went dead.

3

SUBSMASH
Organization for the urgent rescue of a submarine and her company.

Lieutenant James Abbott, R.N., stared at the phone he had just replaced.

What was Unit Seven? And why should GCHQ, which was responsible for the Diplomatic Wireless Service, call up Admiral Howe's night number? Why were they involved if Unit Seven was a naval matter?

Abbott turned the pages of the duty book. There was nothing under "Seven." He leafed through the alpha section. Nothing under "U" either. A slip of paper caught his eye. It was a handwritten note stapled to one of the stenciled pages. Admiral Howe's handwriting.

"Notify me immediately upon receipt of any signals that relate to Unit Seven. Howe."

Big Ben chimed the half hour.

"Notify me immediately..."

Abbott decided to wake the old man in person rather than startle him with the telephone. He entered the corridor and made his way up to the admiral's flat on the top floor. The building gave the impression of being deserted, but most of the upper offices contained duty officers boredly reading within reach of telephones. The admiral's sitting room was a mess; Admiral Howe was one of the untidiest men Abbott had ever known. Abbott supposed that the old man's only bad habit was caused by his never having had a wife to snap at his heels.

He went into the bedroom and gently shook the

frail shoulder. The admiral was awake immediately—an ability he had acquired as a convoy escort commander during the war.

"What is it, James?"

"A message from GCHQ, sir. Unit Seven hasn't reported on schedule. There's a note you've written in the duty book to notify you immediately."

But Admiral Howe wasn't listening. He pushed his bony feet into his slippers and pulled on a dressing gown.

"When did they call?"

Abbott followed the admiral into the sitting room and out into the corridor. The old man could move surprisingly fast.

"Five minutes ago, sir."

Admiral Howe looked anxiously at his watch without slackening his pace. "Why have they left it so long?" he demanded. "Didn't they give at least some sort of explanation?"

The white-haired old sailor's concern was infectious; Abbott looked extremely worried when he replied that they hadn't.

No, thought Admiral Howe—they wouldn't. No one other than himself and those members of the Admiralty Board who had a "need to know" knew anything about Unit Seven and its mission. The Soviets knew of course. But they didn't know they were supposed to know.

Admiral Howe lowered himself into his chair and gazed at his aide.

Abbott sensed that this wasn't the right moment to speak. In truth he was shocked by the change in the old man. The driving vitality that was always present, no matter what the time of day or night, had gone. The good-humored sparkle in the eyes was no longer there; the weathered face was now pale and drawn.

Admiral Howe was experiencing the once-familiar crawling sensation at the base of his spine: the wedge of fear that had warned him of a U-boat's proximity before his ASDIC operator had detected it. The enemy no longer flew the swastika—but the sensation was the same.

Wearily Admiral Howe said to Abbott: "Get me the Subsmash operational directives."

It was then that Lieutenant Abbott began to have an inkling of what Unit Seven was.

4

SATSCAN
An operation specially mounted to listen for radio signals relayed from a communication satellite.

On the plains of San Augustin near Socorro in New Mexico stands the VLA (Very Large Array) of the world's largest steerable radio telescope, owned and operated by the United States Radio Astronomy Observatory. The twenty-seven dishes, each with an area of five hundred square yards, are capable of functioning as one dish twenty miles in diameter.

At 09:00 hours local time, after a series of exchanges between the observatory's director and the Ministry of Defence (Navy) in London, the mighty radio telescope was doing just that. But instead of listening to the electronic uproar from 50,000 light years away at the center of the galaxy, the twenty-seven antennae were locked onto the United Kingdom's Skynet III military communications satellite poised in geostationary orbit 22,000 miles above the equator.

Apart from the position of the satellite and a channel frequency, the astronomers were given no information; if signals were heard, they wouldn't be able to decode them—all they were required to do was listen. So they obligingly tuned their sensitive receivers, and listened.

Silence.

Similar scenes were repeated throughout the southern hemisphere; South Africa, Australia, and New Zealand listened intently for even the faintest electronic scratching from the ether and heard nothing. Even the U.S. Navy's modest tracking facilities on remote islands in the South Pacific were required to listen and to report. Like all the others, they heard nothing.

The "thank you" signals poured out from London.

The largest and least-publicized Satscan operation ever mounted had been an abysmal failure.

5

HOSTILE ICE
Ice over two meters thick with no ice skylights thus preventing a missile-carrying submarine from using communications system or deploying weapons.

It was twenty-four hours since the submarine *Asteria*, otherwise known as Unit Seven, had failed to report.

Apart from the abortive Satscan operation, nothing had happened. Lieutenant James Abbott was baffled. Why hadn't a search-and-rescue operation been launched? Why hadn't the various NATO commands been alerted? And, above all, why had Admiral Howe automatically assumed the worst from the moment the submarine had failed to report? There hadn't been a panic the time when the *Sovereign* had been late with a report; everyone had rightly guessed that the submarine had failed to find a skylight during the North Polar hostile ice season. News of the *Sovereign*'s overdue transmission had even been released to the press. But in this instance, before Admiral Howe left for Signals Command, he had given Lieutenant Abbott strict instructions that nothing about the *Asteria* was to be disclosed to anyone. "Not even if the Prime Minister himself demands to be told," had been the admiral's exact words.

And so Lieutenant Abbott had spent an embarrassing day issuing a continuous stream of telephone excuses for the absence of his chief from various meetings. One permanent undersecretary had threatened to take the matter higher when confronted by the lieutenant's stubborn refusal to be more forthcoming.

Admiral Howe walked into the office as Big Ben was striking midnight, wearily dropped a bundle of bulging manila files on Abbott's desk, and sank gratefully into his deep leather armchair. Abbott stared at him in concern; he had never seen the old admiral looking so exhausted.

"Can I get you anything, sir?"

Howe shook his head slowly and closed his eyes. "I'll be all right in a few minutes, James. Just a rather wearing day."

"Have you had anything to eat?"

"They gave me lunch in the officers' mess at Stanmore."

"I thought you said you were going to Signals Command, sir?"

"Well I've been to Stanmore as well."

The admiral's tone did not encourage further conversation. Abbott's eyes dropped to the files that had been dropped on his desk. The top one was entitled "Commander V. S. Sinclair-Holmes." The record of amendments columns printed on the cover showed that the file had not been altered for a year.

"He's the *Asteria*'s commanding officer."

Abbott looked up quickly. The intense blue eyes

were watching him from the depths of the armchair.

"I'm sorry, sir," said Abbott hastily. "I thought you wanted me to look at them."

"Of course I want you to look at them," said Admiral Howe testily. "Why else would I dump them on you?"

Abbott said nothing.

"There are thirty-one files there," the admiral continued. "One for each member of the *Asteria*'s company."

Abbott was astonished. "Only thirty-one, You mean officers *and* men?"

Admiral Howe suppressed an angry reply; Abbott was entitled to be surprised. He rose from the armchair and sat on the hard chair in front of Abbott's desk. He rested his chin on his hands, fixed his uncomfortable eyes on the lieutenant and said softly: "Thirty-one men, James. And I want you to become those thirty-one men for the next five hundred days."

Abbott gaped. "I beg your pardon, sir?"

Admiral Howe nodded to the files. "You'll find a microfiche in each file that contains all the correspondence between each man and his family and friends—plus a few enemies in some cases. For example, Mechanician Fisher has been fighting a two-year legal battle with his brother over a house his mother left him. You're to become Mechanician Fisher and you're to continue the battle."

Admiral Howe leaned across the desk and picked up the files one by one. "I want you to become Commander Sinclair-Holmes; I want you to become second officer Lieutenant Bryan Finch, whose wife has a twelve-month-old baby that he's never seen; I want you to become ERA Wall, who's getting a divorce from a wife he's hardly ever seen. In short, I want you to become thirty-one men by perpetuating their correspondence with home for the next fourteen months. Until now, all letters for the men have been sent to a Signals Command box number. In future they'll come to you first. Letters from the *Asteria*'s crew, the letters that you'll now be writing, have been beamed to this country via Skynet and then telexed in the normal way, so you won't have handwriting problems. Just make sure that you get the style right. I've arranged for a microfiche viewer to be installed in here so that you can go over all the previous letters."

Abbott swallowed. "When do I start, sir?"

"Now."

"Why me, sir?"

"Because I can trust you to keep your mouth shut, James. I can also trust you not to begin a love letter with 'Dear Sir or Madam,' which is probably what would happen if I were to give the job to a Main Building scribe."

The admiral moved to the door. "Wake me at ten please, James."

"Why not report the *Asteria* as missing, sir?"

Admiral Howe didn't appear to have heard the question. "Wake me at ten," he repeated.

"Sir," said Abbott firmly. "If you want me to do this, you have to tell me why the *Asteria* isn't being reported as missing."

Admiral Howe considered. Perhaps it might be wise to let Abbott have half the story. He sat down.

"The *Asteria* is not a properly commissioned submarine. She was built by Vickers for the Israeli Navy. Just before she was due to be launched, HMG stepped in and stopped the order and paid Vickers full compensation. So, the government ended up owning a submarine for which it had no real use. Then someone, not me, thank God, had the bright idea of using the *Asteria* to carry out an experimental thousand-day submarine patrol."

Abbott's eyes opened wide. "A thousand days!" he echoed. "I thought it was generally agreed that such a thing was impossible? There'd be psychological collapse of the crew after five hundred days."

"That's exactly what I said at the time. I said that

the thousand-day patrol is a naval strategist's pipe dream and will always be so. But they said: no, we've got a sub, let's give it a try. Hand-picked crew—specially screened for stamina and emotional stability and that sort of thing. I said it would fail but they wouldn't listen." Admiral Howe paused. "It looks like I was right."

Abbott nodded. "No harm in trying, I suppose. So why not admit that the experiment was a failure?"

"We can't," replied Admiral Howe. "We've deliberately leaked information to the Soviets saying that the thousand-day patrol is possible and that this is our second.... That's why you're going to become the *Asteria*'s ghost for the next fourteen months. At the end of that period we'll announce that the *Asteria* is overdue. We'll give an Atlantic position—somewhere exceptionally deep."

"What was her real position, sir?" Abbott's face was impassive as he waited for an answer.

There was a long pause before Admiral Howe replied. "She was tucked up in our Atlantic depot, where she was supposed to be safe."

"Our what?" Abbott was so surprised that he omitted the "sir."

"I didn't like the idea at first," said the old sailor, staring down at the floor. "But they had an answer ready to counter every objection. They had found an ice shelf in the British Antarctic territory that was stable—it wasn't calving icebergs: honeycombed with deep-water caverns hollowed out by summer melt water; easy to convert into a comfortable submarine depot with plenty of room for repair workshops and entertainment facilities."

Lieutenant Abbott gazed at the admiral in astonishment. "But there's a treaty—Antarctica can't be used for military purposes."

Admiral Howe laughed bitterly. "Exactly what I said. But national security outweighed an obscure treaty. I also said that there would be victualing problems but they had an answer for that as well: a phony research base a few miles inland staffed with genuine scientists working on genuine projects to provide the cover, but administer it with service personnel—selected personnel—Royal Marines."

"Perfidious Albion," Abbott muttered. "So what's happened to *Asteria*, sir, if the ice is safe?"

"They thought it was safe," Admiral Howe replied. "Seems like they thought there was something called glacial blockage—buried mountains preventing the ice from moving."

"And now it's moved?"

Admiral Howe nodded. "Several thousand cubic miles, according to the satellite pictures at Stanmore."

Lieutenant Abbott looked disbelieving. "Several thousand cubic *miles*, sir?" he echoed.

"I didn't believe it myself until I saw the pictures—there's now a bay in the coast that wasn't there on the last satellite survey."

"So we're going to mount a subsmash, sir?"

There was a long pause. Admiral Howe shook his head slowly.

"It's not that simple, James. The ice has vanished."

Abbott stared at the admiral. "What?!"

"Normally I detest clichés but this time one is appropriate: the ice—all eight thousand cubic miles of it—has vanished. Vanished into thin air."

6

ICE CORE
Ice sample removed from a glacier or ice cap.

"Well, I think it's madness," said Glen Sherwood

when the white-coated steward had poured their coffee.

Julia Hammond caught Oaf's eye and suppressed a smile. After three years with the Rosenthal Antarctic Survey team she knew enough about Sherwood to know that he disliked changes in his routine. Routine in a place like Antarctica, with either continuous darkness or continuous daylight and the struggle to remember whether the next meal would be breakfast or dinner, was essential if you didn't want to go quietly mad. But now, on the luxury liner *Orion* seventy-two hours out from Sydney and bound for Cape Town, normal periods of day and night had returned.

Oaf gave a booming laugh that caused other passengers at neighboring tables to look up at the giant Norwegian with a mixture of distaste and alarm. He clapped Sherwood on the back. "Still worried about those goddamn core samples, heh, Sherwood?"

The geologist shook his head. "No. I daresay the refrigeration equipment on this nuclear-powered gin palace can cope. I just think record-breaking attempts by ocean liners are irrelevant today."

Julia glanced round the opulent restaurant. There was a noisy gathering of wealthy industrialists and their wives enjoying a joke at the captain's table.

"Maybe they are irrelevant," said Julia shrewdly. "But still a good idea from the owner's point of view if you're way behind schedule and you've got a charter fleet of aircraft laid on at Heathrow to fly everyone home."

Oaf produced a wicked-looking flensing knife with a long curved blade. He was about to probe his teeth with the point when Julia said in a mild voice, "How many times have I told you about that, Oaf? You're not on one of your wretched whaling ships now."

The huge Norwegian looked incongruously crestfallen. He sighed and slid the knife back into its sheath. Julia Hammond was a very forthright young woman and it was best not to antagonize her. He saw Sherwood grinning at him and gave a rich, deep chuckle.

"Sherwood's in no hurry to get back to Southampton. Heh, Sherwood?"

The geologist's grin disappeared. Julia looked interested. "Oh? Why's that?"

Sherwood glared across the table at the amiable, bearlike Norwegian.

"Are you married, Glen?" Julia's tone suggested that she was annoyed at her failure to acquire information about Sherwood earlier. She didn't like mysteries.

"He's married okay," said Oaf, baring his rows of formidable teeth in a broad smile. "He once tell me all about it."

"I *was* married," Sherwood corrected. "Can we change the subject?"

Julia studied Sherwood speculatively. The geologist was uncomfortably aware of her gray eyes fixed on him. "You signed on for three years with Rosenthal in Antarctica to forget?" she asked sarcastically.

Sherwood laughed. "Hell no. I signed on for the same reason we all did—because it was a job and it was well paid. Now that I've confessed all my secrets perhaps we can change the subject."

"Pity they didn't renew our contracts," said Julia pensively.

Sherwood looked at her in surprise. "Who's always going on about how nice it'll be to go shopping in London again?"

Julia shrugged. "There's not that many jobs for marine biologists going."

"Lot of phonies," Oaf mumbled while exploring one of his tombstone teeth with a forefinger that was as thick as a broomstick.

Julia fastened her inquisitive eyes on the giant. "Who? And leave your teeth alone."

"Rosenthal," said Oaf. "Big phonies."

27

Sherwood and Julia exchanged baffled glances. "Oaf," said Julia. "Will you please stop poking at your teeth and tell me what you're talking about?"

Oaf stopped poking at his teeth. "Rosenthal lab technicians."

"What about them?"

"All over Sherwood's height. No glasses. All with good eyesight."

Sherwood frowned.

"Don't be stupid," said Julia with irritation. "Of course they all had good eyesight—they had to pass medicals."

"For height?" Sherwood queried thoughtfully.

Julia hesitated. "Well...I suppose..."

"Phonies," Oaf repeated. "And Brill the biggest phony of them all.'

Julia had always found the chief executive at Rosenthal to be considerate and well behaved. She was quick to strenuously defend him.

Sherwood winked at Oaf and said teasingly to Julia, "Yeah. Everyone on the base noticed your play for him."

Julia controlled her temper. "Brill was the only gentleman on the base among a gang of sex-starved, uncouth so-called scientists whose idea on research didn't extend much beyond trying to find out what I wore in bed at night."

"Don't blame me for your sensitivity over your flannel pajamas," said Sherwood mischievously.

"God give me patience."

"An *officer* and a gentleman," said Oaf abruptly. There was a sudden silence round the table.

"English idiom I learn once," said Oaf in response to Julia's and Sherwood's blank expressions. "Brill an officer. Navy officer." The Norwegian tapped the side of his nose. "I smell 'em. Officers." He would have spat in contempt but sensed that Julia would not have approved. "I tell you something else," he continued. "You ever see in the stores building? No. You know why? Packing crates had marks on them.

That's why the lab technicians never let anyone go in there."

"What sort of marks?" asked Julia.

Oaf made a sketch on a napkin of the short, broad arrow that denoted H.M. Government property. "I see it once when tarpaulin get blown off," the Norwegian explained.

Sherwood leaned forward. "That's interesting. Remember how all of the extreme-weather clothing we were issued had had the labels removed?"

"So what?" said Julia. "Rosenthal purchased government surplus stock. What's wrong with that?"

"Then why try to hide the fact?" Sherwood countered.

Julia turned to Oaf. "So what are you trying to say? That Rosenthal is some sort of military base?"

"No," said Sherwood before the Norwegian could answer. "That would be violation of the Antarctic Treaty. There's a clause that forbids military exploitation of Antarctica. For all their faults, the British government doesn't break international treaties."

"Exactly," Julia agreed. "And, even if they did, what possible military value could Antarctica have to anyone?"

Oaf remained silent.

Sherwood was unable to sleep that night. The atmosphere in the tiny cabin, buried deep in the bowels of the liner, was unbearably oppressive.

He lay in the dark, wondering why it was that a technological breakthrough in efficient air-conditioning, even on a new ship like the *Orion*, had yet to be achieved.

He switched the light on and tried to read a paperback. After five pages he realized that his brain was absorbing nothing of the story. The words were a meaningless blur. He tossed the book onto the dresser and knocked the brochure on the *Orion* to the floor. He reached down to pick it up. Inside was a hastily printed leaflet which outlined details of the proposed record-breaking run. Upon rounding Cape Horn, the *Orion* would be increasing her speed to nearly forty knots and, weather permitting, would maintain that speed for seven days so that the liner would arrive at Southampton on schedule.

Sherwood reread the sentence. Thirty-seven knots for a week! It seemed an incredible figure. He turned to the brochure and read the information on the *Orion* that was included for "the technically minded." Four nuclear reactors...Four turbines ...Maximum speed forty-two knots. Sherwood wondered if the liner had ever been tested at her top speed. He wasn't an engineer but it seemed to him that it was crazy even to consider pushing a largely untried ship to its limits.

He idly leafed through the rest of the brochure and came to a diagram of the ship's decks. It wasn't surprising that he couldn't sleep—G deck was twenty feet below the waterline and immediately above the reactor rooms. He dropped the booklet on the floor, switched the light off and made another attempt to sleep.

Twenty feet below the waterline...

Trust Rosenthal to book the cheapest cabins.

Twenty feet below the waterline...

Sherwood did a mental calculation and worked out that every square foot of hull plate by his head was having to withstand a water pressure of one ton.

7

It had taken Lieutenant James Abbott seven months to overcome his distaste at having to be a husband to twenty-three wives, a lover to six women, and a father of thirty-one children.

The whole business was now a smooth-running operation aided by a giant wall chart that listed birthdays, anniversaries, children's names and ages, together with a mass of detailed information on likes and dislikes. Although Abbott was now familiar with the private lives of every member of the *Asteria*'s crew and could write letters without referring to the chart and a card index, he made a point of always checking his facts first. A mistake, such as the time when he had confused the first names of two wives, could be disastrous.

It was the fifteenth of the month. Mechanician Robertson had always written five hundred words of sleazy syntax on the fifteenth of every month.

Lieutenant Abbott sighed and reached for his notepad.

8

General Nikolai Zadkin of the Intelligence Secretariat placed his huge hands flat on Admiral Turgenev's desk and said in a dangerously mild voice: "So where's that British submarine now, admiral?"

Admiral Turgenev, Commander-in-Chief of the Soviet Black Sea fleet, met the cold Slavonic stare without flinching. He wasn't frightened of thugs like Zadkin. "General. No one seriously believes that the thousand-day submarine patrol is possible. Either your department has made a mistake or you've got hold of some fake intelligence."

"Where's that submarine!"

"The AGI ship lost track of it in the Southern

Ocean. It's virtually impossible to use sonar from the surface in such cold water. Inversion layers bend the beam. The only way to successfully track a submarine without thermal-wake satellite monitoring facilities such as the Americans have, is to use another submarine."

"Locating and monitoring that sub," said General Zadkin icily, "is a number-one priority. It is essential that we find out if the British really have solved the problems of sending men on a three-year patrol or if the crew are relaxing on a depot ship in the South Atlantic."

"That's almost certainly what they are doing," said Admiral Turgenev irritably.

"I need proof!" Zadkin thundered, crashing his fist down on the desk. "Not the opinions of deskbound sailors!"

The last words of Zadkin's insult were drowned by the thunderous roar of eight MIG-25s from the nearby Yevpatoriya airbase.

General Zadkin crossed to the window and shaded his eyes against the brilliant sunlight sparkling on the Black Sea. The fighters wheeled tightly over the Sevastopol naval dockyard and climbed fast, heading south across the Black Sea toward Turkey. The nerve-shattering howl from the sixteen Tumanski engines faded with astonishing speed to a muted thunder as the dwindling jets bored into the distant haze.

General Zadkin watched the shrinking black specks with pride; the Americans had nothing that could match the MIG-25 for speed, rate of climb, and operating ceiling. It had started breaking world records in 1970 and had been breaking them ever since.

He spun quickly round to face Turgenev. "If a submarine is the best thing to use for hunting another submarine in total secrecy, then that's what we'll use."

"We'll need at least twenty to scour the South

Atlantic," said Turgenev impatiently. "We can't spare that many."

Zadkin smiled. "Who said anything about using fleet or nuclear submarines, admiral? We'll use the prototype Delta Two."

Turgenev shook his head. "That's the maddest idea I've heard in a long time, general."

"Remember who you are talking to," said Zadkin mildly.

Turgenev snorted. "I don't care. It's lunacy even to contemplate sending the Delta Two into the South Atlantic. You know their size of course? Eighteen thousand tons. They're designed to cover North American targets from home waters."

"They have the best passive sonar equipment in the entire navy—correct?"

"Yes. But—"

"And they're fitted with SOSUS foxers?"

"Yes," said Turgenev desperately. "But if the Delta Two was detected in the South Atlantic the Americans would regard it as a gross provocation."

"It will be under strict instructions to remain continuously submerged and to keep its SOSUS jammers operational at all times."

"It'll be detected by thermal-wake satellites," said Turgenev irritably. "And another thing—the Delta Two's inertials aren't suitable for position fixing in the South Atlantic."

"Use the Omega system," Zadkin replied smoothly. "I understand that the American and British navies have no scruples about using it in their own submarines, even though it is a civilian system. The very-low-frequency signals generated by the Omega shore beacons penetrate the water to a depth of six meters, do they not? It should not be beyond the abilities of your technicians to equip the Delta with a towed wire antenna so that it can obtain continuous position updating without the need to surface."

"Please listen to me, general," said Admiral Turgenev resolutely. "We need much more oceanographic research before we can risk an eighteen-thousand-ton submarine in unknown waters. If the Delta were to run into a sudden layer of cold water, it would lose trim and shoot to the surface. There's still much—"

"Admiral Turgenev," said Zadkin dangerously, "you will send the Delta Two into the South Atlantic with recordings of the *Asteria*'s signature. I *want that submarine found!*"

9

Julia stared wistfully at the shimmering peak of Table Mountain for some seconds before handing the binoculars to Sherwood.

"It's a bloody shame," she muttered. "I was looking forward to shopping in Cape Town."

Sherwood rested his elbows on the mahogany-capped weather deck rail and focused the binoculars on the distant peak. "You had three hours in Sydney," he pointed out.

Julia gave a sarcastic laugh. She was about to launch into a tirade about not having had a chance to do some proper shopping for three years when she noticed that Sherwood was smiling.

"Are you mocking me again?"

Sherwood lowered the binoculars. His eyes were round and innocent. "Me, Miss Hammond? Now why would I want to do a thing like that?"

Julia's retort was interrupted by a steward. He was very polite: "I'm sorry to disturb you, but we're about to close this deck."

Julia glanced along the deck. Similar requests were being made to the other passengers.

Sherwood took Julia's arm. "Come on. I'll give you a game of electronic tennis. They'll probably close all the open decks once they start this crazy attempt at the record."

"The after deck will remain open," said the steward apologetically. "It'll be out of the slipstream. There'll be extra films, and the entertainment officer is organizing special events."

"Ladies and gentlemen," boomed a nearby public-address speaker. "We are about to increase our speed to thirty-seven knots. The *Orion* is well stabilized— indeed you may find that the ship is much more steady when running at high speed...."

Sherwood snorted.

"... Weather reports are favorable so it looks as if we will be entering Southampton Water in exactly one week from today. We hope you all enjoy your participation in this memorable event."

The speaker clicked off.

"Memorable event," Sherwood repeated sourly.

"It'll be fun," said Julia as Sherwood steered her through the sliding doors and into the glass-enclosed promenade.

"It'll be bloody dangerous."

"Who says?"

"Oaf. He's a good engineer. He said machinery should never have to work flat-out if it isn't essential."

Julia stopped. "I do believe you're scared, Mr. Sherwood."

The geologist looked annoyed. "Of course I'm not scared."

Sherwood was lying; he was scared of the twenty feet that his cabin was below the waterline. He knew it was an irrational fear and that the *Orion*'s owners and captain wouldn't allow the attempt unless they were satisfied that it was safe.

They reached the forward promenade deck over-looking the *Orion*'s bows surging through the white-flecked swell. Julia was about to point out a flock of Cape pigeons wheeling toward the mainland when they both heard the hitherto unobtrusive whine of the

Orion's turbines sharpen so that it could be heard above the incessant piped music. The deck quickened underfoot.

"Sounds like they're turning up the wick," Julia commented cheerfully.

The *Orion* buried her bows in the swell and sent plumes of wind-whipped spray lashing across the foredeck. Excited, chattering passengers gathered along the rail. The next mountainous swell seemed to cause the liner to hesitate. Passengers instinctively recoiled as a maelstrom of spindrift hurled against the glass.

Julia allowed herself to be taken below to the harsh clatter of slot machines in the amusement center. She noticed that Sherwood's hand was trembling slightly as he fed a coin into a slot.

"What the hell's the matter?" she asked.

Sherwood watched the moving spot of light on the screen for some seconds. "There's a door leading off from G deck marked 'Private—Staff only.' Have you noticed it?"

"Yes," said Julia, puzzled.

"It leads to a flight of stairs that comes out on the weather deck."

"So?"

"It might be useful in an emergency."

The next heavy swell caused the entire ship to lurch.

10

The Delta Two class SSBN, the *Podorny*, rolled. It was a gentle roll but it was enough so that Commander Igor Leachinski dived from his bunk and out into the companionway leading to the control room.

Submarines cruising at a depth of three hundred meters do not roll.

"What the hell was that?" Leachinski demanded as he burst into the control room.

The officer of the watch was baffled. "I don't know, captain," he began, and the *Podorny* rolled again. The helmsman just saved himself from slipping out of his chair. There was a sound of breaking crockery from the wardroom. Leachinski was about to order the chief engineer to reduce speed when his blood ran cold: the control-room floor was tilting—the *Podorny* was losing trim. Even before the chief engineer reached the switches that operated the ballast pumps, the *Podorny* suddenly lurched violently and rolled over onto her side. Leachinski tried to save himself by grabbing hold of the back of the sonar technician's chair. His senses reeled, refusing to accept that the familiar control room was turning through ninety degrees. Objects were crashing around him. Men were yelling. There was a smell of burning, and then the lights were flickering.

"Emergency lights!" Leachinski yelled.

"You're sitting on the control panel!" shouted a voice.

The automatic breakers closed with soft clicks—the lights burned steadily. For some seconds there was silence; the turbines continued to hum, driving the *Podorny* along on her beam ends. For the silent, sweating men in the submarine, those seconds seemed to drag on for eternity. There was nothing to do but pray. In the recreation room thirty men lay entangled on a bulkhead that had been the side of the submarine; they prayed amid the smashed remains of the movie projector. In the galley the two cooks, badly hurt by falling against the cooker burners, prayed. Throughout the length of the *Podorny* men prayed while they waited for something to happen.

The two thousand tons of lead poured into the *Podorny*'s bilge spaces began to assert itself. Slowly, the mighty submarine turned about her axis. Men slid down the bulkheads as the floor regained its rightful position. Their training took over: damage reports flowed along the submarine's fiber optic communication system to the control room.

"Missile control center. All systems okay. Category Three damage only."

"Reactor room. Category Three damage. One rating with a suspected broken arm."

"Turbine room. Category Two damage: a fractured HP pipe which we're shutting off now."

Ten similar reports were relayed over the control room's loudspeaker. Leachinski heaved a sigh of relief. There had been no Category One reports—none of the submarine's major systems were damaged. There was no need to order the *Podorny* to the surface. He stared at his white-faced chief engineer.

"What in the name of the Mother of God caused that, chief?"

The chief engineer didn't answer. He pointed dumbly at the depth gauges. Leachinski followed his finger. The depth gauges were reading zero and the pointers on the external light meters were off the scale, hard against the maximum reading stops.

The *Podorny* was on the surface.

Leachinski swore and switched the fin TV camera on. A distant horizon and a blue sky filled the screen. The horizon tilted gently. The motion was repeated underfoot as the *Podorny* responded to the swell.

"Down a hundred!" Leachinski yelled.

"Can't, captain," said the sonar operator.

Leachinski rounded on him. "Why not?"

"Only fifty meters of water under our keel."

Leachinski glared at the sonar operator. "We're in the middle of the South Atlantic, you idiot!"

"See for yourself, captain."

The sonar operator was right: all of the *Podorny*'s independent echo sounders were indicating a depth of fifty meters when they should be showing five *kilometers.*

Leachinski gaped in disbelief.

"Hard echo too," said the sonar operator. "No sub-bottom penetration, so it looks like we're over rock."

For a moment Leachinski's mind raced.

"Stop engines," he ordered.

The submarine had lost way by the time Leachinski stepped out of the fin lift and onto the bridge. The *Podorny*'s hemispherical whale bow, ideal for running at speed when submerged, gave her bad handling characteristics on the surface, and her cylindrical hull, without the stabilizing influence of the hydroplanes now that she was lying stopped, caused her to roll sickeningly through a thirty-degree arc. Leachinski pulled on an interphone headset and plugged the communication jack into one of the pressure-proof sockets. He heard the sonar operator say:

"Depth, forty meters."

Leachinski swept the horizon with his binoculars. There was no sign of land. He listened to the voices from the radio room as the first and second navigation officers went about the business of obtaining a position fix from a satellite and shore stations.

From his position high above the surface, perched on the slender fin, Leachinski peered down at the sea as if hoping to spot a clue that accounted for the shallow water.

"Control room—bridge," said the chief engineer's voice in the headphones. "I don't know if this means anything, but external water temperature is only two degrees above freezing."

Leachinski frowned. If the *Podorny*'s position was correct, the submarine was riding northward on the Benguela Current five hundred miles off the west coast of South Africa. The Benguela, which was an offshoot of the Antarctic West Wind Drift Current, was a cold current. But not that cold. Not thirty degrees south of the equator.

"We've got a fix on two South African Broadcasting Corporation transmitters," said the voice in

Leachinski's headphones. "It looks like the SINS is okay."

Leachinski gave the order to proceed at a cautious three knots.

"Depth steady at forty-eight meters," said the sonar operator.

Leachinski told him to use the forward sonar scan so that the submarine had advance warning of depth variations ahead.

"It's a steady forty-eight meters for three kilometers, sir, and then it shelves away to seventy meters for as far as the beam will reach. Side scan is the same."

Leachinski grunted. Something was seriously wrong with the charts for the South Atlantic. Was it possible that a recent earthquake could have gone undetected? He dismissed the thought: no subterranean upheaval could force the floor of the ocean from a depth of five kilometers to within fifty meters of the surface and not be detected.

"Radar room—bridge."

"Bridge," said Leachinski.

"We're getting a nine-tenths radar map from *Aerios Eight*."

Aerios Eight was a satellite that provided an "over horizon" radar display for Soviet shipping in the Atlantic. It overcame the problem of radar's being unable to see beyond the horizon. Nine-tenths meant that reception was extremely good.

"Anything of interest near us?" Leachinski inquired.

"Nothing ahead, captain. The American nuclear-powered liner, the *Orion*, is six hundred kilometers astern of us. She's just rounded Cape Horn."

Something was wrong with the sea. Leachinski stared down. He heard his voice say: "I thought she was putting into Cape Town?"

"No, captain. She's still with us."

But Leachinski didn't hear the reply. He was

gazing down at the sea in shocked disbelief, hardly able to credit his senses.

"Depth steady at forty-eight meters," intoned the sonar operator's voice.

The fin swayed. Leachinski stared in horror down at the water as it swelled toward him. His throat went dry. His knuckles were white as he involuntarily tightened his grip on the rail. Some spray lashed his face but he didn't notice it. Nor did he hear the warning from the radar room concerning a light aircraft on the *Podorny*'s quarter. One thought dominated Leachinski's bewildered mind.

The sea was turning to honey.

11

"Why's the sea the color of shit?" demanded the CBS News cameraman.

The pilot of the Cessna Skymaster looked down at the sea and shrugged.

"Sand in suspension maybe," he replied in his Afrikaans accent.

"No way."

"So why worry about the sea? You want to film the *Orion*. I take you to the *Orion*. But I don't answer questions about the sea."

The cameraman gazed down through the Cessna's Plexiglas windows. "Sure is odd, though."

"An optical illusion," commented the pilot.

The cameraman screwed a long-focus lens onto his movie camera and looked down at the sea through the viewfinder. The telephoto effect made the sea appear to be a mere fifty feet beneath the aircraft. "It's still the color of shit," he announced.

"So what do you want me to do? Drop a dye marker on it maybe?"

The cameraman said nothing but continued to peer through his viewfinder. He slowly tilted the camera up to the horizon. He stiffened.

"Jesus."

"What?"

The cameraman kept his camera trained at the horizon and made a fine adjustment to the focusing bezel. Without taking his eye from the rubber eyepiece, he said: "There's an enormous submarine about ten miles ahead."

The pilot followed the direction in which the camera was pointing. His trained eyes picked out the white flash of swell breaking where it shouldn't break. He kept his eyes on the target and groped for his binoculars.

"See it?" said the cameraman.

"Yeah, I see it."

The two men stared in fascination at the massive, whale-like hull. The discolored swell seemed to be surging in slow motion across the featureless gray flanks as the submarine punched effortlessly through the heavy seas. The cameraman was familiar with most of the various submarine classes of the world's navies but he had never seen anything like the monstrous apparition that he was now holding in his viewfinder. Unlike most submarines, this one had its slender sail fin located well forward—almost on top of the rounded bows. A heavy sea slammed into the sail and dissolved: the spray seemed to hang in the air before falling back.

"Get over to it," breathed the cameraman.

"What about the *Orion*?"

"Forget it. If that baby doesn't dive, I'm going to run all my footage on her."

The pilot made a slight alteration of course.

The cameraman loaded his camera and whirred the leader through the gate while the pilot tried to call Cape Town to tell them about the submarine. He cursed in Afrikaans as he spun the tuning dial.

"What's the matter?"

"Radio loused up proper," answered the pilot in disgust. "Noise right across the band." He pushed the headphones away from his ears.

"Maybe that's deliberate," said the cameraman thoughtfully.

"You mean that thing's jamming us?"

"We live in a world of sophisticated electronic counter-measures," said the cameraman, raising his camera to his eye.

The pilot muttered an oath. "I thought maybe it was an American job."

"No way."

The giant submarine was now less than a mile away. The two men in the Cessna could see the head and shoulders of a man on the top of the fin. The cameraman swore to himself as he used the height of the man to gauge the size of the submarine.

"Goddamnit—she must be all of five hundred feet long. Please, God, don't let her dive. Take her down lower—I want an oblique." His sentences were a continuous, excited stream.

The Cessna approached the submarine from astern, flying above the curious double wake that is a characteristic of cigar-shaped vessels moving on the surface.

The Cessna pilot had never seen a nuclear submarine before so he was not as awed by the *Podorny*'s size as the cameraman. Even so, there was something frightening about the arrogant way the monster smashed her snub bows through the ponderous swell.

The movie camera whirred.

"Circle right round and come up behind her again!" shouted the cameraman as he twisted round in his seat to hold the mighty submarine in the center of his viewfinder.

The Cessna flashed over the *Podorny* at five hundred feet and banked steeply. The cameraman swung round and aimed across the pilot.

"Look, will you get that thing out of my ear!"

"Right round and come behind her as low and as slow as possible. Jesus—she doesn't seem to give a damn about us!"

It was the most inaccurate statement the cameraman had ever made in his life; Commander Leachinski cared very much about the presence of the little single-engine, twin-boom aircraft and was giving orders to do something about it as it approached from astern for its second pass.

"Lower!" yelled the cameraman, aiming through the wind screen. "Good grief—you can see her missile tubes!"

The pilot presumed the cameraman was referring to the double row of twenty circular marks aft of the submarine's fin.

"Slower!"

The Cessna's stall-warning alarm chirruped merrily.

"If I go any slower, we fall off the goddamn sky!" the pilot snarled.

The aircraft swept over the submarine for the second time. The cameraman frantically changed lenses.

"What a stupid time to take your goddamn camera to bits," the pilot complained.

"Wide-angle. Hell—I've crossed the thread. Do you have to fling her about like that?"

Another man had appeared on the bridge. They kept their faces turned toward the Cessna.

"Here's looking at you, baby," said the cameraman as the film whirred through the gate. "Keep her steady and we might get some usable stills."

The Cessna flashed over the *Podorny* for the third time and banked so steeply that it came close to stalling.

The cameraman spun the wide-angle lens off the camera body and screwed on a zoom lens.

"Okay—now approach her on her beam. Slow as you can. Trail your wheels in the water or something."

"If I do that, we end up on the water, on our back," growled the pilot, but he throttled back and pulled the Cessna's nose up until the aircraft was barely maintaining flying speed.

"Beautiful...Beautiful," breathed the cameraman as the huge Soviet submarine swelled in his viewfinder. He zoomed in on the two men. One of them was holding something on his shoulder: something the cameraman had seen before. What the hell was it? He was too excited by his scoop to think properly.

"What's that guy got?" demanded the pilot.

The Cessna was approaching the *Podorny* at an angle to minimize closing speed. The cameraman rotated the zoom lens to keep the submarine's apparent size constant. He watched the man point the tube. An alarm jangled at the back of the cameraman's mind: Egyptian soldiers during the '73 Arab-Israeli War!

There was a bright flash from the submarine's bridge. The pilot saw it.

"What was that?"

The cameraman didn't answer. He was a professional photographer; his world was the world he saw through his viewfinder. And like a professional he kept filming it until it fell apart.

12

At twenty minutes past midnight, the *Orion*'s wake disappeared.

Sherwood was dozing in a deckchair on the darkened and virtually deserted after deck, sheltered from the slipstream of the *Orion*'s forty-mile-an-hour charge by the ship's superstructure. Four hundred miles to his left was the coast of South West Africa and four yards to his right an unseen couple were giggling—enjoying the hour of tranquillity before the forecast storm. He opened his eyes and looked up at the moon. It was for some, he supposed, a romantic situation: a luxury liner, a tropical night, and the moon sparkling on the swell, adding its luminescence to the ship's glittering phosphorescent wake.

Except that the wake had disappeared.

He leaned forward in his deckchair, puzzled. The *Orion's* phenomenal speed had created a spectacular wake—a trail of luminous turbulence stretching across the sea to the horizon. Now there was nothing but a curious muddy-colored pattern of disturbed water that hardly reflected the moonlight. He crossed the after deck to the rail and looked down into one of the howling eddies created around the *Orion* by its incredible speed. It was then that he noticed the smell—the wet, indescribable smell that he had come to know so well in three years. It was the flesh-crawling smell that Oaf had said could even permeate the stink of blood and blubber from a gutted whale on a factory ship's flensing deck.

"Ice," said a deep voice at his side.

Sherwood jumped, then relaxed. The big Norwegian could move like a cat.

"I thought my nose was playing tricks," muttered Sherwood, angry at having been startled.

Oaf shook his head and leaned on the rail. Both men stared across the water at the yellow wake, their backs to the *Orion's* bows.

"No tricks, Sherwood. That's ice okay. I leave Julie and I go forward. Clear night. No ice. Not in this part of ocean. But I smell it good. I look for you. Your cabin's empty so I reckon you're up here." Oaf flashed his Stonehenge teeth.

"I reckon right, heh, Sherwood?"

"How long ago was it when you first smelled the ice then?"

"Fifteen minutes. Maybe more."

Sherwood looked up in surprise at the impossible hulk towering over him. "Fifteen minutes? You've been able to smell it all that time?"

"I smell good," Oaf replied simply. "And now wake stop shining. That's bad, Sherwood. Very bad."

Sherwood was about to ask Oaf what he meant when the deck suddenly heaved. There was a tremendous crash from forward followed by a series of thunderous concussions that seemed to rip through the ship with the speed of an express train. The force of the *Orion*'s deceleration would have thrown Sherwood back against the superstructure had not Oaf's huge arm quickly circled his waist and held him in a viselike grip. The rail Oaf was gripping with his other hand bent under the load as the *Orion* ground to a shuddering halt. The pulverizing shock waves that slammed through the length of the ship merged into one sustained explosion that seemed to last forever. People were screaming. The air was filled with flying deckchairs, lengths of rope—everything that hadn't been secured. Numb with shock and unable to comprehend what was happening to his orderly world, Sherwood saw the two lovers tumble from their hiding place as the deck became the side of an erupting volcano. The man went through the rails and must have fallen to the weather deck. The girl managed to grab a stanchion for an instant, but the force of her fall and the steepening deck angle broke her grip. She fell into the yellow sea that seemed to be racing up toward Sherwood. Oaf was yelling something, his arm holding Sherwood in an anaconda grip so that he could barely breathe. There was a heavy crump of more explosions mingling with hideous screams echoing from an air-conditioning duct. The deck heaved again.

"Got to get to the lifeboats!" Oaf yelled above the cacophony of tearing metal that seemed to come from below. "You hear me, Sherwood? Lifeboats!"

Sherwood nodded dumbly. He felt curiously

detached from the pandemonium around him.

Oaf grabbed Sherwood's hands and wrapped the fingers round the rail.

"You get good hold before I let go!"

Sherwood nodded and tightened his hold on the rail. He felt Oaf's grip on his waist relax and nearly panicked when he saw the sickly yellow sea at the end of the slope that had been the deck. His fear drew on unsuspected reserves of strength as he clung in terror to the rail.

"You okay?" shouted Oaf.

Sherwood heard himself croak: "I'm okay."

"I find rope and good lifeboat. I come back."

The moon went behind a cloud. Sherwood, holding on to a rail he couldn't see, cried out in fear.

But Oaf had gone. He was completely alone save for the anguished cries from the air-conditioning duct. Then there was a man's faint voice from the passenger address speakers—as if the amplifiers weren't receiving full power. His ankles twisted painfully as he tried to keep his body upright on the remorselessly canting deck. He could hear the struggles and desperate cries of those who had been swept overboard.

The deck gave another shudder. Someone nearby was shouting through a bullhorn but he couldn't make out what was being said. Something about lifeboats.

The moon reappeared. Sherwood was again seized by panic when he saw how steep the deck had become. Something hit him. He shrank back in fear. It was a rope.

"You pass it under rail and throw back to me," called out Oaf's reassuring voice from the shadows of the companionway that led down to the aft weather deck.

Sherwood groped blindly with one hand for the end of the rope. He gathered it clumsily into a coil and tossed it in the direction of the Norwegian's voice. He felt the rope tighten.

"Okay," said Oaf. "Now you come down rope like monkey."

Sherwood's feet slipped from under him when he transferred his hold from the rail to the rope. He half-fell, half-slid along the rope until he felt Oaf's huge fingers close on his forearm and haul him to his feet.

A flare arched high into the black sky and exploded into dazzling light suspended from a drifting parachute. The strengthening wind of the threatened storm carried them the length of the crippled liner. Four more flares sailed up. The night became day beneath the brilliant magnesium suns.

"That's better," Oaf growled. "Follow me, Sherwood. I've found a raft."

Sherwood stumbled down the steps behind the Norwegian. He found himself walking on the ridges of stairs that were now virtually horizontal.

"Bloody queer, eh?" said Oaf over his shoulder.

Sherwood slipped again. Oaf cursed in Norwegian and picked Sherwood up as though he were a rag doll. He reached the end of the steps and turned toward the port weather deck that seemed to be towering over the two men, so steeply was the *Orion* listing to starboard. Oaf set Sherwood down and pointed up. He saw Sherwood's bewildered expression, cupped his hands against the geologist's ear, and shouted above the uproar of screaming passengers and bellowing bullhorns from the starboard side.

"We gotta go up," Oaf yelled. "Come on, Sherwood. We move pretty damn quick!"

Sherwood followed Oaf's finger to the edge of the deck, where the bulwarks were etched against the scudding moonlit clouds.

"That's the wrong way!" Sherwood screamed. "All the lifeboats will be jammed up there!"

"Raft!" Oaf shouted back, "Easy to launch down side of ship. And no big crowds going crazy. Come on!"

The *Orion* gave a sudden lurch. There was renewed screaming from the far side of the ship. Sherwood shut the noise out and concentrated on climbing up the weather deck. The ascent was made easier by many teak deck planks that had been forced from their seams by the enormous twist that had been induced throughout the length of the liner's hull. He reached a lifeboat davit and pulled himself to his feet. The seemingly endless climb had left him exhausted. Oaf had one leg over the bulwark and was hauling on a rope that disappeared into the shadows.

"Need help, Sherwood. You pull as well."

Hardly knowing what he was doing, Sherwood braced himself against the davit and tried to grasp the rope. His arms were jerked back by the force of the Norwegian's pulls.

"Heave, damn you," Oaf growled.

More flares blazed a windswept path into the sky above the dreadful scene and burst into light. Sherwood's arms were aching from the climb up the deck but he pulled as hard as he could. There was a bulky liferaft pack attached to the end of the rope.

"Got to get it over side, Sherwood. Come on."

"Christ, Oaf. For God's sake let's rest a minute."

"Plenty of time to rest in raft."

The two men lifted the heavy canvas pack onto the bulwark and balanced it there while Oaf felt for its inflation lanyard.

"Okay, Sherwood. Now we heave smart on three. One...two...three..."

The pack tumbled down the side of the *Orion*'s hull, trailing the lanyard. Sherwood felt sick as he looked down the *Orion*'s sloping flank at the evil yellow sea. The pack hit the surface with a splash that couldn't be heard. Oaf jerked the lanyard. The floating bundle swelled and burst its specially weakened fasteners. Bright orange fabric appeared. It spread out into a disc some twenty feet in diameter and then the rim of the disc began to inflate until two-foot-high sides to the raft were formed.

Oaf lashed a length of rope to the lifeboat davit and tossed it down to the raft.

Sherwood shook his head. "I couldn't do it, Oaf. You go without me."

Oaf pushed the rope into Sherwood's hands. "You bloody climb down or I throw you down!"

Sherwood was desperate. "Oaf, I can't do it!"

The giant Norwegian moved menacingly toward Sherwood. "You go first. Bloody now! You go backward and you don't look down!"

Sherwood took the rope and reluctantly swung his legs over the bulwark. He did as the Norwegians said and was surprised to discover that the descent wasn't as difficult as it looked despite the steadily rising wind that clutched at his clothing. He paid the rope out mountaineer fashion as he walked backward down the long slope to the waiting yellow sea. He had one bad moment when air pressure inside the hull blew a porthole glass out of its mounting right beside him with explosive force.

After two minutes his feet had crossed the waterline and he found himself walking on the coppery anti-fouling paint that had been exposed by the *Orion*'s heavy list. The rope vibrated. He looked up. The huge bulk of Oaf was swaying down toward him. He could now hear the dull boom of the swell hurtling itself against the steel hull. The life raft lifted and fell away. Sherwood timed the next heave and allowed himself to drop the last six feet into the water.

The intense cold was like a thunderbolt. It jarred the breath from his body. He lashed out in panic, terrified that the sudden shock was going to make him faint.

Oaf succeeded in dropping straight into the life raft. It was a credit to its makers that his 280-pound bulk didn't go through the fabric floor. He grabbed Sherwood by his collar and waistband and rolled him inboard. The geologist lay on the floor of the raft coughing up the freezing sea water he had swallowed while Oaf pounded his back with rib-shattering, sledgehammer blows.

"For Christ's sake, Oaf," Sherwood spluttered. "You'll kill me."

Sherwood pulled himself into a sitting position. He had been in the water for less than thirty seconds but he was shivering uncontrollably and his teeth were clattering like clockwork castanets. Oaf held up the arm he had plunged into the water to grab Sherwood.

"Pretty bloody cold, eh, Sherwood? Three minutes kill a man."

Sherwood shook his head. If someone made a statement he disagreed with he would dispute it, no matter what state he was in. "You'll argue on your deathbed," his mother used to say.

"Benguela Current, Oaf. Cold—but not that cold."

"Current don't matter a damn," Oaf muttered. "If it's cold like that it kills. Pretty damn quick too. You get down out of the wind."

"Now look," Sherwood disputed. "If I say—"

"I say I throw you back," Oaf growled. "Too damn small."

Sherwood stared uneasily at the giant. Oaf flashed his row of monolithic teeth in a broad grin. The geologist forgot the agony of the cold and laughed.

"Thank you for everything you did, Oaf."

Oaf made no reply but stared up at the canting bulk of the *Orion*.

The moaning wind was blowing the life raft away from the liner.

"Pity about woman," said Oaf. "She damn good. Not enough in world."

"You mean Miss Hammond?"

Oaf nodded. The moon made a brief appearance through the gathering storm clouds. The liner's mass reminded Sherwood of a huge Celtic burial mound.

"Good at what?" inquired Sherwood, half guessing what the Norwegian's answer would be.

Oaf's answer was a broad, knowing grin.

Sherwood heard some faint screams. He looked up the mountainous incline. The life raft was fifty yards from the liner. It no longer looked such an impossible climb. He turned to Oaf.

"We were all on G deck on this side, weren't we?"

"Sure. Two decks below waterline."

Sherwood pointed to the *Orion*'s exposed waterline. "But above the waterline now, Oaf. Is there a torch in that pack?"

Oaf opened the life raft's survival pack. He pulled out the raft's insulated roof and its tubular aluminum support, two folding paddles, water containers, and packs of food. There was even some fishing tackle. The torch was sealed into a watertight bag that Sherwood ripped open.

"Come on, Oaf. Paddle back to the side."

The two men assembled the paddles and steered the life raft back to the *Orion*. Sherwood shone the torch beam on the porthole that had been blown out by air pressure. The rope they had used to descend the liner's side lay alongside it.

"What are you thinking of, Sherwood?"

"I'm small enough to squeeze through the porthole to check her cabin. What was its number?"

"G12. Sherwood, you're crazy. Maybe she's in a lifeboat."

"And maybe she isn't." Sherwood jammed the torch into his pocket.

Oaf shook his head and paddled the life raft cautiously into the water seething against the liner's hull. Sherwood clutched the life raft's sides, watching for an opportunity to grab the rope.

The swell lifted the life raft. Sherwood tensed and jumped. His fingers closed thankfully around the rope. He pulled himself up the *Orion*'s side while Oaf watched anxiously, fending the raft away from the stricken hull with a paddle. Two minutes later Sherwood had wriggled through the opening and had disappeared.

Sherwood was surprised by the silence in the ship. He switched the torch on and walked downhill into the passageway. E deck was deserted. He found the stewards' companionway and picked his way carefully down the crazily inclined stairs—walking half on the corners of each tread and half on the bulkhead.

G deck, two deck levels below E deck, was a different story; there were terrible moanings from within the cabins. The people inside heard Sherwood trip over something. Suddenly the trapped passengers were screaming and beating on their doors. Sherwood tried to open one but it was firmly jammed in its frame by the *Orion*'s distortion.

He walked along the tilted passageway, steadying himself with one hand and flashing the torch on the cabin numbers.

G20...G19...Seven more doors to G12.

His feet splashed through water. Warm water. He flashed the torch ahead. The passageway was sloping down. G12 was at the end of the passageway with the water up to its door handle. Why the hell was it warm when the water outside had been freezing?

Then he remembered the nuclear reactors.

The water was up to his waist outside G12. Supposing it was radioactive? If it was, it was too late. He tried the door. It was either jammed or locked. He banged on it.

"Julia?"

He could hear her crying.

"Julia! Is the door unlocked?"

A distraught voice answered: "No. It's stuck. I can't get it open."

"Hold the handle down!" Sherwood called.

There was a movement inside the cabin. The handle twisted down.

"Like that?" There was hope in her voice.

Sherwood threw his weight ineffectually against the door. It was useless—the water absorbed most of his effort and the *Orion*'s heavy list meant that he had to exert upward. Maybe a drop kick...

He braced his spine against the opposite bulkhead and lashed out at the door with both feet. The shock jarred his whole body. The door splintered inward. Julia winced with pain as she helped drag the door open; her fingernails were torn and bleeding from her desperate hammering and clawing at the unyielding door. She collapsed into Sherwood's arms.

"I thought no one would come," she croaked, her voice hoarse from shouting.

The *Orion* trembled. The list was getting worse. Sherwood grabbed Julia's hand and dragged her into the passageway. He didn't notice her grimace in pain as his fingers closed on her lacerated nails. "Come on! We've got to move fast!"

Ten minutes later they were at the open porthole. Sherwood peered out. The weather had worsened: the wind had reached near gale force and was hurling mountainous seas against *Orion*'s side. Oaf had rigged the life raft's cover. He had it open and was fending the life raft away from the liner's abrasive steel plates. He grinned with relief when he saw Sherwood's head.

"Can you climb down this rope?" Sherwood asked Julia.

She looked down and saw the heaving yellow seas crashing against the liner's flank. Her voice didn't betray her terror. "Yes I think so."

"You sure?"

His tone annoyed her but she said nothing and allowed him to help her squeeze through the porthole. The breaking seas drowned her cry of pain as she grasped the rope. Her hands were slippery with blood and she would have lost her grip had Sherwood not seen her hands and grabbed her.

"You'll have to hang on to me!" he yelled.

"I'll be okay!" she shouted back defiantly.

"You won't. Let me do the climbing—you hang on to me!" He put an arm around Julia's waist and did his best to emulate Oaf's viselike clasp while hanging on to the rope with his other hand. "I've got you," he panted. "You take some of the weight if you can, but I've got you."

Julia decided not to argue. Despite her torn hands she felt certain that she could climb down the rope unaided. Naturally she was grateful to Sherwood for coming back for her but resented his automatic assumption that she was a helpless female.

Inch by painful inch, Sherwood began the nerve-wracking backward walk down the rope while supporting Julia's weight. He was halfway down when both of them were swamped by a freezing sea breaking against the hull. The impact swept Sherwood's feet from under him. In terror, he felt his hold on Julia's waist slacken. At the precise moment he tried to renew his grip, another wave roared up the side of the hull and slammed into them. Sherwood gave a scream as Julia was torn away. For a wild moment he thought she would fall into the madly spinning life raft. Oaf's mighty arms plunged toward her. But it was too late; her helpless body tumbled head first into the foaming caldron of yellow water.

Sherwood let the last few yards of rope burn through his fingers. Oaf was screaming obscenities at him. He landed on top of the giant Norwegian just as he was swinging the life raft round to where Julia had hit the water and disappeared.

Oaf swore bitterly at Sherwood and tossed him contemptuously across the life raft. "Stupid bastard, Sherwood!" he snarled.

"I couldn't help it! I swear I couldn't help it!" Sherwood pleaded in desperation.

But Oaf wasn't listening. He was staring at the honey-colored water—searching for Julia—calling her name. He saw something and started paddling frantically with his hands while roundly cursing Sherwood in a mixture of Norwegian and English.

"Come on, Sherwood! You help!"

Sherwood snatched up a paddle but Oaf tore it out of his hands and threw it down.

"You push wreckage out of the way!"

For five minutes they searched—Oaf sometimes churning the freezing water to foam whenever

56

something caught his eye and Sherwood fending away the debris that was hemorrhaging into the sea from the hidden wound in the doomed liner's hull.

Oaf pointed suddenly. "Hey, Sherwood! We both paddle like stink!"

There was no time to hunt for the paddle; Sherwood plunged both hands into the water and followed Oaf's example. The cold was an agonizing thunderbolt. His numbed hands felt as if they had been amputated. The wind had risen to a shriek. It whipped spray off the broken sea that lashed his face with bull-whip ferocity. He paddled blindly, obeying Oaf's bellowed orders like an android.

The Norwegian lunged his great bear frame forward. There was a sudden flurry of violent movement.

"Okay, Sherwood. You stop paddling. Get cover shut fast."

Sherwood opened his eyes. Julia was lying in the bottom of the raft. Her face was the ghastly pallor that he had seen once before when a Rosenthal laboratory technician was brought back to base three days after his Sno-Cat had broken down. He stared guiltily down at the pathetic body. She was lying very still.

"Is she dead, Oaf?"

"What the hell do you care, Sherwood?" the Norwegian growled. "Just get cover fixed good. Keep out wind."

Sherwood zipped the cover closed and extended the center tube to provide more headroom. He hung the torch from a clip.

Oaf was cradling Julia's head in the crook of his great arm. He gently prised her jaw open. "You push down on her chest every time I stop blowing," he commanded.

He forced her lips into a pout and covered her mouth with his own. He blew steadily into her lungs for three seconds then raised his huge head. Sherwood pressed down on her sternum.

"Both hands!" roared Oaf. "And hard! You won't hurt her!"

Oaf blew again and Sherwood pressed down with both hands spread across Julia's breasts. Her body felt like ice through the thin material of her blouse. There was a faint sound of air rushing past her frozen lips.

Oaf blew and Sherwood bore down on her chest again.

The two men settled to a steady rhythm. Blow ... press. Blow ... press ...

Fifteen minutes passed. The gale worsened. They tried to ignore the life raft's crazy motion.

Blow ... press. Blow ... press ...

Two more agonizing minutes slipped by.

Sherwood felt a flicker of life beneath his aching fingers. He looked up at Oaf in exaltation. "She's alive, Oaf! She's alive! I felt her heart beat!"

Oaf grunted. "Heart going all the time. First time it start going stronger."

Sherwood's misery was forgotten. He grinned happily at the Norwegian. "She's going to be all right, isn't she? She's going to live!"

"Maybe. Maybe not" was the laconic reply as Oaf started unbuttoning Julia's blouse.

"What the hell are you doing?" Sherwood demanded angrily.

"You get jeans off, Sherwood." Oaf looked up at the geologist. "Come on! You want her to die?"

Oaf leaned Julia forward and peeled her blouse off while Sherwood struggled with the zip on her saturated jeans. Oaf swore with impatience. Sherwood grasped both sides of the material and ripped the fly open. Oaf held Julia off the bottom of the life raft while Sherwood rolled the jeans down to her knees. Her face was fixed in a mask of death. There was a lacework of raw-looking veins visible beneath her transparent skin. He pulled the jeans clear of her feet.

Oaf tore the wrappings off the survival-pack

blankets and spread one out on the life raft's floor. He pulled his sweater and shirt off and started to wriggle out of his trousers.

"Get undressed, Sherwood. Everything off."

"Why?"

"Just do it! Got to get her warm. Only hope."

Sherwood struggled out of his clothes while Oaf pulled Julia against himself. The giant Norwegian's body was a mass of thick, tangled hair from chest to groin. He grinned at Sherwood as he arranged the blankets.

"Come on. Sherwood. We make a sandwich with this little one in the middle, heh?"

Sherwood suddenly understood. He knew from the brief survival course he had attended before leaving for Antarctica that warmth was the best immediate treatment for exposure, although no mention had been made of Oaf's method.

Oaf reached up a gorilla-pike arm and switched off the torch.

Sherwood eased himself up against Julia. She was facing him, folded like a child into the matted curve of Oaf's hard body. He shivered as the frozen nakedness of her thighs and breasts greedily sucked the warmth from his body.

He lay still in the darkness, listening to the sounds of the storm and Oaf's stentorian breathing. A reassuring ghost of air from Julia's lungs brushed against his shoulder. He put his hand on her waist. Julia's presence reminded him of his wife. He wondered what Clare was doing; whether there had been a letter waiting in Cape Town; whether he would survive... Whether Clare would care...

Very soon he slept.

13

SACLANT (Supreme Allied Commander Atlantic (NATO)
The wartime task of SACLANT is to ensure the security of the whole Atlantic area and to deny its use to an enemy.

The matter was sufficiently urgent for Admiral Brandon Pearson, SACLANT, to be flown in his Hustler bomber direct from his headquarters in Norfolk, Virginia, to the Anti-Submarine Warfare Research Center at La Spezia in northwest Italy.

He and his aide, Captain Rolf Hagan of the Marine Corps, were taken straight to the submarine "signature" library and played a sonar recording that had been made by the U.S. Navy oceanographic research ship *Eureka* at a range of seven hundred miles. Computer analysis showed that the "signature"—the sound fingerprint—of the mysterious submarine matched recordings that had been made in the Soviet Navy's trials area in the White Sea. It was conclusive proof that one of the Russian's monster eighteen-thousand ton Delta Two class nuclear submarines was loose in the South Atlantic.

Pearson chewed on a cigar as he listened to the various experts arguing about Soviet reasons for sending their latest piece of largely untested nastiness into his patch of ocean. He was a broad, powerful man in his late fifties with a relaxed easygoing air that inspired confidence. He was tough, resourceful and efficient. Apart from his qualities of leadership, he had an uncanny insight into the Soviet mind, acquired when he was junior liaison officer in Moscow during the closing stages of the Second World War. He could also speak fluent Russian.

He was worried. He couldn't think of one good reason for the Russians to send a Delta Two into the Atlantic. What was the point when its SS-N-8 missiles had the range to wipe out every North American city without the submarine having to stray from home waters? Why risk an untried weapon such as the Delta Two where it was far from help if an emergency arose?

Hagan read his thoughts. It was something the captain was getting good at. "Maybe it's a provocation probe, sir?"

Pearson shook his head. "They use their old Novembers for that so that they alarm the press and not the Pentagon."

Something else was worrying him: the submarine had been heard in the same area that the *Orion* had gone down in. He bit on his cigar and summed up with a six-word sentence that made up in conciseness what it lacked in finesse: "Those bastards are up to something."

14

SARAH (Search And Rescue And Homing)
A buoyant, self-righting, automatic radio transmitter that broadcasts a continuous homing signal on the international distress frequency 2182. Standard equipment in lifeboats, life rafts and the like.

Pale daylight was filtering through the life raft's cover when Sherwood woke. There was no sensation in his body; he was paralyzed with the murderous cold that had clawed its way through the insulated floor and was now gnawing into his vitals.

He could feel nothing except that the raft was now still.

The danger point is reached when you no longer feel the cold.

He fought his protesting brain into full wakefulness.

Julia's face was the color of death. Her mouth was open but she didn't seem to be breathing.

"She die soon," said Oaf's voice.

Julia's deathly appearance frightened Sherwood badly.

He eased his body away from her and placed his hand on the now gray skin beneath her breasts. There was an almost inperceptible movement as her lungs gradually filled.

Sherwood gently lifted an eyelid. The gray lusterless eye stared at him accusingly.

You killed me. You let me fall because of your stupid masculine ego and you killed me.

Oaf was dressed. He knelt beside Julia. "She die soon," he repeated. "Big pity, Sherwood. Kid good screw."

Rage welled up inside Sherwood at the Norwegian's words. He looked up into the deep-set blue eyes under their shaggy brows and was about to say something scathing, but Oaf sensed his anger and said quickly: "I only screw her, Sherwood. You dropped her."

Sherwood said nothing. He tucked the blankets round Julia's cold body and got dressed.

"How long have I been asleep?"

"Three hours, Sherwood."

"For God's sake, Oaf, there must be something we can do for her. We can't just sit and watch her die."

Oaf shrugged. "No heat. She need heat bad."

"Well, Christ—we could burn some wreckage or something!"

"No wreckage," said Oaf simply.

"The sun, you idiot!"

"No sun."

Sherwood reached up to the roof zip.

"You let heat escape," Oaf commented.

Sherwood ignored him, pulled the zip open, and stood up.

Oaf was right; there was no sun. Only a thick, cloying fog. So thick that it didn't even swirl. Visibility was less than four yards. The honey-colored water was strangely still and silent.

There's always an ocean swell.

"What the hell are we going to do, Oaf?" asked Sherwood despairingly.

"I've set the SARAH," said Oaf. He stood beside Sherwood and pointed to the little floating radio transmitter that was tethered to the life raft by a cord. "Like goddamn fools we forget it. Someone hear it soon maybe."

"I wonder how far we are from the *Orion*?"

"We come a good way north in the storm," said Oaf.

"Nothing makes sense," said Sherwood, staring down at the water. "The water temperature; this yellow stuff, whatever it is. And now fog and no swell."

Oaf spat. "Men make rules for the sea, Sherwood. And sea always breaking them, heh?"

There was a strange noise from the depths of the fog. A whistling sound like the breathing of an unimaginable sea monster. Sherwood felt the hair prickling on the back his scalp.

"What the hell's that?"

The noise was repeated: a flesh-crawling half-moaning, half-sighing that made Sherwood's chilled blood run even colder. Then there were a series of heavy splashes that seemed to get louder—as if some malignant creature of the depths were swimming toward them with long, purposeful strokes. Ripples were spreading out of the freezing fog from the direction of the terrifying sound. The life raft began to rock with a rhythm that quickened with Sherwood's heartbeat. Oaf's razor-sharp whaler's knife had appeared in his gnarled, hamlike fist.

But Sherwood knew that it would be useless

against the thing that was coming for them from the fog.

15

TAT 12 (Transatlantic Telephone cable)
4000-channel voice highway linking South Africa and the United States. Same cable pattern as used in the United States—France TAT 6.

The *New York Times* sub-editor watched the story unfolding on the teleprinter.

...FOG STILL MAKING IT IMPOSSIBLE FOR HELICOPTER CRUISER SPRINGBOK TO OPERATE ITS WASP HELICOPTERS IN THE SEARCH FOR ORION SURVIVORS. SOUTH AFRICAN WEATHER EXPERTS BAFFLED BY THE PERSISTENCE AND DENSITY OF THE FOG WHICH IS NOW COVERING TEN THOUSAND—REPEAT—TEN THOUSAND SQUARE MILES OF OCEAN IN THE DISASTER AREA. SOUTH AFRICAN PREMIER TODAY DESCRIBED ORION LOSS AS WORST PEACETIME MARITIME DISASTER SINCE TITANIC. A SPOKESMAN FOR THE

The teleprinter stopped abruptly in mid-sentence.

At the same time, all over the United States, all telephone conversations with South Africa were cut without warning, leaving thousands of angry subscribers on both sides of the Atlantic shouting uselessly into their phones.

Ten minutes later, the telegraph cable was also cut.

Frantic engineers in Cape Town and New York carried out resistance tests on their respective ends of both cables and established that the breaks had inexplicably occurred in the three-mile-deep Cape Basin off South West Africa. It was baffling because oceanic cables are usually safe, lying in dark tranquillity on the abyssal floors of the oceans. Only where they are exposed to trawls and the tides in the shallow coastal waters over the continental shelves are they likely to suffer damage.

Even more extraordinary was the fact that the cables had been cut in approximately the same position from which the *Orion* had broadcast her distress calls.

16

"Shut up, Sherwood!" Oaf hissed. "You shut up so I listen!"

Sherwood fell silent. He felt a bitter resentment for the way the big Norwegian had automatically assumed command.

Oaf listened intently to the deadened, eerie noises coming out of the fog. He swore suddenly, jammed the long whaler's knife back into its sheath and thrust one of the folding paddles at his companion.

"Come on, Sherwood! We paddle like stink!"

It was an order Sherwood was more than willing to obey. He snatched the paddle from Oaf and drove it into the water. Fear gave him strength. He spun the life raft round.

"That way!" yelled Oaf, jabbing a huge finger in the direction of the sound and arresting the life raft's motion with his own paddle.

Sherwood stared at him. "Are you crazy?"

Oaf ignored him, swung his paddle into the water and propelled the life raft through the water with effortless sweeps. "Come on, you lazy shit, Sherwood! Paddle like stink!" He suddenly grabbed Sherwood by the shoulder and held his paddle up in a threatening gesture. "You paddle like stink or I kill you!"

Sherwood did as he was told and started paddling, letting Oaf do the steering.

The hideous noise drew nearer.

A minute of arm-breaking effort passed. Oaf signaled to Sherwood to stop paddling. The big Norwegian strained his sensitive ears into the fog, turning his head to the left and right to get a bearing. The noises were louder and the ripples had become small waves.

"How far?" whispered Sherwood. How far to what?

"Fog play trick," answered Oaf. "But pretty near maybe. Paddle."

Sherwood paddled. He glanced down at Julia. Her face was changing from its deathly white to an ashen gray. He was certain that she was now dead.

The terrifying breathing noise was less than twenty yards away. Then there was a sudden explosive hiss that sounded like superheated steam escaping from a safety valve. It was followed by the sound of rain. Warm spray blew in Sherwood's face. He paddled without thinking. He was reaching the point where he no longer cared very much what happened to him.

There was a tremendous splash. A second later the life raft was nearly turned over in the maddened turmoil of enraged water.

Sherwood was thrown across Julia's body. He heard Oaf screaming: "Paddle back! Paddle back!"

The life raft span round as Oaf frantically back-paddled.

Then Sherwood saw it: a ghastly double-headed specter of childhood nightmares rearing into the fog. For a terrifying second it was poised high against the fog-diffused daylight. Despite his fear, Sherwood's scientific instincts asserted themselves: he estimated that the two heads spanned at least sixteen feet. Oaf was yelling at the top of his voice but Sherwood was too transfixed by the apparition to heed what the Norwegian was saying.

There was a savage hissing. The two heads swooped down and smashed into the water. As Sherwood fought to remain in the bucking life raft, he suddenly realized what the apparition was.

The twin flukes of a blue whale's tail.

"We get down the side of him!" Oaf was shouting.

The life raft circled clear of the giant mammal's tail as Oaf drove his paddle through the water.

"Why get near the bloody thing at all?" Sherwood shouted.

Oaf didn't answer. He steered the life raft alongside the creature's fluted flank. Sherwood was convinced that the Norwegian was crazy. He knew that Oaf had seen many whales close-to during his days as a whale catcher and lemmer so why risk going near this animal when it might sound at any moment?

"Him near dead," said Oaf as if he were reading Sherwood's thoughts.

The tail rose again. The motion was sluggish.

"How do you know?"

"He's beached," said Oaf. "His own weight crushing him so he can't breathe properly."

"You mean, we're in shallow water?" asked Sherwood incredulously.

Oaf pointed at the whale's curving hulk, which looked like an overturned ship. "Lot of him out of the water. He's beached okay."

Air blasted out of the creature's blow hole. Sherwood felt an eddy of warm, fetid air on his face. The smell was appalling. He was nearly sick.

"How the hell can we be in shallow water?"

Oaf shrugged. "You're the scientist, Sherwood." The Norwegian jerked the aluminum roof-support tube out of its mountings and examined it critically, flexing it to test its strength.

The life raft drifted near the creature's absurdly

small eye, which was gazing uninterestedly at Sherwood. Oaf steadied himself by resting one hand on the whale's side while gripping the aluminum tube with the other hand. With one swift movement, he drove the makeshift harpoon into the whale's eye. He then placed his palm on the end of the tube and rammed the entire five-foot length deep into the creature's body and held it there.

Nothing happened for some seconds; perhaps the whale was already on the point of death. Then, with graceful slowness, the tail lifted high into the fog, and instead of slamming down on the water, gently lowered itself so that there was scarcely a ripple.

"Dead now," said Oaf unnecessarily. Without waiting for an answer, he jumped onto the whale's back, produced his flensing knife, and started to work the blade into the thick blubber.

Sherwood watched, transfixed. "Do you think you'll be able to eat it all, Oaf?"

"Tie raft to harpoon," the Norwegian grunted.

Sherwood did so. "Now what?"

"Get girl up here bloody quick."

"Why, for Christ's safe?"

Oaf didn't pause in his work. He pushed a hand deep into the mountainous corpse. "Do it."

Sherwood tried to be gentle as he dragged Julia's lifeless body to the side of the raft and propped her up. The blanket fell away. He tried to push it back into place.

"Don't need blanket," said Oaf. He reached down with one blood-covered hand and grasped Julia under the armpit.

The two men lifted her frozen naked body onto the whale's back.

"Need paddles and a life jacket," said Oaf, pointing into the life raft.

Sherwood passed them up. Oaf took them and held out his hand. "Need help," he said.

Sherwood grasped the hand, which was slippery with whale blood, and allowed himself to be hauled onto the whale's back beside Julia.

Oaf went back to work on the two-foot-square section of blubber he was hacking off the corpse. Sherwood watched in fascination as the Norwegian's swift knife strokes sliced through the tissue. Oaf gestured.

"Get hold and pull."

Sherwood helped tear the section of thick blubber clear. The underside felt pleasantly warm in his frozen fingers. He began to understand what Oaf was planning. The knife went down into the flesh, releasing a strong, sickly odor and clouds of steam as the cold fog combined with the warm air rising from the wound. Oaf made a long cut and wedged it open with one of the paddles. Sherwood did the same with the other paddle. Life-giving heat poured out from the interior of the dead whale through the gaping incision in its body.

Oaf took a deep breath and pushed himself head first into the whale, holding his knife above his head. There was a heavy gurgling noise. Oaf wriggled backward out of the hole. The upper half of his body was covered with the hot, thick blood from the severed artery that was filling the gaping wound like a cistern.

The Norwegian wiped the blood away from his eyes and pointed at the life jacket.

"So she don't slip down too deep. Fix it round her tits."

Sherwood tied the life jacket round Julia's chest and the two men lowered her body feet first into the bath of hot, steaming blood until she was immersed to her neck. Oaf eased the paddles out so that the sides of the incision closed on Julia and held her firmly.

"Many years ago," said Oaf as he splashed the blood out of his hair with icy sea water, "a man try walking on grease ice and he go through. We fish him out half dead like girl. We shoot a sea elephant, slit belly open, and put man inside." Oaf grinned. "Two hours later he was walking about again but he stink terrible for weeks."

Sherwood sat down on the whale's back. He hadn't realized until now just how exhausted he was.

"You ought to take over the Rosenthal survival course, Oaf."

Oaf spat into the sea. "Them old women never been outside London."

Sherwood watched Julia's face. It was serene. "Will she live?"

"We know in an hour. Maybe more. Maybe less."

It was less.

To the delight of the two men, color was returning to Julia's face after thirty minutes.

Fifty minutes after she had been placed in the whale, with the strengthening sun dispersing the fog, Sherwood realized that Julia's eyes were open. She was watching him with a quizzical expression. The life jacket under her chin restricted her vision; all she could see was the sky. Her voice when she spoke was sweet music: "Hallo, Mr. Sherwood. Where am I?"

Sherwood stared at her. "Oaf!" he yelled. "Oaf!"

The Norwegian scrambled out of the life raft onto the whale's back and knelt beside Julia. He kissed her, placing his huge arm around her head. Sherwood turned away, leaving them to talk. He wondered how Oaf would tell her about the whale. Jealousy was an emotion he had no experience of. He climbed back into the life raft. Oaf had been cleaning the aluminum tube he had used as a harpoon. Sherwood reached down into the water with it. The end of the tube struck the sea bed before the icy water had reached his shoulder. He forgot his jealousy of the moment as he pondered the phenomenon of such shallow water in the Cape Basin. Although the bottom felt like rock through the aluminum tube, he twisted it back and forth in the hope of obtaining a sample.

There was the distant beat of an engine. Oaf

started dancing up and down on the whale's back, waving the bright yellow folding paddles like semaphore flags.

Sherwood looked up. The fog was clearing rapidly. Silhouetted against the pale sky, with its absurd undercarriage resembling the wheels of a tea trolley, was an anti-submarine Wasp helicopter with Royal Navy markings. It was losing height as it homed in on the automatic radio signals from the life raft's SARAH beacon.

It was within two hundred yards when Sherwood remembered to look at the end of the tube he had ground into the sea bed. His breath was melting the curious off-white, powdery substance. He stared at it. Several seconds passed before he realized what it was.

Ice.

17

The ITN news presenter adopted a grave expression as he replaced his phone.

"We've just heard," he told the television camera and fifteen million people throughout the United Kingdom, "that three more survivors from the *Orion* have been found today by a helicopter from the British frigate *Snow Tiger* that is helping the South African navy in the search and rescue operation...."

Admiral Howe dozed in front of his television. The news presenter's voice washed over him. He was exhausted after a long day in his Whitehall office. The room was its usual mess.

"... the three—Julia Hammond, a marine biologist from South London; Glen Sherwood, a geologist from Kingston-upon-Thames; and Oluf Johansen, a

Norwegian engineer—were returning to Southampton after a three-year tour of duty with the Rosenthal survey team in Antarctica...."

Admiral Howe was suddenly awake at the mention of the Rosenthal Base and paying close attention to the rest of the news presenter's words. Mention of Rosenthal by the media always made him nervous.

"The extremely high death toll is due to the exceptionally low temperature of the water. South African oceanographers have admitted to being baffled by the icy sea, which is only one degree above freezing...."

The last sentence stunned the old sailor. It's not possible, he reasoned. Not after seven months.

Then he remembered just how much ice was missing. His arthritic hand shook as he dialed Lieutenant Abbott's number.

"And now for the rest of the news...."

But Admiral Howe wasn't interested in the rest of the news.

18

George Fielding, a normally easygoing retired bank president from Houston, was beginning to get irritated by the South African naval officer questioning him politely in the *Springbok*'s sickbay as the cruiser headed for Simonstown.

"Look," said Fielding. "Let's take it from the top again. Shortly after midnight I went up on the weather deck for air. It was closed to passengers but I stepped over the rope."

"Wasn't it cold, sir? The *Orion* was doing thirty-seven knots."

"Chilly," said Fielding. "But I didn't pay much attention."

"And you saw this white track in the water at thirty minutes after midnight?"

"Torpedo track," Fielding corrected.

The naval officer sighed.

"Just before the ship was blown apart," Fielding finished.

"Sir," said the naval officer earnestly. "I want you to think very carefully. Are you absolutely certain it was a torpedo track you saw?"

"Yes," said Fielding without hesitation. He had said the first time that he had seen a torpedo track and he wasn't a man to change his mind once he had made it up. Maybe the white pattern that had flashed on the surface for a few seconds had been irregular but he had read somewhere that modern torpedoes didn't have to run straight—they weaved about as they homed in on their target. *Time* magazine had run an article on them: that was good enough for George Fielding.

"Did you see bubbles from this...this torpedo track, sir?"

The banker stared at the naval officer. "Hell, no. Since when did modern torpedoes use compressed air?"

It was the naval officer's turn to stare. He looked at Fielding in surprise.

"I know what a cavitation track looks like," Fielding stated stubbornly. "I was on the old *Nevada* in Pearl Harbor."

The naval officer was desperate. It was vital to convince the elderly businessman that he could be wrong. In twenty hours the *Springbok* would be docking. Simonstown was swarming with journalists from all over the world, eager to interview the *Orion*'s survivors.

"Look, Mr. Fielding, you *must* be mistaken. Why would anyone want to torpedo the *Orion*?"

"I saw a tinfish," Fielding insisted. "And if it wasn't a torpedo exploding outside the *Orion*'s hull, how is it that that pod of whales were thrashing

73

about half-stunned on the surface smashing up all the lifeboats except ours?"

The naval officer was writing up his report an hour later in the wardroom when his commanding officer walked in and sank wearily into a chair. He looked across at the officer.

"I've just been talking to that Japanese shirt manufacturer. He was on the port weather deck at the time. You'll never guess what his crazy theory is about the sinking."

"That the *Orion* was torpedoed?" ventured the officer.

The captain gaped at his subordinate.

"Yours said the same?"

The officer nodded unhappily.

"Hell," breathed the commanding officer.

19

It was the first time that the press officer had a written statement to read to the sweating journalists packed into the suffocating conference room at Simonstown. Hitherto, the press conferences had been informed question-and-answer sessions.

He held a sheet of paper in his hand and waited for the snap of camera shutters to die away. He had never bothered before. The room quieted. There was only the soft whir of movie cameras as he spoke.

"It was decided at ten this morning to extend the search and rescue operation by another seventy-two hours—until the same time on Wednesday. The number of survivors still stands at twenty-three. Twenty on the *Springbok* and three on the British frigate *Snow Tiger*. Both ships have excellent hospital facilities so that the survivors can remain aboard until the search is called off."

There was a loud groan from all the journalists.

"Does that mean we won't be able to see them for three days?" demanded a Canadian.

"Yes," said the press officer.

"Supposing we charter a helicopter? Will we be able to land on the *Springbok* or the *Snow Tiger*?"

The press officer smiled self-effacingly. "I'm very sorry, ladies and gentlemen, but the helicopter-handling facilities on both ships are fully committed to their own machines during the search."

The answer was too glib. Journalists always get suspicious when they think they're being frozen off a story.

Ralph Kroll of CBS News had a question: "What search, Mr. Stevasson?"

The press officer looked surprised. "I don't understand your question, Mr. Kroll."

The cameras swung toward Kroll.

"Forgive me, Mr. Stevasson," said Kroll, pinning his victim down with thirty years' experience in dealing with officials, "but I was under the impression that no actual searching was involved—that your choppers had only to home in on the lifeboat beacons."

The press officer hesitated. His mind raced. "There might be people in the water," he pointed out.

Kroll nodded. "Dead from exposure like the seven hundred bodies that you've recovered so far?"

The press officer smiled. "And there's the possibility that there's a lifeboat somewhere whose occupants haven't switched on their beacon because they don't know what it is."

"There is that possibility, of course," Kroll admitted. "Even if the operating instructions are etched on each beacon in eight languages, including Chinese and Japanese."

"We can't take chances with people's lives," said the press officer evenly.

Kroll made a note and then looked up at the press officer with a puzzled expression.

"Is there any connection between the loss of the *Orion* and the arrival of the NATO Supreme Allied Commander Atlantic here in Simonstown?"

There was a stir in the room. The journalists looked gratefully at Kroll.

"I have no information," said the press officer, glancing at his watch.

Kroll's innocent blue eyes opened wide. "Maybe I can enlighten you then, Mr. Stevasson; his Hustler is right here on the Simonstown airbase. I recognized its tail markings. Everywhere that Hustler goes, Admiral Brandon Pearson goes too. Perhaps you'd be good enough to tell us why he's here—save all these ladies and gentlemen having to file home a lot of speculative copy."

The press officer's reply was tinged with hostility. "I have no information."

The sleepy blue eyes remained fixed on him. "And I guess that goes for news about my colleague whose plane has disappeared?"

"I'm sorry. I have no information."

Kroll maintained his innocent expression. "Would you care to comment on the rumor that a helicopter of the South African Navy spotted the wreckage of a light airplane on the water and recovered a body? A body clutching a movie camera?"

"I have no information," the press officer repeated doggedly.

No one in the room believed him.

20

The tourists were pressed six deep against the railings of Buckingham Palace, watching the changing of the guard. Lieutenant Abbott accelerated past a laden coach. Admiral Howe was deep in thought at his side, paying little attention to Abbott's conversation.

"I keep thinking of this seven-month period between the loss of the submarine and the sinking of the *Orion*," said Abbott. "I don't see how the ice could've been the cause. It just doesn't seem possible."

"You heard those experts," muttered Howe, rousing himself.

"But they wouldn't commit themselves, sir."

"Do they ever?"

The two men fell silent. Abbott concentrated on his driving. Admiral Howe spoke first.

"It's lucky those three Rosenthal survivors are on one of our ships."

Abbott turned his head. "What does it matter what ship they're on, sir? They don't know anything about the depot."

"No. They don't know anything. But I don't like the idea of Rosenthal personnel being subjected to press probing and publicity."

"But none of the survivors have seen anything unusual, sir."

"We've only the South Africans' word for that. Our three survivors are trained observers, and one of them, the girl, is an oceanographer. I don't want them talking to the press—not newshounds of the caliber that the agencies have sent to Simonstown."

"Then how do you propose to stop them, sir?"

"We need time on this operation, James."

"But how can we stop them talking to the press?" Abbott persisted.

Admiral Howe considered for some moments. "We'll have to think of something, James."

21

Pearson and Hagan recognized the face of the dead CBS News cameraman as soon as the cover was pulled back.

"Yes, I know him," said Pearson. "I know most of them by sight. You didn't drag me here just to identify a body, Mr. Differing?"

"No, admiral." The South African Defense Minister waited for the naval doctor to move away. "You know, this guy was hanging on to his camera so tight that the doctors who examined his body had to break two of his fingers. Now we know why. Film was ruined by sea water getting into the magazine through the core but there's four meters at the end which maybe will make your flight worthwhile."

The South African spoke quickly. Hard Cape Town vowels. He ushered his visitors to the door. "They've shown me how to use the projector in the lecture hall."

"Holy cow," Pearson muttered to himself in the darkness.

"My sentiments exactly," said Differing.

There was an eighteen-thousand-ton Soviet Delta on the screen. The picture was so vivid, so compelling, that Pearson had no difficulty in imagining the surging roar of breaking water as the mighty submarine drove its massive bullet-shaped bow contemptuously through the heaving yellow sea. Its sheer physical presence breathed icy life into the time-worn, half-forgotten phrases coined during the uneasy fifties and sixties: Megadeath...Overkill...Flash zone...Primary fire zone...

The picture zoomed in on two men on the slender

fin. One was pointing a tubular device up at the approaching camera.

"A Soviet Grail shoulder-launched anti-aircraft missile," said Differing. "Watch carefully."

There was a bright flash from the two men standing on the submarine's fin. Differing slowed the projector down. A series of clicks punctuated each frame change. A pencil-slim, flaring rocket jerked up toward the camera. The screen went blank.

Pearson broke the silence that followed when Differing had restored the lights. "Why in hell didn't it dive before the airplane got close? They've got over-horizon radar facilities."

"Simple," said the South African. "Our guess is that it was towing several thousand meters of hawser with a telephone cable cutter on the end."

Pearson lit a cigar. "And they'd use their latest and largest submarine?"

"Sure. Six miles of hawser takes up space."

"It's a pity that the clip didn't show the sub's stern," said Pearson pointedly.

Differing smiled thinly. "You can have the original film back, admiral. Your own experts will confirm that it was damaged by sea water. The only thing we can't account for is the unusual color of the sea. It's not a color processing fault. We were careful."

Pearson thought for a few moments. "You've interviewed *all* the *Orion* survivors?"

"Except three scientists returning from Antarctica. The British frigate *Snow Tiger* picked them up. They'll be in Simonstown tomorrow."

"I want to talk to *all* the *Orion* survivors before drawing conclusions such as you've drawn, Mr. Differing."

Differing looked pained. "We're going on the eye-witness accounts of two reliable people, admiral. One of them is a fellow citizen of yours who knows all about being torpedoed. And the survivors who didn't see the torpedo tracks will tell you all about the pod of whales that were struggling on the surface, smashing up lifeboats. It's obvious that the explosion occurred outside the *Orion's* hull."

"What about the freezing water, Mr. Differing? You have a neat theory for that as well?"

The South African shrugged. "Freak conditions, admiral."

Pearson inhaled deeply on his cigar, carefully choosing his words. "Assuming the Soviets did sink the *Orion*, have you asked yourself why they should do such a senseless thing?"

"There was the sinking of the *Athenia* on the first day of the last war," said Differing. He paused before adding in an expressionless voice: "It seems to be the modern way of starting them these days."

22

Reduced to unparaphrased plaintext, the signal printed out on the British frigate's secure-channel data-link line-printer read:

ACQ LONDON TO COMMANDER LEYSDOWN, SNOW TIGER. CONGRATULATIONS YOUR RESCUE ROSENTHAL PERSONNEL. IMPORTANT THEY HAVE NO CONTACT PRESS OR PUBLIC. DO NOT RETURN SIMONSTOWN. LT. JAMES ABBOTT ON WAY TO YOU TO ADVISE. REMAIN ON PICKET.

23

"Ice?" exclaimed Julia. She would have laughed but Sherwood was serious. "Are you sure?"

"I know what ice looks like," Sherwood answered.

"Even inside a roof support tube?"

Sherwood refused to reply. Julia didn't blame him. As a scientist, Sherwood wouldn't make claims unless he was sure of his facts. She gazed pensively down at wake foaming out from under the *Snow Tiger*'s transom, carefully studying the frigate's dancing shadow on the broken water. She apologized but Sherwood quickly brushed it aside.

"I want to say sorry to you," he said.

"What for?"

"For dropping you into the water. It was childish of me not letting you try to climb down that rope."

Julia laughed to ease his embarrassment. "Forget it. I've been dropped by men before. I don't suppose it'll be the last time. And no permanent damage has been done. As a matter of fact, the ship's surgeon paid me a dubious compliment by saying that I'm as strong as a horse."

Sherwood laughed. "Some horse."

Julia didn't seem to hear him; she was screwing up her eyes to look at the sun. "Have you told anyone else about the ice?" she asked.

"No."

She returned her attention to Sherwood. "Why not?"

"I didn't think anyone would believe me."

"Then why tell me?"

"I thought that you might be able to offer some sort of explanation. I'm damned if I can come up with one."

Julia thought for a few seconds, then glanced up at the sun again. "*If* it was ice, it doesn't make sense. Maybe it was ice from the *Orion*? Wait a minute—what about your core samples in the liner's refrigeration hold? They ran into several tons of ice, didn't they?"

"Yes, but—"

"There's your answer—some submerged wreckage from the *Orion* with some of your ice cores must've

81

drifted with the life raft and you stuck the life raft's roof support tube in one of them. Simple. Say thank you."

"I suppose that is a possible explanation," Sherwood conceded.

"You should be grateful to me for setting your mind at rest," said Julia, grinning.

"But it doesn't explain the unusual color of the sea or its near freezing temperature."

"I'll give you a real mystery to ponder on," said Julia. "Ask yourself why this remnant of our once glorious navy turns a few degrees to port every thirty minutes so that we're steaming in a huge circle."

Puzzled, Sherwood looked up at the sun.

It was in the wrong place.

24

NORAD—North American Air Defense Command
Joint U.S.-Canadian organization to defend the North American continent against surprise attack from over the polar regions.

Admiral Brandon Pearson was furious. Captain Hagan was the nearest to receive his wrath. It was virtually unheard-of for a NATO country to invoke the "urgent national business" clause to pull out a ship without prior notification.

"No explanation?" he barked.

"No, sir."

"You told Northwood that I want to talk to those three survivors they've got on the *Snow Tiger*?"

"Yes, sir. They said that they're very sorry, but the *Snow Tiger* is unable to return to South Africa at the moment."

Pearson grunted. "Trouble from their goddamn left, I suppose. Okay. Fix me a chopper—I'll fly out to the *Snow Tiger* myself."

Hagan hesitated. "Before you do, sir, I think you ought to look at this signal from the *Johnson*." He held out a buff signal envelope. "The carrier has reported that ten bottom-fixed sonobuoys in the South Atlantic Seaguard barrier have ceased functioning. They suggest using one of NORAD's magnetic anomaly detector 707s to plug the gap until new sonobuoys can be dropped into position."

Pearson spun round quickly, his face shocked. "*Ten* buoys?"

Hagan nodded. "That's what I thought. Maybe the Soviet sub wasn't just cutting telephone cables."

Pearson thought quickly. The Soviets *were* cooking something. Something big. Something that made his flesh crawl. Ten buoys! That meant there was a gap in the barrier that the entire Soviet Navy could sail through undetected. He started firing orders.

"I'm going straight out to the *Johnson* now. Tell them I want their strike command combat control center in a go condition by the time I arrive and the conference-secure satellite channels to Washington, Norfolk, Mons, and Northwood checked out and cleared for immediate operational use. I also want all SSBN set to AQ readiness. After that, you're to fly out to the *Snow Tiger* and talk to those three *Orion* survivors—you know the sort of questions I want asked. That is all."

Hagan was dismissed. He saluted and left.

Outside the office he collected his reeling thoughts. In sounding general stations throughout his command, the admiral was calling an Alert.

A low-key, unendorsed Alert maybe.

But still an Alert.

25

SILENT RUNNING
A condition aboard a submerged submarine in which machinery noise and crew movement are kept to a minimum to avoid detection by passive sonar.

The *Podorny* was running blind at a depth of three hundred meters when she collided with the frozen cliff beneath the sea.

There was no warning; her forward scan sonar had been switched off to reduce noise. Her off-watch crew, under severe movement restriction, were watching a movie in the forward missile room and listening to the sound track through headphones.

They died immediately—crushed into instant oblivion by the cataclysmic inrush of the Atlantic as the *Podorny*'s unstoppable eighteen-thousand ton momentum split the submarine like a self-opening sardine can.

At the moment of impact, Commander Igor Leachinski was radioing the *Podorny*'s position to Sevastopol through a surface-trailed antenna wire. The sudden deceleration threw him against the communications room bulkhead. And then the countless tons of water were upon him, driving the breath from his lungs and the life from his body in one devastating blow that swept through the length of the submarine in less than three seconds.

The concertinaed remains of the *Podorny* hovered for timeless, silent moments against the edifice that had completely destroyed it. Then, with seemingly infinite care, they grated down the face of the submerged cliff on the first stage of their three-mile last voyage to the abyssal floor of the Angolan Basin in the South Atlantic.

Thousands of irregular headstones of every conceivable size came bobbing to the surface, marking the *Podorny*'s grave. They twisted and jostled in the long, easy swell.

Then they began to melt.

Ice.

26

The British frigate *Snow Tiger* made another of her imperceptible alterations of course as Julia sat in the vacant chair between Oaf and Sherwood. Oaf was sound asleep and snoring. The afternoon sun was warm and agreeable. Sherwood looked inquiringly at Julia as she made herself comfortable.

"Did you see the captain?" he asked.

"Yes. He said that they're searching for an *Orion* life raft that's been seen in this area by a scheduled SAA flight. I asked him why none of the men on watch were using binoculars and he said that their radar was more sensitive. He's not certain when we'll get to Simonstown."

Sherwood glanced at the *Snow Tiger*'s deserted helicopter deck. "Is that what the Wasp is doing—out searching?"

Julia shrugged. "How should I know?"

"It's odd."

"What?"

"That helicopter's been gone since this morning— at least twelve hours. As its duration is two and a half hours it must've landed somewhere. Why didn't it take us with it?"

Julia shaded her eyes and stared at the horizon. "Talk of the devil..." she murmured.

They watched the distant black dot that was swelling against the blue background.

"I know what caused your yellow sea," said Julia casually.

"Oh?"

"Ostracods."

"Now why didn't I think of that? What are they?"

The dot became the unwieldy shape of a Wasp helicopter.

"They're microscopic organisms that live at depths of two to three thousand meters. A sudden change in the sea temperature kills them and they come to the surface in their countless millions and turn the sea a muddy yellow color. I remember reading about a nine-day press wonder when the liner *Corinthic* steamed for several days through a sea of honey. It must have been ostracods."

The Wasp approached the *Snow Tiger* from astern.

"What sort of temperature change?" Sherwood persisted. "An increase or a decrease?"

"Either." Julia had to raise her voice to make herself heard above the uproar from the helicopter turbines.

Oaf stirred in his sleep but amazingly failed to wake.

Sherwood was too preoccupied to pay any attention to the Wasp as it lowered itself onto the helicopter platform.

He was thinking about ice.

27

From: Minister of Defense, Chairman of Military Council.
To: All First Deputy and Deputy Ministers of Defense.

Subject: The loss of the submarine *Podorny*.

Instructions are to be issued to Admiral Turgenev, Commander-in-Chief, Black Sea Fleet, that the recovery of the *Podorny* is *absolutely vital* irrespective of cost or the undoubted difficulty. There must be no repetition of the *Glomar Explorer** incident we experienced when Howard Hughes and his CIA minions stole one of our submarines. The Black Sea Fleet has the deep ocean recovery vessels and the necessary heavy surface units to establish a significant naval presence in the area where the *Podorny* went down. Such a presence will be essential to deter over-inquisitiveness by American-controlled NATO forces who consider the Atlantic their own territory.

Once the recovery task force is in position, the Americans will guess immediately what has happened and will watch carefully for a chance to recover the submarine themselves. For that reason, the salvage vessels *must* be provided with *continuous* protection and logistic support.

Admiral Turgenev is to be provided with all the facilities necessary to execute the recovery of the *Podorny*, including the authority to release our new Kiev-class carriers to assist in the provision of air cover.

Admiral Turgenev heaved a sigh of relief when he read his instructions—no blame for the use of the Delta submarine had been steered his way. Thank God he'd ensured a wide distribution of his memo to General Zadkin in which he had deplored the assignment of a Delta to the unknown waters of the South Atlantic.

With any luck, General Zadkin's star should now be on the wane in Moscow.

---

*Project Jennifer: the recovery by the CIA in June 1974 of a lost Soviet Golf-class submarine that had sunk in the Pacific.

28

Lieutenant James Abbott was wearing a civilian suit and an apologetic smile that he hadn't allowed to slacken for an instant since he had landed on the *Snow Tiger* an hour earlier. He was surprising himself with his acting ability. He introduced himself to Julia, Sherwood, and Oaf as the Rosenthal Foundation's new scientific establishment officer and quickly explained the purpose of his visit. As expected, the three survivors were incredulous.

"You want us to go back to Antarctica?" echoed Julia.

"That's right," said Abbott, smiling easily at all three in turn. "But only for a year. Until your replacements get the feel of your work. I was appalled when I discovered how inexperienced they were. A complete administrative foul-up, the whole thing. They didn't even hire an engineer to replace Mr. Johansen." Abbott smiled at Oaf. "At least, not an engineer with your experience of working in polar conditions, Mr. Johansen."

Oaf grunted.

"So we'd be extremely grateful if you'd return on the supply flight that'll be refueling in the Azores. The Navy has agreed to fly you there from the *Ark Royal*."

"When?" asked Sherwood. His voice didn't betray his excitement at the prospect of returning to Antarctica.

"Now," said Abbott, maintaining the smooth, friendly smile. "Naturally we'll increase your pay. Will thirty percent be okay? Should be a tidy sum in your accounts when you get back to England."

"I don't think I'll ever see a shop again," said Julia forlornly.

Captain Rolf Hagan's helicopter touched down on the *Snow Tiger* late that afternoon and was told that the three *Orion* survivors had left for the *Ark Royal*. He was also told that his helicopter couldn't be refueled because the supply pump to the platform deck had broken down and that repairs wouldn't be completed until the following day.

"Okay," said Hagan to the *Snow Tiger*'s first officer. "Maybe you'd refuel her with cans? I've got to get to the *Ark Royal* and then return to the *Johnson*."

The first officer was extremely apologetic. "I'm terribly sorry, old boy, but the captain's a fearful stickler over the rules about loose fuel on the platform." His tone became consolatory. "But he sends his compliments and says he'd be delighted if you'll be our guest of honor for the night. Unlike American ships, we do carry an excellent selection of liquid refreshment."

The offer appealed to Hagan's Irish instincts.

"We'll explain the situation to the *Johnson*," concluded the British officer with a dazzling smile.

Hagan had no alternative but to accept.

29

The President of the United States listened, grim-faced and silent, as the Defense Secretary summed up the growing list of Soviet provocations while his advisors sitting along each side of the conference table made notes.

"Item one—definite," said the Defense Secretary. "The Soviets move a flotilla of Delta Two SSBs into the Atlantic."

The Defense Secretary paused to polish his gold-rimmed spectacles. "Incidentally, Mr. President, those SSBN's now account for eighty-five percent of all submarine-borne ballistic missiles at sea."

No one commented. The Defense Secretary went back to his list.

"Item two—definite. They kill an American citizen—a CBS cameraman—with a surface-to-air missile. Item three—probable. They sink the United States-United Kingdom liner, the *Orion*. Item four—definite. They destroy a major section of the South Atlantic sonobuoy barrier. Item five—definite. They cut the United States to South Africa transatlantic telephone cable. And, as we've just heard, four more telegraph and telephone cables linking us with the African continent have also been cut in succession. And finally, item six—definite. The Soviets are working around the clock bringing their entire Black Sea fleet and auxiliary supply fleet to a condition of strike-readiness."

"Including their new Kiev carriers," added the President.

"Yes, Mr. President."

Everyone was silent. They had all said their piece.

It now remained for the President to make his decision.

"Admiral Pearson will be in Washington within the hour," the President stated. "Are we all in agreement with Professor Galland that the admiral is the best man for this task?"

There was a murmur of assent.

The President considered for a few moments before speaking again.

"Very well, gentlemen. We will adopt the professor's suggestion to first give the Soviets the chance to back down without losing face. There will be no issuing of dramatic statements to the press or appearances before the nation. Let us pray to Almighty God that the Soviets seize the opportunity we are offering. If they don't, and they continue with their present senseless course, then they will learn that the consequence of extreme and persistent provocation is that the time inevitably comes when we are provoked."

30

It was spring in Antarctica.

Sherwood sat at the rear of the RAF Hercules's unsoundproofed freight cabin staring down at the hummocked and rafted pack ice of the unending Weddell Sea. Julia and Oaf were playing their twentieth card game; there hadn't been much else to do during the long flight from Graham Land.

The low, returning sun cast long distorted shadows across the ridged ice field that never melted. So clear was the pollution-free atmosphere that it was impossible to judge whether the distant ice cliffs rising out of the sea ahead of the Hercules were five miles or fifty miles away.

"Beautiful, isn't it?"

Sherwood looked up, startled. Julia was sitting in the seat opposite.

"Glad to be back?" she asked.

"I don't know. I suppose so."

"Will your wife mind? You being away for another year?"

"No."

"I would—I'd probably divorce you."

"She has."

They both lapsed into silence and gazed out the window. The Hercules was nearer the soaring ice cliffs and taking a straight line across a vast bay. The bleak edges of the cliffs captured the northern sun and stood out with razored sharpness against the cold, blue sky. Immediately below the freighter the pack ice was disintegrating—honeycombing into regular slabs like the baked mud of a dried-up river bed.

"Rotten ice," commented Julia. "Bit early in the year for the pack ice to be breaking up, I would've thought."

Baffled, Sherwood could only nod as he stared down at the frozen sea.

Oaf joined them. "What do you make of that, heh, Sherwood? Field rotting early."

"Maybe it's a freak warm current?" said Sherwood.

Julia was skeptical. "This far inside the convergence?"

"Excuse me a minute." Sherwood rose and threaded his way through the narrow passage created through the crates of supplies destined for the Rosenthal Base. He opened the door leading to the flight deck.

Squadron Leader Merrick, the Hercules's captain, turned round in his seat and genially welcomed Sherwood to the "front office." The atmosphere on the flight deck was stifling—all the crew seemed to be smoking foul-smelling pipes.

"Top of descent checks start in thirty minutes if you're after a progress report," said Merrick, exhaling a cloud of smoke. He nodded to his co-pilot. "Paddy's been onto Rosenthal. They say the landing strip's in good condition so we should have a reasonable landing—no skidding halfway to the South Pole this time."

Sherwood laughed. "I've come to beg a small favor. We're flying over a large bay. Do you know if it's shown on your charts?"

"Our charts were drawn up for Captain Scott," said Merrick shortly. "They're pretty useless. We don't need them. Mike navigates with his inertials. Just as well really. He couldn't read a chart to save his life."

Mike was absorbed in an instrument check and refused to be baited.

"Could you draw me a radar map of the bay please? Nothing too elaborate—just an outline of the coast will be fine."

"No problem," said Mike, flipping switches below the radar screen on the navigator's panel.

The sparkling cliffs Sherwood could see ahead were reproduced as a glowing, irregular line on the radar screen.

"Intermediate range ought to do it," said Mike.

He twisted a knob and the entire bay appeared on the screen. It was a simple matter to place a piece of thin paper over the display and trace the coastline with a pencil.

"There you are," said Mike, handing the sheet of paper to Sherwood. "One map of the bay. It's roughly a hundred and eighty miles across by ninety miles deep. Isn't modern technology marvelous."

Sherwood thanked the navigator and agreed that it was.

Merrick jabbed the stem of his pipe down at the approaching cliffs. "Something odd down there. Lots of Sno-Cat tracks. Looks like it's been busier than Hyde Park Corner."

Sherwood followed the direction in which Merrick was pointing. The plateau along the top of the cliffs was scarred with the parallel herringbone marks that Sno-Cat grousers made.

"That's odd," said Sherwood. "We were never issued enough fuel to reach the coast. Brill had strict rules."

"Don't blame him," Merrick commented as he tapped out his pipe. "Sorry, old boy. Got to throw you out now. Top of descent in a few minutes."

Sherwood thanked the squadron leader and left the flight deck. He closed the door behind him and studied the map of the bay. It was triangular-shaped . . . 180 miles by 90 miles . . . 8,000 square miles of melting pack ice that had no right to be melting. The theory that had been pushing to the back of his mind ever since the *Orion* disaster, because it was such a crazy half-baked notion, began to assert itself again. Sherwood was annoyed with himself for even considering it. It was the sort of theory that could result in his reputation's being laughed into oblivion.

And yet, in a way that was almost too terrifying to contemplate without a sensation of sickness in the pit of his stomach, it was one of those improbable theories that fitted the equally improbable facts.

31

The two men met for a discreet lunch in the Rib Room of the Mayflower Hotel in Washington, D.C. They spent the three courses reminiscing in Russian about their wartime experiences. They also enjoyed the meal.

Admiral Pearson offered his guest a cigar after their coffee had been served and said: "How do you like Washington, Max?"

The other man sensed that his host was about to come to the point. "Anna likes it," he replied cautiously.

Admiral Pearson inhaled on his cigar as he considered his words. "Would it surprise you, Max, if I tell you that this meeting is at the request of the President?"

The Soviet official's face remained impassive. "Possibly," he conceded.

Pearson grinned at the understatement. "I want to talk to you about the Black Sea fleet buildup at Sevastopol, Max. I don't suppose you know anything about it, so I'll do the talking."

"Wait a minute," interrupted the Russian, his voice losing its friendliness. "I had to get the ambassador's permission to have this lunch with you."

"Of course," said Pearson.

"I was told not to discuss political or current military matters."

"You don't have to," Pearson replied. "What did your ambassador say about listening?"

The Russian shrugged.

Pearson stirred his coffee. "This is an informal meeting, Max, so that views can be informally exchanged."

Max smiled and shook his head. "What you really mean, Brandon, is so that the United States can make its own views known without having to commit itself in public. Correct?"

Pearson came straight to the point. "We have evidence that the cruise liner *Orion* was sunk by a Soviet submarine."

The Russian nearly choked. He stared at the admiral for a few seconds and then laughed. "No wonder you don't want to commit yourself in public if those are the sort of accusations you're throwing about."

"Furthermore," said Pearson, "we have irrefutable proof that one of your SSBN's, operating in the

95

South Atlantic, shot down a light aircraft and killed an American citizen." Pearson reached into his jacket pocket and slid a package across the table. "You can keep that, Max. It's a film of the incident, and the last few frames show the launching of one of your Grail missiles at the airplane the film was shot from."

The Russian opened his mouth to protest but Pearson silenced him by holding up his hand.

"Just hear me out, Max," said Pearson. He pointed to the package. "You'd better put that away."

Max pocketed the film and remained silent, waiting patiently while Pearson relit his cigar.

"There are a number of other provocative actions your country has carried out," said Pearson, dropping his match in the ashtray, "which I'm not prepared to discuss just yet."

"I've no idea what you're talking about," the Russian said sulkily.

Pearson smiled. "Sure you don't, Max. I'll list some of them for you: you're operating a fleet of Delta Twos in the Pacific and the South Atlantic; you're drafting in a lot of surface units into Sevastopol and bringing them to operational readiness, and fast."

"Maybe they're getting ready for an exercise," said Max, leaning back in his chair and regarding Admiral Pearson with hostility.

"You've recently unloaded in the neighborhood of six hundred thousand tons of war material at the deep-water ports of Maputo, Beira and Porto Amelia in Mozambique," continued Pearson. "Plus another half a million tons at Luanda in Angola. You've also built an airstrip outside Luanda which is long enough to handle your long-range Antonov transports, which you're already using for a squadron of Yak 28 interceptors."

Max shrugged but said nothing.

"We're not arguing about your presence in Africa," said Pearson. "If we did, you would say that you are there at the invitation of the Angolan and Mozambique governments." Pearson bit down on his cigar and clasped both hands together on the table. He leaned toward his guest. "What we're concerned about, Max, are those Kiev carriers at Sevastopol."

The Soviet official looked contemptuous. "Those *cruisers* are part of the planned strength of our Black Sea fleet, admiral. We've made no secret—"

"I don't give a shit what they are, Max," Pearson interrupted. "I'm telling you this—if one of those carriers, or any aircraft carrier for that matter, passes through the Bosphorus Straits and pokes its bow into the Sea of Marmara, we'll sink it."

The Russian's face went white. He carefully replaced his coffee cup on the saucer and stared at Pearson.

"You'll what?"

Admiral Pearson repeated his statement and sat back, watching his guest carefully. The Soviet official opened his mouth to speak, and shut it again. Pearson waited patiently for him to collect his thoughts. The Russian recovered quickly. He toyed idly with his napkin and said flatly: "As you well know, admiral, the Black Sea is landlocked and we have a right of access to the Mediterranean through the Bosphorus."

"Bullshit," Pearson observed dryly in English.

Max stood up. "Thank you for the lunch, admiral. It's a pity it's been spoilt for me by your afterdinner conversation."

"Sit down, Max," said Pearson crisply. "I'm not through. And I don't suppose for one minute that your ambassador will thank you if you go running back to him with half the story."

"If your government has anything to say," the Russian replied harshly, "he can always be summoned to the State Department."

"They'll deny everything. That's why you'd better sit down and hear me out."

The Russian hesitated. He met the shrewd blue eyes and subsided back into his chair with an air of arrogant resignation.

"Nothing you say can change the fact that we have a right of access through to the Mediterranean."

Admiral Pearson smiled amiably. "Sure you have, Max—the 1936 Montreux Convention. It must be one of the oldest arms-control agreements still in force."

Max folded his arms. He was back on safe ground. "I'd forgotten its name but I remember that it grants our warships unhindered passage through the Bosphorus."

"Except aircraft carriers," said Pearson.

"That's nonsense."

Pearson eased the ash off his cigar. "I've spent this morning going over the approved translations of the Montreux Treaty with a team of State Department linguists. It's there in several languages, Max—English, Russian, French, Turkish, and German. No aircraft carriers may pass through the Bosphorus Straits. And your country is a signatory to that treaty." Pearson grinned at the Russian's bewildered expression. "None of the translations define an aircraft carrier but our lawyers are of the opinion that 'any warship that carries aircraft or is capable of carrying aircraft' is a definition that will stand up in any international court."

Max shook his head. "You're forgetting something, admiral—the Soviet Navy does not possess aircraft carriers."

Pearson snorted.

"Listen," said the Russian angrily. "The Kiev-class ships are submarine-intercepting cruisers."

"Sure. Sure. That's what you told the world when you sent your first Kiev through the Bosphorus. We didn't kick up a fuss then but we are now. As far as NATO is concerned any warship in the Soviet navy that can deploy aircraft—whether fixed-wing or rotary-wing—is an aircraft carrier."

"Including helicopters?" asked the Russian coldly.

"I said, rotary-wing."

"Helicopters hadn't been invented at the time the treaty was signed," said the Russian angrily. "So how can it possibly be interpreted as including them?"

"Well now," said Pearson easily, "we thought you might throw that one at us so we've done a little scratching around in the Library of Congress. A Frenchman, Paul Cornu, flew a helicopter in November 1907. And, before that, Leonardo da Vinci sketched the idea for one in 1488. Even earlier is the unknown artist who painted a Madonna and Child in 1460; the Christ Child is shown holding a toy helicopter." Pearson grinned. "Take a trip to the museum at Le Mans if you don't believe me. Of course, the father of the modern helicopter was a countryman of yours—Igor Sikorsky. He was designing and building helicopters in Russia before the First World War so you can't say that in 1936 you knew nothing about them."

The Russian said nothing.

Admiral Pearson hunched his shoulders over the table. "So you go back to your ambassador, Max, and tell him that if any Soviet carrier, and that includes destroyers fitted with a helicopter platform, as much as shows its nose in the Marmara—we'll sink it."

The Russian's scalp went back. "This isn't 1962, Brandon. The Soviet Navy is now the most powerful fighting force in the world. And how do you think the rest of the world will react to the news that the Americans are once again resorting to imperialist blackmail?"

Pearson shrugged. "The same way that the world will react to the news that the Soviet Union flouts international agreements. Maybe a few African countries might have second thoughts before they enter into treaties with you. And besides, this is going to be a NATO action—every country in the organization has agreed to it."

"Do you think we'll accept a situation in which a

third of our navy is bottled up in the Black Sea?" the Russian demanded.

"Two-thirds," Pearson amended.

"Well?"

"You should've thought of that before you started embarking on a violation of international agreements," Pearson replied cheerfully. "Cheer up, Max. They don't still shoot the bearers of bad news, do they?"

Two hours later an Aeroflot jet left Washington with one passenger on board—the Soviet Ambassador to the United States. He had told newsmen at the airport that his sister had been taken ill. Fourteen hours later, after a refueling stop at Shannon Airport in the Republic of Ireland, the Tupolov touched down at Moscow Airport. There were no customs formalities; a black, chauffeur-driven Zim drove the ambassador direct to the Kremlin.

All through the long flight, the ambassador had been too preoccupied to alter his watch from Eastern Standard Time.

32

Angus Brill, chief executive at the Rosenthal Base, nearly had a heart attack when Sherwood first showed him the sketch map of the bay. Studying it carefully for a few minutes while Sherwood made his request gave him time to recover from his initial shock. His voice had its normal cheerfulness when he managed to speak.

"Of course you saw Sno-Cat tracks, Glen. I authorized an expedition there about two months ago."

Sherwood looked puzzled. "But from the number of

tracks, it looked like more than just one expedition—it looked as if there had been regular trips back and forth."

Brill's heart nearly stopped beating. He prayed that his voice sounded annoyed when he said: "I hope those young devils haven't been wasting fuel again. You scientists are all the same—you've no idea how much a gallon of diesel is worth once it's been flown out here."

"But you'll let me go out to the bay?"

Brill thought for a moment. "I agree that, if the pack ice is melting prematurely, then it ought to be investigated. But I really need you to work on the replacement of those ice cores that went down with the *Orion*. Did you know that we all prayed for you when we heard the news? Dreadful business. Dreadful. I can't tell you how pleased I am to have you, Julia, and Oaf back with us—even if it is for only a few months."

Sherwood tried to interrupt but Brill took him gently by the arm and was leading him to the door as he spoke.

"Look," said Sherwood. "I could do the trip with just one cat...."

"But it's still a round trip of six hundred miles, Glen. I honestly can't spare the fuel—even for one cat." Brill paused. "Maybe later on during the summer if consumption between now and then doesn't get out of hand as it did last season."

"But it might be too late then," Sherwood protested.

"I promise to see what can be done as soon as possible," said Brill sincerely.

Sherwood sighed. "Can you answer me one thing, Angus?"

"If I can."

"Why don't we get our supplies from Australia or New Zealand? Wouldn't it be cheaper than having the RAF fly the stuff all the way from England?"

Brill chuckled as he opened his office door. "You

know, Glen—that's exactly the same question I asked headquarters when I first took on this job. Apparently it's some mutual back scratching they've fixed up with the Ministry of Defence—we need the supplies and they need the training flights." Brill pumped Sherwood's hand for the second time and guided him into the corridor. "Anyway, it's really nice having you back. I only hope that you don't find having to go back over your old work too much of a bore."

Sherwood was alone in the corridor before he could open his mouth to reply.

Brill returned to his desk and sat down. God, what a mess. But at least he could congratulate himself on his smooth handling of a potentially explosive situation. He stared down at his desk top deep in thought; then suddenly realized to his anger that Sherwood had taken the sketch map of the bay with him.

33

ICE WISE
A modification of reinforced bows and protected propellers that enables a ship to operate in low-density ice fields.

The United States Navy oceanographic survey ship *Eureka* drove her 10,000-ton bulk through the decaying pack ice of the Southern Ocean and into the teeth of a freezing 120-mile-an-hour gale that blew with the ferocity of 10,000 demented bread knives. The crazed ice floes splintered and ground along the length of the hull as if seeking a weakness so that they could tear the ship's side out. The screaming wind whipped spray off the broken sea and flung it across the *Eureka*'s superstructure. The steel drained the spring warmth from the water and froze it into a steadily thickening layer of sea ice that clung to masts, radio and radar antennae, and lifeboats. The steel shrouds that supported the satellite tracking dish were four times their normal thickness and severely weakened by the cold and the strain thrown on them by the research ship's sickening eighty-degree roll.

To Captain Rolf Hagan, hanging on to a deckhead safety strap in the heated wheelhouse, it seemed inconceivable that any ship could take such punishment for two unrelenting weeks, as the *Eureka* had done on this vital mission into Antarctic waters.

Deke Sutherland, the commanding officer, turned to Hagan after a brief conference with the deck officer. He seemed to have made up his mind about something.

"We can make another fifty miles but no more. Not in this weather. And this ice field is getting worse."

"How near does that get me to Rosenthal Base?" asked Hagan.

"Three hundred miles."

"That's no goddamn good," Hagan replied shortly.

"Don't blame me for the weather."

Hagan bridled. "You said you would get me within helicopter range of Rosenthal, captain."

The *Eureka* shook as an ice floe, forced onto its edge by the plough-like action of the bows, cartwheeled slowly along the ship's flank before falling back to the sea. For the thousandth time in two weeks, Sutherland wondered why it was so important that Hagan should get to see the three *Orion* survivors.

"No," said Sutherland. "I said I'd get you within range of Rosenthal, weather permitting." He jabbed a thumb at one of the spinning glass discs that afforded a clear view through the wheelhouse windows. "Even if I got you to within two hundred miles of Rosenthal, you wouldn't be able to fly off your chopper in this shit."

The *Eureka* corkscrewed into a trough separating two mountainous seas and splintered an ice floe. Spicules raked the wheelhouse windows like grapeshot.

"Jesus Christ," Hagan muttered. "How much longer can this last?"

Sutherland shrugged.

"What's the weather forecast, for God's sake?"

"There isn't one," said Sutherland. "Not in these latitudes. And the satellite-tracking antenna can't be moved until we get a steam hose on it—it's frozen up."

"To think this is spring," Hagan muttered.

"Sure it's spring," Sutherland replied. "And it'll be summer in a few weeks. But this weather is manufactured at the South Pole, where it's winter all the year round."

The bridge interphone shrilled. The deck officer lifted the handset off its hook.

Hagan thought for a moment. "Okay. We ride this out until it eases up."

Sutherland stared at him. "Are you crazy? This could blow for another month. Two months. You'll louse up our schedules."

"We ride it out," Hagan repeated.

Sutherland pointed to Hagan's helicopter lashed to the platform. The machine was encrusted with ice. Long stalactites were forming on the drooping rotors, dragging them even lower. The rotors flexed and twisted in harmony with the *Eureka*'s savage motion.

"What state will that chopper be in after a few more days of that sort of treatment, Captain Hagan?" Sutherland demanded.

"My orders are to interview those survivors," Hagan said doggedly. "And your orders are to obey my orders."

The deck officer approached the two men. He

saluted Sutherland with one hand and hung on to a safety strap with the other.

"Ensign Katz reports that he's raised Rosenthal, sir. Their radio operator says that he misunderstood our earlier signals and has stated that the three *Orion* survivors are *not* at the base."

Hagan nearly let go of his strap in his anger. "How the hell did that misunderstanding arise?"

"Because Glen Sherwood, Julia Hammond, and Oaf Johansen used to be members of the Rosenthal team," the deck officer explained. He paused and glanced from his captain to Hagan. "Rosenthal's chief executive sends his sincere apologies and hopes that we haven't been too inconvenienced."

Sutherland began to laugh. He turned to Hagan. "So what are your orders now, Captain Hagan?"

34

Julia opened her shutter. A laboratory technician was checking the double doors on the Sno-Cat building to ensure that they were locked. She watched him leaning against the gale-force wind as he trudged back to the accommodation block.

"Well, I think it's you two who are being unreasonable," she said. "You're forgetting that Brill has overall responsibility for the success of every project and can't possibly authorize the release of fuel just so individuals can go off on trips to satisfy their curiosity."

Oaf pared a huge thumbnail with his flensing knife. "That's why everyone's in Antarctica, heh? Curiosity."

"Oaf's right," said Sherwood. "An extraordinary phenomenon has been reported that's within range of this base, therefore Brill ought to allow a visit."

"How can he if there's not enough fuel?"

"Plenty of fuel," Oaf said without looking up.

Sherwood nodded to the double-glazed window. "Trouble approaches."

The laboratory technician had altered course and was walking toward Julia's unshuttered window. He stopped, pushed up his goggles and pointed to his watch. Julia sighed and closed the steel shutter. One of the base's standing orders during the continuous-daylight months was that all shutters were to be closed by 10:00 P.M. It was Brill's conviction that health on the base was improved by observation of normal periods of night and day.

"How do you know there's plenty of fuel?" asked Sherwood.

"Once I go into the Sno-Cat shed. Drums of diesel to the roof."

"Weren't you caught?" Julia inquired.

Oaf bared his gleaming teeth. It was supposed to be a smile. "No. Like Sherwood—I was curious."

"How much diesel was there?" asked Sherwood, trying not to sound excited.

Oaf thought for a moment. "How far to that bay? Three hundred miles? Six hundred miles the round trip?"

"About that."

Oaf considered. If the going was easy the Sno-Cats could average five miles per gallon fuel consumption. He toyed with his knife and murmured: "They won't miss a hundred and fifty gallons—fifteen drums."

Sherwood warmed to the big Norwegian. Oaf could always be relied on to make a decision without a lot of argument.

"And how about you, Julia? Fancy a trip to the beach?"

"It won't be a picnic. You're both crazy."

Sherwood nodded. "That's right, love. No doubt Brill will skin us alive when we get back."

"We'll take sixteen drums," said Julia firmly. "One for luck. We'll need it. And food and extreme-cold-weather clothing. And climbing gear in case we can't find a way for the Sno-Cat down those cliffs."

Oaf gave a mischievous grin. "No trouble."

Brill thoughtfully removed his headphones and lifted the arm off the record. An unexpected visitor would have automatically assumed that the chief executive was listening to his beloved Chopin.

Brill remained deep in thought for some minutes. The conversation between Sherwood, Miss Hammond, and Oaf was, he felt, one of those events that he would have to report to London.

35

Admiral Howe was sitting on his favorite bench in St. James's Park when Lieutenant Abbott tracked him down and sat beside him. He gave the admiral an internal post envelope.

"Sorry to disturb you during lunchtime, sir, but this has just arrived from GCHQ."

Admiral Howe broke the nylon seal and unfolded the message: a typical Cheltenham plaintext printout—a yard of paper for a hundred-word message.

He read it quickly, then a second time slowly. Abbott was bursting with curiosity. Let him. This was something that he couldn't be told.

By the time Admiral Howe had reached his office, he had mentally composed a reply to Brill. It would be a message that Admiral Howe knew he would be ashamed of for the rest of his life, but it had to be sent. He half hoped that Brill would disobey orders but it was unlikely. Brill was an officer who didn't disobey orders. Which was why he had been given the job in the first place.

36

AWACS (Airborne Warning and Control System)
A continuously airborne fleet of battle manage-
ment centers with a primary function of
providing advance "over-horizon" warning on
the movements of enemy aircraft and surface
ships.

The AWACS was flying at 55,000 feet in "friendly"
Turkish air space but its radar beams were slanting
down through "unfriendly" air space to the Soviet
naval base at Sevastopol on the landlocked Black
Sea.

It was 03:00 hours local time when the long-
expected event happened: five of the AWACS's radar
plots indicated that a blip had detached itself from
the Crimean peninsula and was heading southwest
with incredible slowness.

The AWACS's precision radar beams narrowed—
increasing their intensity and eliminating the
background "clutter" from dockyard buildings and
cranes. There was little sound within the Boeing's
air-conditioned, soft-lit interior as the crew set the
computers to work to analyze the flood of incoming
data. There wasn't even the click of key switches; the
glowing control panels responded to the touch of the
human finger and not the pressure.

The beams probed the Soviet ship, evaluating its
lengths, its beam and hull profile, and even its bow
wave.

The electronic interrogation proceeded at the
speed of light. Line by line, the results materialized in
silence on the AWACS's cathode ray tubes and

simultaneously on the screens before Admiral Pearson in the *Johnson*'s strike-command combat-control center:

0300
TARGET + KIEV CLASS CARRIER
POSITION + ZONE BS GRID SQUARE 8900
COURSE + 326 DEGREES
SPEED +2 KNOTS
SECONDARY OBSERVATIONS + NO FIXED OR ROTARY WING
AIRPLANE DEPLOYMENT ON FLIGHT BACK
ETA BOSPHORUS AT PRESENT COURSE AND SPEED + 100 HOURS

The carrier was creeping across the Black Sea, just as Admiral Pearson had predicted it would. The Russians weren't accepting the situation but they were creating a hundred-hour lead time.
Four days.
Time enough for a lot of talking to be done.

37

Julia, Oaf, and Sherwood were singing above the roar of the diesel as the Sno-Cat raced across the plateau at twenty miles an hour.

They were now a hundred miles from Rosenthal. Stealing the five-ton bright yellow vehicle had been unexpectedly easy—no laboratory technicians had been around when they had opened the double doors of the motor transport hut. Oaf had set the Sno-Cat's inertial navigation instruments while Sherwood and Julia filled the fuel tanks to capacity. Ten sealed drums of diesel fuel were stacked conveniently near the Sno-Cat. These would be needed for the return journey. Oaf had helped lift them into the Sno-Cat's stowage bay.

No one had come to investigate when the Perkins diesel engine coughed into life—the eternal winds that shrieked round the cluster of low buildings effectively cloaked the roar of the engine and the sound of the track grousers as they crunched into the hard snow.

Oaf had steered the Sno-Cat away from Rosenthal, keeping the transport hut between the vehicle and the accommodation buildings. Only when they were four hundred yards away did he open the throttle and circle round until they were heading on the correct course for the mysterious bay in the coastal ice shelf.

"I don't think I can sing any more," announced Julia.

"I know some Norwegian whaling songs," said Oaf.

He was voted down.

The Sno-Cat thundered on across the flat, white wilderness. The upper snow layers were frozen into a hard pan that made easy going for the track-laying vehicle. The warmth and humidity in the cab caused Oaf's snow goggles to keep misting up. He gave up trying to wipe them and pushed them up on his forehead, squinting against the glare caused by the low sun reflecting off the ice.

"What about crevasses?" asked Julia.

"I've drilled this area for three years," said Sherwood. "The ice cap's as solid and stable as Gibraltar. We'll have to start taking it easy when we're within a hundred miles of the coast."

"Why's that, Sherwood?" demanded Oaf.

"Two reasons," said Sherwood. "First, I was never allowed enough fuel to survey near the coast; and second, without the self-buttressing effect of ice, there are more likely to be crevasses in the coastal area."

The vivid yellow machine charged on over the featureless frozen landscape.

The three escapers eventually tired of trying to make themselves heard above the sustained reverberation of the engine in the enclosed cab and fell silent.

An hour of seemingly unending monotony passed.

Julia was about to suggest that they stop to stretch their legs and eat, when the ice suddenly opened up beneath the Sno-Cat. She was thrown forward against the windshield. She screamed as the cab tilted down. Oaf threw the tracks into reverse and slammed the throttle open. The diesel's note rose to a howl—the frenzied grousers ground the snow to powder as they bit down deep into the edge of the three-mile-deep chasm. But it was too late: the remnants of the snow bridge collapsed under the Sno-Cat's five-ton mass and its momentum carried it over the brink. The headlights sprayed parallel beams of quartz iodine light into the awesome fissure in the ice cap. As the Sno-Cat plunged down, Julia realized, foolishly, that she was staring at a ribbon of exposed Antarctic continent.

38

The Lucas grapnel's jaws closed round the silent transatlantic telephone cable and held it securely. Three miles above, a switch was thrown on the cable-laying and repair ship. An electrically operated blade on the complex grapnel sheared through the cable on one side of the jaws. A power winch began turning, lifting the cable from the abyssal darkness of the Angolian Basin.

An hour later, engineers began collecting around the winch, watching the lifting hawser climbing out of the water and waiting for the cable to appear. Many of them were the same engineers that had helped lay the cable three years previously. TAT 12 was their baby.

It was 3:25 P.M. when the grapnel broke the surface. The cable end was passed around a capstan and the cable carefully coiled in one of the ship's circular holes as it came aboard.

The first repeater appeared an hour later. Externally, it was nothing more than a bulge in the cable; internally, the 4,000-channel voice amplifier represented the most advanced technology in the world. There were over 150 repeaters in the cable, strung out like beads across the ocean floor. They were built with painstaking care and were designed to last a hundred years without attention. Failure of one of the $150,000 repeaters would put the entire cable out of action.

The second repeater appeared the following morning at breakfast time. The winch operator stopped lifting and sounded the alarm. Engineers abandoned their meals and poured onto the deck to investigate.

The senior engineer stared speechless at the suspended repeater. Its armor sheathing had been ripped open and its components, more carefully selected than the gems in the crown jewels, were hanging out. Some of the delicate solid-state circuits had been torn completely away, and the cable seals, which were capable of resisting a water pressure of several tons per square inch, had been savagely torn from their housings. It was a similar story with the visible length of cable hanging from the sheaves; the heavy insulation was lacerated as if it had been flailed in a giant threshing machine. So deep were some of the cuts that the teredo tapes had been sliced right through to expose the reinforcing jute yarn.

The senior engineer gave the order to restart the winch. During that day, eighty miles of wrecked cable and two more disemboweled repeaters were coiled down into the cable ship's hold.

Lifting continued throughout the night under the

glare of floodlights. The damage to the $50-million voice highway got progressively worse. At one point the two-inch-diameter cable was virtually sliced right through.

It was 4 A.M. when the senior engineer was awakened and told that the winch strain gauges were indicating that the severed end of the cable had finally been reached and was now being lifted off the floor of the South Atlantic.

With over a hundred miles of mutilated cable in the hold, the senior engineer was certain of one thing: the damage could not possible have been caused by a human agency.

39

"Keep still," said Oaf through clenched teeth. "You both keep pretty damn still."

Julia and Sherwood remained frozen in the positions they had fallen into. Sherwood's arm was trapped painfully against the side of the cab. The Sno-Cat had plunged twenty feet into the narrowing chasm. The roof had gouged deep into the ice and spun the vehicle round so that it was now facing upward toward the band of gray sky.

"We move one at a time," said Oaf. "But we don't even breathe."

It took the three an hour to shift their positions. Miraculously, none of the windows had been broken in the fall; it was the slender aluminum window frames supporting the roof panel that were preventing the vehicle from crashing down into the depths of the crevasse.

They arranged themselves on the seat, staring upward like three Apollo astronauts waiting for lift-off.

Moving with infinite care, Sherwood reached for the radiotelephone handset.

"Won't be any good," said Julia. "Even if the aerial's not been torn off, you won't get a signal out down here."

"Maybe," Oaf muttered. "But it's worth a try."

The radiotelephone was dead.

"So what do we do now?" Sherwood demanded.

"I go out," said Oaf. "I climb around back and open stowage bay—release oil drums to lighten her. We have to do that first."

Julia thought of the bottomless gulf she had seen for an instant when the Sno-Cat had gone over the edge.

"You'll have to let me do it," she said.

"Don't talk crazy," said Sherwood.

"I weigh the least," Julia pointed out. "My weight moving about isn't so likely to dislodge anything."

Sherwood started to argue but Oaf cut him short. "She's right, Sherwood."

Julia groped cautiously under the seat for her extreme-cold-weather mittens and pulled them on. She stood very slowly while Oaf released the windshield catches.

"We better all put cold-weather clothing on before I open this," said Oaf.

Two minutes later, Oaf pushed the windshield open inch by inch until the opening was wide enough for Julia to ease herself through. Freezing air knifed into the cab.

"Close it again," Julia ordered when she had climbed out.

To Sherwood, such an action would seem like abandoning her.

"No!" he shouted hoarsely.

"For Christ's sake, shut it!" Julia repeated as she gingerly tested her weight on the upturned track guards.

Oaf was about to pull the windshield down when Sherwood reached up to stop him.

114

"No! Leave it open!"

The sudden movement caused the Sno-Cat to rock. There was a harsh scream of metal slicing into ice. A side window cracked like a pistol being fired. The report echoed along the crevasse. Julia threw herself flat across the Sno-Cat's snub radiator grille and clung to the power winch. The side window exploded to granules of glass that rattled down the side of the hanging vehicle and fell into the black void. Julia heard them clattering into the echoing darkness. Hypnotized, Sherwood and Oaf stared at the slowly buckling roof pillar. Another side window disintegrated. Julia could see where the track grousers were pressing into the ice wall—they were slipping—forcing up ridges of ice.

The Sno-Cat fell.

Oaf pushed Sherwood against the floor. The roof caved in and all the remaining windows, including the windshield panels, shattered. The sides of the chasm seemed to close in on Julia like the jaws of a gargantuan vise. Then there was silence. The inverted Sno-Cat had stopped its mad backward plunge.

Julia opened her eyes and stared in horror at the flattened cab. She could have reached out and touched the frozen sides of the abyss. She called out in panic: "Glen! Oaf!"

"Don't move, Sherwood," Julia heard Oaf's voice growl from the depths of the mangled cab. She cried out in relief.

"Can you hear me, Oaf?"

"I can see you," the Norwegian replied.

Julia realized that a shaggy face was watching her through a tear in the folded metal.

"Are you hurt?" she asked.

The face moved away. The Sno-Cat swayed.

"Hey, Sherwood," said Oaf's voice. "You hurt?"

"No . . . I don't think so."

Julia forgot her own predicament and offered a silent prayer of thanks. Moving with extreme care, she turned around until she could peer into the yawning fissure down one side of the crushed cab. The crumpled remains of the door were rammed deep into the scored ediface. It was obvious that the other side would be the same. The Sno-Cat swayed again. One of the trapped men was trying to open a door. There was a grinding sound. At that moment Julia saw with horrifying clarity the perilously narrow ice ledge that was barely supporting the stricken Sno-Cat.

"NO!" she screamed with an anguish that sprang uninhibited from her soul. "NO! NO! NO! Don't move! Whatever you do, *don't move!*"

The starved acoustics in the ice maw seized her voice and snatched it into the depths, hurling it gleefully from wall to wall as they drained its strength.

Julia took five minutes over lifting herself onto one knee. She steadied herself against the power winch and turned her head up. The razor edge of the chasm sliced the sunlight into its component colors. She estimated that the Sno-Cat had fallen fifty feet.

"Listen, Oaf. I've got an idea."

Oaf's puzzled face appeared at the opening.

"You'll have to shift your weight to the right-hand side of the cab," Julia said. "That's *your* left. The cat should be more stable. But for God's sake do it slowly."

There was no reply. Julia felt the vehicle give a slight tremble. Two minutes later, Oaf's voice said: "Okay. What now?"

"Can you reach the climbing gear?"

There was a pause. Another tremble. Then: "Yes."

"Pass them out to me one at a time. The rope, the pitons, and ice axes—everything."

"What are you thinking of doing?" asked Sherwood's voice.

Julia told him. Sherwood started protesting. Oaf told him to shut up. One by one, the items of

116

mountaineering equipment were passed through the opening to Julia.

"And the spades."

Oaf eased the sharp-pointed ice spades through the narrow gap. Julia carefully spread all the items out so she could pick them up one at a time without making unnecessary movements. It took her ten minutes to prepare for the climb. She was forced to remove the heavy mittens so that she could adjust and secure the harness. She had forgotten the cold until she saw a strip of skin from the ball of her finger adhering to one of the metal quick-release fasteners. With the harness in place and trailing two ropes from the small of her back, she was ready. She stood, held a piton against the ice face, braced herself, and swung the hammer.

For the rest of her life, Julia was to have great difficulty remembering details from that grueling fifty-minutes climb. Occasional subliminal scenes would come back to her: hanging by the safety harness from a single piton while swinging the hammer above her head; transferring her weight to an ice axe and straightening her legs to gain another six inches. But she retained a clear impression of the searing cold that seeped continuously through her protective clothing. The cold was part of lying utterly exhausted on the ice near the lip of the crevasse.

She closed her eyes and rolled onto her back. Maybe the extreme-cold-weather parka had thicker insulation in its back panels, for the cold didn't feel so bad. Even the bright sun on her face felt warmer. She pulled off a mitten and let the warm shingle of the Dawlish beach trickle through her fingers. Her parents took her to Dawlish every year despite Dad's grumbling about the railway track that ran along the top of the beach. She could hear a train coming—the wail of twin-tone air horns getting louder, rising to a frenzied shrieking that seemed to blast from the bowels of the earth.

Then she remembered. Freezing water was dripping from her hand. She opened her eyes. There was no sign of the beach—only the white desolation. But the howling siren continued. She rolled onto her stomach and peered over the brink of the crevasse. Her brain reeled as she stared down at the Sno-Cat's headlights; she felt as if she were clinging helplessly to the edge of a cliff with the strange vehicle charging toward her—its horn blaring for the final yards of its headlong suicide rush. Then she saw the two ropes snaking down from her safety harness. One of them was tied to the two long-handled ice spades. She waved feebly and began hauling the spades up.

She removed the harness, anchored it with a piton and began digging a trench in the ice with one of the spades, first loosening the ice with the axe. It took her thirty minutes to complete the task. The finished trench, thirty yards from and parallel to the chasm, measured five feet long, six inches wide, and three feet deep.

The simplest part of the operation was cutting a slit with the ice pick from the center of the trench to that part of the brink immediately above the trapped Sno-Cat.

She grasped the second rope leading down to the vehicle and called out: "I'm ready to haul up now! Release the clutch on the winch!"

The cable drum on the Sno-Cat's power winch turned slowly as she hauled the cable up. She used the ice pick to embed the cable into the groove. The free end that emerged into the trench was tied firmly around the hafts of two spades. The spades were then laid in the trench and buttressed hard against the trench side.

Julia stood back and studied her handiwork. There seemed no reason why the makeshift T-shaped snow anchor couldn't take the Sno-Cat's five-ton weight; the hafts on the steel spades, now lying in the trench, were thicker than the ten-ton breaking strain winch hawser.

She crawled to the edge of the brink and looked down. She thought she could see Oaf's eyes through the opening in the torn metal.

"Ready, Oaf. But there's about six feet of slack that you'll have to take up first."

There was a movement inside the crushed cab. The Sno-Cat rocked slightly.

"Okay," Oaf's voice answered. "If this bastard will start. Pretty crazy angle, heh?"

"Pretty crazy," Julia agreed, her voice tight.

The Perkins diesel fired on the third attempt. The vibration dislodged ice that rattled hollowly down into the abyss. Julia screamed in horror as the Sno-Cat fell. The winch hawser gave a sharp musical note as it snapped taut.

"Start the winch!" Julia screamed, and then she almost sobbed with relief when she heard the crunch of the gearbox and saw the winch drum start turning. Without stopping to see if the Sno-Cat was climbing the cable, she raced back to the trench. The two spades, with the lifting cable lashed round their hafts, were pulled up hard against the side of the trench. Everything about the T-anchor looked right—the Sno-Cat couldn't possibly drag the spades through the thirty yards of ice between the trench and the brink.

There was an echoing crash from the crevasse. Julia ran near to the brink, threw herself down flat on her stomach and looked over the edge. The diesel's roar was sweet music.

There was another crash and the sound of tearing metal. The Sno-Cat was pulling itself clear of the frozen jaws!

Even as Julia stared down, she could see that the machine was inching toward her—inexorably winding the cable round the drum and climbing, like a giant yellow spider hauling itself up a strand of silken web.

Powdered ice jetted from under the grousers as the Sno-Cat's tracks scored into the side of the chasm.

The hawser had pulled itself firmly into the ice like a wire cheese slicer.

She went back to the trench. Her heart nearly stopped when she saw the two spades. The knot tied around the hafts was slowly flattening them and the spades were distorting into a V-shape with the apex driving into the side of the trench. As she stared aghast, she realized that the spade hafts were tubular and not solid as she had supposed.

The Sno-Cat's power winch appeared above the edge of the crevasse. Above the roar of the diesel was the sharp twanging noise made by the rigid hawser as the changing angle jerked it out of the ice. The tracked vehicle seemed to be climbing into the air. Julia threw herself down and began frantically packing loose ice around the spades that were grating up the side of the trench and slowly closing like dividers. She even tried jumping on the spades to force them down, but it was useless—her weight was no match for the five-ton force being exerted by the Sno-Cat's bulk. The sides of the trench crumbled as the now wedge-shaped spade hafts drove into the ice. Julia cried with despair and frustration. She tore off the mittens and used her fists to beat the ice down. Then she transferred her blows to the slowly buckling spades, heedless of the intense pain as the cold welded her skin to the metal and tore it away in strips.

There was a crash from behind her. Turning round was her last conscious action. The spades jerked free—flailing the icy air as the tension in the hawser was unleashed. A flying handle struck her on the temple.

Then there was a black nothingness.

40

The President of the United States regarded the Defense Secretary thoughtfully and said: "If the Chairman is still not offering anything, John, why should I speak to him again?"

"He's on the line now, begging you to see reason."

The President pointed to the sheaf of papers and cables lying on his desk. "Tell him that his country will have to appeal to virtually every member of the NATO alliance. How long before that carrier reaches the Bosphorus?"

"Fifty-two hours."

The President nodded. "Tell him that it is his country that has to see reason. That it is *his* country that is about to violate an international agreement."

The Defense Secretary moved to the door.

"I see no reason to withdraw the orders issued to Admiral Pearson," the President concluded.

41

MIRVOS (Multiple Independently-Targeted Re-entry Vehicle Orientation Satellite)
Active satellites which provide mid-course guide for multiple-warhead intercontinental ballistic missiles.

With forty hours to a major East-West confrontation, four unmanned rockets were launched from Andrews Air Force Base at intervals of ten minutes.

The first one jettisoned its spent main booster at an altitude of 100 miles and continued climbing on its second-stage rocket until it reached 180 miles. Its target was a Soyuz satellite which had been launched, unannounced, eighteen months previously.

The orbital injection maneuver was successfully completed; the ground controllers' computers and instruments told them that their rocket, moving at 18,000 miles per hour, was closing on the Soyuz satellite at 5 miles per hour on a matching orbit.

After five minutes of precision jockeying with retro-rockets, the U.S. rocket was within three feet of the Soviet satellite.

A panel set into the nose of the rocket slid open and the payload, millions of copper dipoles, the size and shape of darning needles, were slowly ejected so that they clung in a dense cloud around the satellite, effectively screening all incoming and outgoing command signals.

There would be no permanent damage to the satellite. But for two hundred hours, until the million-mile-an-hour solar wind eventually swept most of the dipoles away, the Soviet MIRVOS would be useless.

During the next two hours, the other three Soviet MIRVOS satellites were similarly disabled.

42

There were two reasons why Admiral Pearson had selected the British Leander-class frigate H.M.S. *Swiftfire* for the task of disabling the Soviet aircraft carrier should it try to enter the Sea of Marmara from the Bosphorus. First, the small warship workhorse had been on a visit to Turkey and was already in the Marmara when the crisis erupted. Second, the

Swiftfire had an ideal weapon—a single anti-submarine Wasp helicopter. The use of such a small torpedo-carrying machine launched from one of the smallest ships in the NATO force gave the West a propaganda advantage if the attack on the Kiev carrier was eventually carried out—the Soviets would be made to look foolish if they started screaming about imperialist bullying.

With twenty-five hours to confrontation, the *Swiftfire* was operating in "closed down" condition. Her decks were deserted. All hatches and doors were closed and sealed, and the windows of the enclosed bridge heavily shuttered. The *Swiftfire* was a ghost ship. Even her long-range warning radar antenna was still; all the information the *Swiftfire* needed was pouring into her electronic warfare office from the Boeing AWACS which was maintaining a continuous watching patrol in Turkish airspace to the east. Her Seacat surface-to-air missiles mounted on top of the helicopter hangar were poised for action.

The *Swiftfire*'s principal warfare officer was now in overall command of the warship's weapon systems and had the authority to issue "requests" to the captain. He, like all the technicians and ratings manning the consoles in the darkened computer room and electronic warfare room, was wearing a white one-piece Nuclear-Biological-Chemical protective suit complete with hood and tinted nuclear flash visor. The air supply throughout the ship was provided from an independent system so that the ship could continue to fight at maximum efficiency even if her combat zone became saturated with intense radioactive fallout.

"PWO, *Swiftfire* to *Johnson*," said the principal warfare officer.

Admiral Pearson glanced at the voice-print screen. It had taken the computer a thousandth of a second to analyze the British officer's voice, compare its inflection and tonal qualities, and display on the screen:

"Go ahead, *Swiftfire.*"

"Phase Four achieved, sir."

"Very good, *Swiftfire.* Continue to the ten-hour threshold."

The PWO acknowledged and cleared the circuit. Admiral Pearson spun his swivel chair round and studied the floor-to-deckhead glass map of the North and South Atlantic that dominated the *Johnson*'s combat control center. At the foot of the map, in Antarctic waters, was the marker for the research ship *Eureka* that Hagan was aboard. He wished Hagan were with him and cursed the continuing weather conditions that had prevented his aide's return. Interviewing the *Orion* survivors now seemed an unimportant and fruitless enterprise. Admiral Pearson turned his chair back to face his control console and leaned toward the microphone. He pressed the key that connected him with the *Johnson's* meteorological officer.

"Any change in the conditions in the *Eureka*'s area?"

"Checking now, sir."

There was a pause while the met officer checked the latest satellite weather pictures.

"Yes, sir. Looks like a significant improvement. The gale has moderated to Force Seven and is getting better all the time."

Pearson grunted and called up the communications room.

"Keep trying to raise the *Eureka*. When you do, tell Captain Hagan that I want him back on the *Johnson* as soon as possible."

Pearson next spoke to the *Johnson*'s logistics officer, who confirmed that with in-flight refueling and a fast transport from the U.S.S. *Guam*, Hagan could be back on the *Johnson* within ten hours.

Admiral Pearson's next task on Washington's

orders was to upgrade the alert status of the United States' nuclear submarines. It was an order which, until then, he had given only during exercises. He said a simple but heartfelt prayer to himself, and said into the microphone: "All SSBN designated in combat radial Charlie-Hotel-Foxtrot to set condition ISQ readiness."

Translated from the jargon the order was: "All missile-carrying nuclear submarines get ready for war."

43

"Hey, Sherwood! She's awake!"

Sherwood abandoned the Sno-Cat's radio that he had been attempting to repair and crawled into the tent beside Oaf. Julia's hands and head had been expertly bandaged by Oaf. She was sitting in the sleeping bag and staring wide-eyed at Sherwood.

"Now I believe it," she said to Oaf.

"Believe what?" asked Sherwood.

"That we're not all dead. What happened?"

Sherwood caught Oaf's eye. The Norwegian shook his head. "I've not told her, Sherwood."

"Told me what? Speak."

"You hit your head."

"I guessed. Where are we? How far are we from base?"

"Three hundred miles," said Sherwood apologetically.

"Now listen," said Julia reasonably. "How can we be that distance from Rosenthal? That was the distance to the coast."

The two men looked at each other for mutual support. Before they could move to stop her, Julia ripped back the tent flap and gaped in astonishment at the pack ice some fifty yards from where the tent was pitched on the shale-strewn beach. She groaned.

"The coast," was Sherwood's unnecessary explanation.

Julia made no reply. She turned her head to gaze at the Sno-Cat parked a few yards away under the soaring ice cliffs. The vehicle's wrecked cab had been cut away. She could see twin grouser tracks down a plunging fold in the ice cap.

"And we managed to find a safe route down," said Oaf triumphantly.

Julia closed her eyes and muttered something that sounded like a request to God to give her patience. She opened her eyes and, carefully choosing her words, said: "Why is it that, knowing the mess we were in, you two idiots—or rather imbeciles—*didn't turn back to base!*"

Sherwood nodded vigorously. "A good question. There's a good answer—you climbed up the wrong side of the crevasse. Not that we're complaining, mind," Sherwood added hastily. "We think you did very well to do what you did, don't we, Oaf?"

"Better than a man," agreed Oaf. It was the finest compliment he could pay a woman.

Julia was in no mood for flattery. "Have you found out why that pack ice is melting?"

"Yes," said Sherwood. "You won't believe this but—"

"Good. I feel fit enough to travel, so we'll break camp right now and start back."

"We can't...."

"We damn well will. We might have to make a long detour to avoid that crevasse." Julia started to struggle out of her sleeping bag, but Sherwood restrained her.

"Julia. It's no use. You might as well rest."

She angrily shook Sherwood's hand off her arm.

"You tell her, Oaf."

"Not enough diesel for return," said Oaf simply. "Enough for fifty mile—maybe more but not much.

I've just found out that spare drums are full of petrol—no good in a diesel engine. Wrong markings on the drums."

Julia sat back suddenly and stared at Oaf. "Are you sure?"

Oaf nodded unhappily.

"And the radio's busted," said Sherwood. "It can receive but not transmit."

There was a long silence.

"So we start walking," said Julia dully.

"When you've rested."

Another silence.

"So what's causing the pack ice to melt?"

"It's not melting," said Sherwood. "But it is breaking up. Quite fast too."

"Why?"

"The entire beach and seabed in the bay are lifting."

"What!"

"The same sort of thing is happening in some parts of Norway and Scotland but much more slowly. The land is still recovering after having been compressed by the weight of the ice cap and glaciers during the last ice age."

Julia frowned. "But why is it happening here?"

Sherwood pointed to the sweeping curve of razor-sharp ice cliffs that bordered the bay. "Those cliffs are unweathered. New. This bay wasn't here until quite recently—last Christmas or therabouts." He paused. "This camp and that ice field is where eight or nine thousand cubic miles of ice was standing. And now it's gone."

44

While crowds gathered along the shores of Istanbul's Golden Horn peninsula and lined the great bridge that linked Europe and Asia to watch the Kiev's stately progress through the Bosphorus, a hundred miles away on the Sea of Marmara the British frigate H.M.S. *Swiftfire* began her final preparations to cripple the Soviet warship.

Shortly after midday, the frigate's hangar door was opened and two men wheeled the Wasp helicopter out onto the *Swiftfire's* tiny helicopter deck. They quickly unfurled the rotors and swung the folding tail into the open position.

There was a small torpedo hanging beneath the Wasp. Its warhead had been set to detonate at a depth of sixty feet beneath the Kiev's stern. A depth calculated to stop the carrier by wrecking her stern gear without causing injury or loss of life to her crew.

45

"Sabotage," announced Julia.

Oaf and Sherwood peered at the printed circuit board that Julia had removed from the Sno-Cat's radiotelephone.

"If you look closely you can see where someone has snipped three wires to remove a component. Probably a transistor. We should've tested the set before leaving."

"There wasn't that much time," commented Sherwood dryly.

All three stared down at the tiny board that was smothered with electronic components.

"Well," said Julia at length. "If we had a soldering iron I suppose we could try a transistor from the receiver board."

Sherwood shook his head. "Even if we could repair it, who would hear us? We'd never get a signal out over those cliffs."

"Twelve-volt soldering iron in the toolbox," remarked Oaf.

"And wire cutters?"

"Sure."

"But it's useless," said Sherwood. "No one will hear us."

46

The oceanographic research ship U.S.S. *Eureka* heard them.

An ensign caught up with Captain Hagan as he was about to board his helicopter on the first stage of the long flight back to Admiral Pearson on the *Johnson*.

"Captain Hagan!"

Hagan had one foot on the helicopter's boarding steps. His pilot was holding the door open. Hagan turned. The breathless ensign was clutching a piece of paper. He saluted clumsily.

"A message from Captain Sutherland, sir. We've just picked up a distress call. Very weak. Three members of the Rosenthal survey team are stranded on the Coats Land coast and we can't hear anyone answering them...."

"So?"

The junior officer held out the piece of paper. "Their names and position, sir."

Hagan glanced at the message. He sat down abruptly on the helicopter steps and gave the ensign a suspicious look. "Is this your captain's idea of a joke?"

"No, sir."

Hagan handed the paper to his pilot. "Can we make that position if this hole in the weather holds?"

The pilot disappeared into the helicopter and reappeared with a chart. He looked doubtful. "It's a seven-hundred-mile round trip, sir."

"Okay," said Hagan impatiently. "So it's a long way. Can we make it?"

"Just about, sir. If you stay behind."

"Okay," said Hagan wearily. "Go get them."

47

BUS
The final stage of a submarine-borne Trident missile which carries a set of MIRV nuclear-fusion warheads up to targeting height.

The scene being enacted on the U.S.S. *Virgil Grissöm* was being duplicated on all the Trident nuclear submarines. It was a scene that was enacted once a week, but this time there were illuminated signs displayed in the nuclear submarine's various control centers; signs that flashed on and off at one-second intervals—a frequency calculated to create a sense of urgency without causing irritation:

THIS IS NOT A DRILL....THIS IS NOT A DRILL. ...THIS IS NOT A DRILL....

The weapons officer placed his face against the soft rubber visor and rotated the unmarked combination wheel. One by one, the glowing digits appeared: his wife's birthday in reverse prefixed by the first two numbers of his home address ZIP code. He cleared the display and pulled the safe's outer door open. Next, the executive officer pressed his eyes to the visor and spun his combination. The two men did not know each other's combination.

THIS IS NOT A DRILL.... THIS IS NOT A DRILL....

The executive officer opened the inner safe and removed the two identical keys. He gave one to the weapons officer. The two men returned to their respective stations: the executive officer to the command center and the weapons officer to the missile control center three decks below the command center. They moved through the carpeted, air-conditioned passageways in total silence.

THIS IS NOT A DRILL.... THIS IS NOT A DRILL....

Once in his control center, the weapons officer opened his safe. Inside were two triggers similar to a Colt 45's. One red, one black. The black trigger was for drills. The weapons officer selected the red trigger. He closed the safe and surveyed the row of technicians hunched over their consoles, saying nothing. The usual ebb and flow of good-natured banter had died when the submarine had been set to an ISQ condition and the signs had started flashing:

THIS IS NOT A DRILL.... THIS IS NOT A DRILL....

"Assign Missile One," the weapons officer ordered the weapons supervisor.
"Assign Missile One," the supervisor repeated woodenly for the benefit of the weapons center voice recorder. He pressed the button that started a computer checkout of Trident Missile One's control

systems. Targets were automatically assigned to each MIRV, depending on the submarine's position; the BUS's orbital trajectory was planned so that it could sprinkle its warheads to maximum effect.

The weapons officer inserted the firing key in the fire control box and turned it. He then screwed the red trigger into place. For psychological reasons the missile fire-control mechanism had been designed to resemble the stock of a handgun. It was felt that yet another button did not convey sufficient emotional regard for the control's significance.

Without turning around as he always did on the weekly drill, the weapons supervisor said: "Missile One assignment initiated."

The weapons officer flipped the intercom switch to the captain in the submarine's command center. "Missile assignment program initiated, sir."

The captain acknowledged and stared at the first of the many target lists that were appearing on a screen: names of cities, large towns, small towns. Some names he recognized, some he did not—spelled out in phonetic English with the Cyrillic version indented underneath. His firing key was in his left-hand pocket. It would remain there until the President's scrambled voice was received on four separate radio frequencies, reassembled by the submarine's computers and submitted for voice-print identification. Until the President had given the order and the captain had inserted his firing key, none of the Tridents could be fired. In the meantime, there was little to do but wait and try to ignore the flashing signs that repeated:

THIS IS NOT A DRILL....THIS IS NOT A DRILL- ....THIS IS NOT A DRILL....

48

The President of the United States was sitting in a soundproof glass booth, feeling like a contestant in a TV quiz show except that the stakes were the lives of a sixth of the world's population.

His mouth was dry. He poured another glass of water from the carafe and sipped, watching the soundless activities on the other side of the glass. The vast room was filled with senior officers from all the services. There were at least twenty phone conversations in progress but the President could see only lips moving. The wall map, showing the positions of the NATO and Warsaw Pact forces, was for the benefit of the humans in the room: the computers didn't need wall maps—the information on it was out of date by the potentially disastrous margin of five seconds.

His mouth was dry.

There was a marker that indicated the Kiev carrier crawling through the Bosphorus. Another marker in the Sea of Marmara was the British frigate tensely lying in wait for it.

His mouth was dry. He poured some more water. An army general was watching him. He managed to keep his hand steady.

A flashing light appeared on the wall map. Another Soviet Yankee-class nuclear submarine had been pinpointed, two hundred miles off Long Island. Anti-submarine helicopters would be tracking it with dipping sonar. The President had been a helicopter pilot and had once tracked a submerged Yankee for three hours. During that time the Russian captain had done everything within his command except perform underwater somersaults in his frantic efforts to shake off his remorseless pursuer. After three hours of twisting, abrupt changes of depth and course, sometimes stopping dead, then making off at thirty-five knots, the Russian had managed to escape by plunging beneath a layer of cold water that had bent the beam of the dipping sonar through twenty degrees. After that there had been another two hours' fruitless casting about over five hundred square miles of ocean—but the Russian sub had vanished.

Damn Yankees.

His mouth was dry.

Another glass of water.

"Your voice must sound quite natural when you give the order, Mr. President."

How the hell could anyone be expected to make his voice sound "quite natural" when giving such an order?

He bumped the microphone with the carafe. A dozen pairs of eyes turned toward the booth.

His mouth was still dry.

Damn Yankees.

49

The Kiev-class carrier moved through the late-afternoon haze like a gray ghost. The most formidable ghost ever to move on the surface of the Marmara. It was the Soviet Navy's first aircraft carrier—the result of thousands of hours spent by intelligence-gathering trawlers in the vicinity of American and British carriers; photographing them, measuring flight-deck lengths, height above the water, underwater hull form. One had even passed suicidally under the bows of the *Ark Royal* to see how quickly the British warship could maneuver.

Admiral Turgenev had transferred his flag to the Kiev. He knew about the British frigate and that it was still in the Marmara long after its Turkish visit was supposed to be over. It wasn't hard to guess why. For four days, as the Kiev had made its way across the Black Sea, the admiral had prayed that the politicians would see sense and would order him back to Sevastopol. Now, as he leaned on the bridge rail and studied the *Swiftfire* through his binoculars, it seemed too late. No one was going to yield.

He estimated that the British frigate was twenty kilometers away—straight ahead. The frigate's Wasp helicopter appeared to have been wheeled out of the aft hangar. The haze made it impossible to determine what was happening on the frigate's decks. They'd know in the radar room—at that range they'd be able to pick up even the slightest movement of the Seacat missile launchers.

A junior officer approached and saluted. "The captain sends his respects, sir. The helicopter on the frigate has started its motor. The chief radar officer has reported that its rotors are turning."

Turgenev returned the salute. His reply was drowned by the shrill clamor of the general quarters alarms sounding throughout the aircraft carrier.

He raised his binoculars. The Wasp was lifting away from the British warship. Slung between the machine's four oversize wheels was the unmistakable cigar shape of a torpedo.

50

The *Eureka*'s doctor bandaged Julia's hands in the research ship's sick bay while Captain Hagan fired questions at Oaf and Sherwood. The geologist's answer to his last question had staggered him.

"The *Orion* was what?"

"It's possible that it was sunk by a submerged iceberg," Sherwood repeated.

Hagan seemed unable to speak for a moment. "Do you seriously expect me to believe that?"

"I'm certain it was an iceberg," said Sherwood stubbornly. He wished he had kept quiet but Julia had insisted that he should make his suspicions known.

"A submerged iceberg?" said Hagan sarcastically.

Sherwood glanced at Julia but she avoided his eye. "It's up to you to stand up for yourself. No one else can believe in something for you," she had told him.

"It's submerged because there's a mountain in it—perhaps several. They were sheared away when they could no longer resist the ice-cap loading." Sherwood paused. It wasn't easy to talk with Hagan glaring at him with undisguised hostility. "At calving it would've measured about a hundred and eighty miles by ninety miles—triangular-shaped. Around eight thousand cubic miles of ice if it stayed in one piece."

Hagan had a glazed look. "I've a mind," he said hoarsely, "to fly the three of you back to where we found you."

Sherwood decided that it would be easier to back down and said: "It's only a theory, captain. I'm not saying that—"

"No!" said Julia angrily. "It's not. There are too many facts that fit: the freezing water where the *Orion* went down; the color of the sea—everything!"

Hagan remembered the curious hue in the CBS film. He frowned. Then there was the mystery of the freezing water that had killed so many after they had escaped from the liner. "What about the fog? Can your iceberg explain that too?"

"Warm air—cold sea," said Oaf, speaking for the first time.

Hagan was beginning to feel uncomfortable. Every time one of these three spoke they touched a sensitive nerve. "Okay," he said. "So where's this berg now?"

Sherwood thought. "This is where guesswork creeps in, but going on when the *Orion* sank and the slowness of the current, I'd say that it's moving in the general direction of the Cape Verde Islands."

"Drifting below the surface?"

"Yes. It must be. Until it drops the mountains, of course—then it'll surface. But even submerged it shouldn't be too difficult to locate. All you've got to do is base a team on the Cape Verde Islands with a helicopter so that they can systematically block-search the ocean for the iceberg's trail of low-salinity sea water—it'll be shedding millions of tons of fresh water each day."

Hagan decided that Sherwood was mad.

"I've just thought of something," said Julia.

So's she, thought Hagan.

Julia looked thoughtfully at Sherwood and said: "Is the iceberg touching the ocean floor as it moves?"

"It's possible," Sherwood admitted. "But there may not be any seismic indication because there's a layer of sediment on the ocean floor that's several hundred meters thick."

"But the sediment is dense enough to support the weight of telephone cables, isn't it?"

"Yes," Sherwood agreed, wondering what Julia was leading up to.

"There you are then," said Julia triumphantly. She turned to Hagan. "If Glen is right, sooner or later his iceberg is going to cut a transatlantic cable."

Julia's words had an immediate effect on Hagan. The color drained from his face and he stood abruptly. With a curt "Wait here" he moved quickly to the door and was gone.

51

"It's a report from Western Electric," said the Secretary of State's voice over the booth's speaker.

"They say that their repeaters in the TAT 12 United States-South Africa transatlantic telephone cable could not have been damaged to the extent that they were by a human agency. They cite the damage to repeater 133 as a typical example—"

"I'm not interested in details," interrupted the President curtly. "I want to know if we have sufficient grounds to call off this operation."

"There's something else, Mr. President. Western Electric says the mysterious cutting of cables has happened before. On November 18, 1929, most of the telegraph cables between America and Europe were cut one by one. A similar event happened even earlier in 1888, when several cables to Australia were cut. That led to Australia's mobilizing her navy. In both cases the cause was never discovered."

The President watched the activities in the room for some seconds before replying. The latest development was a polar patrol of twenty long-range Tupolev 95 bombers flying dangerously close to U.S. territory. NORAD were preparing to deal with them if their courses became Alaskan intrusive.

"The operation continues," he said.

52

Admiral Pearson acted on his own initiative in ordering that a ship-to-ship communication link between the American and Russian aircraft carriers be opened when he heard that the Russian ship was flying Admiral Turgenev's pennant.

Silence fell in the *Johnson*'s combat control center when Admiral Pearson picked up his phone.

"Good afternoon, Admiral Turgenev," he said in Russian. "This is Admiral Brandon Pearson speaking."

"Good afternoon," said the Russian politely.

"I'm sorry that you have not heeded our warnings and that you've gone ahead and violated the Montreux Convention."

"I'm not at liberty to discuss the matter," said the Russian coolly.

"If you turn back—"

"That is out of the question," said Admiral Turgenev. "The Soviet navy has merely exercised its right of passage through the Bosphorus."

Admiral Pearson listened patiently as the Russian outlined the background to the Montreux Convention.

"Have you requested permission to turn back?" Admiral Pearson asked, not expecting his opposite number to reply to the question.

He was surprised when the Russian said: "Yes. Just before we entered the Bosphorus."

"Can you see a British Wasp helicopter near you?"

"Yes. It is hovering six kilometers on our starboard quarter. We are watching it carefully." The Russian officer's tone was flat. Disinterested.

"It's waiting for my order to attack you," said Pearson simply.

A signals ensign, holding a sealed envelope, tried to approach Admiral Pearson but was intercepted by a lieutenant.

"It's from the admiral's aide on the *Eureka*," the ensign explained. "Captain Hagan. He says it's important."

"What did it say?"

"I don't know, sir. As it was classified, I sealed it as it came off the printer without reading it."

"Where is the *Eureka*?"

"In the South Atlantic. Its exact position is given in the header code."

The lieutenant took the envelope from the ensign. He considered it unlikely that a message from a research ship several thousand miles away could be of sufficient importance to warrant disturbing the admiral at this critical stage of the operation.

"Okay," the lieutenant said to the ensign. "I'll see the admiral gets it when he's free."

The ensign saluted and withdrew. The lieutenant dropped the envelope on a nearby console's working surface and promptly forgot it.

Admiral Pearson transferred the phone to his right ear. The Russian had made no reply to his previous statement. "Do you hear me, admiral?"

"I heard you," said Admiral Turgenev after a long pause. "If you do behave in such an aggressive manner, we have been instructed not to retaliate. But I very much doubt if similar instructions have been issued to the rest of our armed forces."

"Listen," said Pearson earnestly. "I'm prepared to avert this clash by canceling the operation and resigning my job if you're prepared to do the same by ordering your carrier to turn back."

"Resign my job?" the Russian echoed incredulously.

"Does it matter what happens to us?" said Pearson doggedly. "What the hell does it matter what happens to us just so long as our actions give everyone some breathing space?"

"We train our officers to obey orders," said Turgenev.

"Bullshit. You train them to use their initiative— just as we do."

"You obey your orders," said the Russian, "and I'll obey mine." There was a click and a hiss of carrier wave in Pearson's headset.

Pearson muttered to himself and dropped the phone back on its cradle. He ignored the no-smoking signs and lit a cigar. He looked up and met the eyes of the control officer, who was regarding him speculatively.

"Nothing from Washington?" asked Pearson.

"Nothing, sir."

Pearson inhaled on his cigar. He suddenly felt very old. For the first time in his life he regretted his choice

of career. He looked at the digital clock and said:
"This order timed at nineteen-zero-ten Zulu Time.
Initiate the attack."

53

The words spoken by the Wasp pilot as he gave a
running commentary on his attack approach were
heard in every major command center throughout
the NATO alliance. Every head of state was
listening; every general, admiral, and air marshal.
The crisp, even tones of the British pilot gave no
indication that he was aware of his distinguished
audience.

"Ten thousand yards," he said into his microphone.

He maintained a constant fifty feet above the sea
without referring to the Wasp's ground proximity
radar.

"ASI indicating six-zero knots . . . Reducing to four-
zero now."

The pilot kept his eyes fixed on his objective. If the
Soviet carrier, now looming larger with every
passing second, made the slightest alteration to her
speed or course, he was to break off the attack
immediately and await further instructions. At two
thousand yards, he was to drop the homing torpedo.

"Eight thousand yards. I have excellent visual
contact."

The President sipped from the glass of water.

"Six thousand yards," said the speaker in the
glass booth.

Strange that my pulse should be normal, thought
the President.

"Five thousand yards," said the speakers in the
Johnson's combat control center. "No sign of any

flight-deck activity. It looks deserted."

Admiral Pearson beckoned to the lieutenant he had seen take the envelope from a signals ensign while he was talking to the Soviet admiral.

"Four thousand yards," intoned the speakers.

"Sir?"

"What was the message?"

The lieutenant looked blank.

"You chased an ensign away just now."

The lieutenant's face cleared. "Oh yes, sir. That's right—there's a message for you from Captain Hagan."

"Three thousand yards," said the Wasp pilot. There was a perceptible quiver in his voice. There was something surrealistically beautiful about the serene carrier nosing its way gracefully through the clear, blue water.

His hand went to the torpedo release control. He knew exactly where it was—there was no need for his eyes to flicker from his magnificent target.

At 2,500 yards he released the safety catch.

At 2,300 yards he made the final course correction so that the torpedo would run true even if its acoustic homing controls failed.

The water was a blur beneath the Wasp. A red light flickered and then glowed steadily: the torpedo's detonator was already sensing the magnetic anomaly of the carrier's 45,000-ton presence.

"Positive gauss indication," said the pilot. "Two thousand one hundred yards. Dropping now."

He was about to operate the torpedo release control when a voice crashed urgently in his headphones: "Abort! Abort! Abort!"

The pilot hesitated. The Kiev's towering bulk swelled toward him. "Codeword!" he shouted, his fingers tensed on the release.

But before he had finished the word, the voice was urgently repeating: "Icarus! Icarus! Icarus!"

The pilot sheered away from the Soviet warship.

54

The tension between East and West slackened as quickly as it had begun. Neither side offered nor expected apologies. Service men and women throughout the Warsaw Pact and NATO alliance countries whose leave had been suspended were allowed to go home. Bombers were recalled, submarines returned to their billets, and border infantry movements halted.

It had been the thirteenth major alert since August 24, 1949—the day the North Atlantic Treaty had come into force.

There was a final touch of irony: five hours after the British Wasp helicopter had abandoned its attack on the Kiev, the Soviet aircraft carrier developed a serious steering-gear fault and was forced to turn back to Sevastopol.

PART TWO:

menace

CAPE VERDE ISLANDS
Group of fifteen mid-Atlantic volcanic islands
off northwest coast of Africa. Part of the central
Atlantic intrusive ridge that stretches from
Iceland to Tristan da Cunha. Portuguese.
Sugar, fruit, and tourism. Pop.: 300,000. Former-
ly a listening center for a "Seaguard" array.

The ice moved. It moved slowly northward; an
unseen, undetected harbinger of death.

Julia picked her way past the umbrellas that
speckled the beach like acne and sat on the sand
beside Sherwood. He opened an eye.
"Well?"
"We start work tomorrow. The instrument package has arrived. You lower it into the water for five
seconds and get an instant reading."
Sherwood said nothing. Lying on a hot beach was
something he had dreamed about in Antarctica.
Julia made herself comfortable. It was two hours to
sunset and still blindingly hot on the west-facing
beach.
"Where's Oaf?"
"Swimming somewhere."
Julia shaded her eyes. She had to look virtually
directly into the sun but she could pick out Oaf
swimming with long, easy strokes some twenty yards
from the surf that was indifferently demolishing
shrieking children's sandcastles. There were about a
hundred people in the water.
"Have you drawn up the search schedule?" asked
Julia.

Sherwood yawned and sat up. "I'll do it tomorrow morning. Never do today what you can put off till tomorrow."

A zephyr rustled the lunch wrappers of a nearby English family. The sudden breeze started a newspaper and sent it scudding for cover under an outcrop of rocks.

"Hey, Sherwood!" Oaf bellowed from the water. "Come and swim, you lazy bastard!"

"His manners are impossible," said Julia, noticing the disapproving look from the English mother.

The breeze strengthened slightly. Sherwood pulled a towel around his shoulders and watched Oaf swimming. "I've not noticed you complaining."

"Oaf's great advantage is that he is totally devoid of complications," said Julia with an impish smile.

Oaf trod water and swore loudly at some children who were splashing him.

Julia shivered. "There's a mist coming in. Look."

A bank of gray cloud, looking strangely out of place against the blue sea and sky, was seeping from the south across the water and dissolving the horizon.

Julia shivered again. "It's gone a bit chilly."

"Sunset soon."

"Yes, but it didn't do this the same time yesterday."

A dog was running along the tideline, chasing after pieces of driftwood thrown by its owner. It suddenly sat down in the surf, lifted its head to the darkening sky and bayed mournfully. Nearby children squealed in delight.

Julia heard one of the English children say: "Daddy, look! The sea's changing color!"

"That's because the sun's going down."

Julia was about to comment on the mist that had completely obliterated the horizon, when the dog's baying became a continuous, blood-curdling howl of fear.

"You don't know if there's rabies in these islands,

147

do you?" said Sherwood, apprehensively eying the terrified creature that was dragging its hindlegs through the surf and ignoring the soothing noises its frantic owner was making.

Julia felt her scalp crawl. She and the dog had sensed that something was terribly wrong.

Then the child was yelling excitedly. "Daddy! Mummy! Look! Look! The sea's turning to blood!"

A hundred yards out to sea several dolphins leaped high into the air, their tails thrashing wildly. They fell back and flailed the water white. Men, women, and children in the water were suddenly screaming in terror and jerking their arms and legs convulsively. People ran down the beach and plunged into the sea to rescue their children but were immediately seized by the same hideous paroxysms as soon as their bodies were immersed.

Julia and Sherwood stood and stared aghast at the terrible scene, knowing instinctively that there was nothing they could do.

A maddened dolphin bored blindly through the ferment of screaming, struggling people. Its sharp snout, moving at forty miles per hour, rammed into the small of a man's back with the full force of the creature's four-hundred-pound mass. The man's spine snapped like a piece of dry spaghetti. He died instantly but the nerve cells in his disrupted brain kept firing repeatedly, causing his dead arms to continue their savage spasms. He moved slowly through the seething mass of the dead and the dying. In death he had acquired an ability that had eluded him in life: he could swim.

Oaf's deep, guttural bellows carried across the blood-red water. The bodies of the children who had splashed him were floating face down within reach of his mighty, pounding fists.

Sherwood took a blind step forward. Julia reached for his arm. Without taking her eyes off the nightmare before her, she said quietly: "There's nothing we can do, is there?"

They stood motionless, side by side letting the sight and sound of the horror before them etch deeply into their memories.

2

The dead man gave the Portuguese army truck a friendly wave.

The motor convoy stopped. Six pairs of headlights lanced along the silent beach littered with the glistening corpses of dead fish. A searchlight on the leading truck probed the dead man. He waved again, moving a huge, hairy arm with a curious jerking motion. Oaf was dead; the macabre reflex action was caused by post-death cerebral rhythms that continued to surge through his poisoned brain.

Four men jumped down from the leading vehicle's tailboard: two soldiers carrying a folding stretcher, an army doctor and a black-gowned priest. The sea whispered mockingly at the group as they approached the dead man. They stepped over a tuna fish and carefully skirted a hammerhead shark that was lying on its side, its crescent jaw gaping and a pectoral fix twitching.

The soldiers set the stretcher down beside the giant dead man, staring apprehensively at the body while the doctor listened to his chest. The corpse lifted an arm, which became entangled in the doctor's stethoscope. The doctor pinned the arm down with his knee and nodded to one of the soldiers.

The priest faltered in his droning recital of the last rites. He licked his lips nervously and continued reading, holding his book at an angle to trap the light shining from the trucks. The soldiers reluctantly passed a leather strap around the shaggy corpse and fastened the buckle securely.

The doctor completed his examination and straightened up. Without being ordered, the soldiers lifted the heavy body onto the stretcher and carried it back to the waiting convoy.

Oaf's body was the sixty-third recovered from the Cape Verde beaches that night. Few of them had required so much effort to carry.

They were mostly children.

3

Admiral Howe absently tossed pieces of bread to a squabble of London starlings as he listened to Abbott making his report. It was amazing that those three had turned up on the Cape Verde Islands but he was confident that they knew nothing about the missing submarine *Asteria*. If Brill was certain then that was good enough.

"But my big worry," Abbott concluded, "is that sooner or later I'm going to make a serious mistake in the crew's correspondence."

Admiral Howe threw the last piece of bread. "You're coping admirably, James."

"There have been minor errors, sir," Abbott confessed. "Luckily I've always managed to explain them away in subsequent letters."

The starlings moved aggressively in on a St. James's Park drake who had a whole slice of bread to himself. Admiral Howe watched their antics with amusement.

"Well, you won't have to worry for much longer, James. It's been decided to abandon the operation. The *Asteria* will be posted as missing as soon as a favorable opportunity arises."

4

Sherwood looked on as Julia drew a column of the red-tinted seawater into a pipette and carefully smeared a few drops on to a clean slide. The nuns who ran the hospital on Cape Verde had agreed to let her use their tiny laboratory.

She was about to place the slide under the microscope when her hands suddenly started trembling uncontrollably. Sherwood gently disengaged her fingers from the slide and pressed the palm of her hand to his lips. He had remained at her side that morning throughout the three hour mass burial service. The only time her outward calm had nearly collapsed was when she had bent over Oaf's open coffin to give the shaggy giant a farewell kiss.

"Sometimes it helps if you cry a little," said Sherwood softly.

Julia shook her head and turned back to the work bench. "I'm okay now." Her voice was expressionless.

Sherwood reluctantly released her hand. Julia placed the slide under the microscope and stared through the eyepieces for some seconds before indicating that Sherwood should look.

He peered down at the thousands of magnified creatures that resembled delicate, transparent bells.

"Are they the ostracods you told me about?" he asked.

"No."

"What then?"

"They're a dinoflagellate—*Cymnodinium breve*," said Julia dully. "A sudden drop in sea temperature kills them and they release a mild nerve toxin into water. Quite common in the Gulf of Mexico where they cause the so-called red tides."

"And they caused...?"

"Fish swimming through the red bloom are killed as their nerve axons start firing—their entire nervous systems are disrupted."

Sherwood straightened up and eyed the flask of sea water. "Is that stuff still dangerous, Julia?"

Julia stared out of the window at the distant blue sea. "No. The toxin decays rapidly in sunlight."

"But if it's only a mild toxin, then how—?"

"Take another look," said Julia. "I've never seen such a concentration of them."

Sherwood looked through the microscope again at the myriads of bell-like organisms.

He found it impossible to believe that they could turn the ocean into a deadly nerve gas.

5

Supreme Allied Commander Atlantic, Admiral Brandon Pearson was a better listener than talker. He sat very still in his cabin on the aircraft carrier *Johnson*, asked only the occasional question and nodded his head from time to time to encourage Sherwood to keep talking. Nothing in his face betrayed his reactions to the geologist's theory concerning a gigantic submerged iceberg. Just once, when Sherwood repeated his figure of eight thousand cubic miles of ice, did Pearson catch Hagan's eye. That was the only lapse. The Marine captain was sitting on a chair near the door making notes. Julia had said her piece and was silent.

Pearson held up a hand. "Wait a minute, Mr. Sherwood. Tell me how your berg reached the Cape Verde Islands from Antarctica."

"My belief is that it was carried on the West Wind Drift Current in the Southern Ocean, then picked up by the Benguela Current that flows northward up the coast of South West Africa, and is now being pushed northwest across the Atlantic toward the Eastern Seaboard of America by the North Equatorial Current."

A tap at the door broke the silence that followed. Hagan answered it and returned to his seat reading two signals.

Pearson tipped his chair back and steepled his fingers. "And what's your estimate of your berg's present size?" He had used the expression "your berg" in all the questions put to Sherwood.

"I'm not sure, sir," Sherwood answered after a moment's thought. "We've no information on the behavior of submerged icebergs and virtually none on the temperature or direction of subsurface ocean currents. I've based my guesswork—and that's just about what it is—on the known movements of surface currents."

Pearson stood. "Thank you for seeing me, Miss Hammond, Mr. Sherwood. I'd appreciate it if you would agree to remaining awhile on the *Eureka* until we've investigated further."

The interview was over.

"And you believe them?" Pearson fired at Hagan a minute later, when Julia and Sherwood had left.

"Yes, sir. That's why I sent them to Cape Verde in the first place."

"My God, I've been asked to swallow some things in my time," Pearson muttered. "Did you get down everything Sherwood said?"

"Yes, sir." Hagan passed the two signals to Admiral Pearson. "These came while you were talking to him." Hagan gave a ghost of a smile as he spoke.

The SACLANT read the first one. It was from the Scripps Institution of Oceanography. They had completed their own tests on the Cape Verde sea-water sample and confirmed Julia Hammond's findings. In addition, they cited the incident at Miami Beach in February 1969 in which several bathers had suffered dinoflagellate brain damage.

The second signal was from the Naval Space-Surveillance Center at Dahlgren, Virginia:

YOUR REQUEST INFORMATION LARGE ICEBERGS. LARGEST SEEN PHOTOGRAPHED BY ESSA-3 SATELLITE DURING 1967/1968. BERG REMAINED IN WEDDELL SEA. FIRST SEEN ORBIT 4699 ON OCTOBER 11 1967. LAST SEEN ORBIT 6408 ON FEBRUARY 27 1968. SIZE 175 KILOMETERS BY 111 KILOMETERS. BERG DESIGNATION—GIANT TABULAR. ...

Pearson broke off reading. His eyes met Hagan's. "Only a few kilometers smaller than Sherwood's iceberg," said Hagan, reading Pearson's thoughts.

6

FLIP
Floating Instrument Package

From: Walter J. Krantz
      Department of Transportation
      U.S. Coast Guard (3rd Coast Guard District)
      International Ice Patrol Headquarters
      Governors Island
      New York, N.Y. 10004

To: Admiral Brandon Pearson, SACLANT, U.S.S. *Johnson*.

Dear Admiral,

Reference: Conversation transcript—yourself/G. Sherwood/J. Hammond.

We have read. We have considered. And we are skeptical. Our experience of icebergs is limited to Greenland bergs, in particular those bergs calved in Baffin Bay and swept into the North Atlantic shipping lanes by the Labrador Current. These are the icebergs that concern us. Occasionally a large berg drifts as far south as Boston and we've heard from contacts in South Africa of an Antarctic berg that was sighted off Cape Town in 1955, so there's no doubt that icebergs can and do drift exceptionally long distances. But it is impossible for any iceberg, Arctic or Antarctic, to survive long enough to cross the equator. We are astonished that Mr. Sherwood (whom we recall served with us for a period as an IIP observer) should believe that such an unprecedented event has taken place. Ask Mr. Sherwood why the calving of eight thousand cubic miles of ice did not leave a seismic fingerprint and why the inevitable wave disturbance was not registered by FLIPS owned by Scripps and the British IOS.

A detailed analysis of all Mr. Sherwood's points will be with you within twenty-four hours. We are not qualified to comment on Miss Hammond's remarks concerning ocean toxin level increases caused by the death of plankton.

Sincerely,

(Signed)
Walter J. Krantz
Deputy Vice-Commander, International Ice Patrol

7

"Sit down, Mr. Sherwood," said Admiral Pearson affably as the geologist was shown into his cabin. Sherwood sat in the indicated chair. His original awe at meeting the Supreme Allied Commander had faded. He now felt irritated at being shuttled back and forth by helicopter between the *Eureka* and the *Johnson.*

"There's a flaw in your theory about your giant iceberg," said Pearson. "A serious flaw."

"I'm surprised you've found only one," said Sherwood evenly. "Personally, I don't care if you find a thousand and one flaws."

Pearson ignored the comment. "Experts on icebergs say that eight thousand cubic miles of ice taking to the water would cause a seismic disturbance. They've been going over the records. There's been no significant earthquake activity in Antarctica for several years." He unwrapped a cigar while waiting for Sherwood to answer. "Well, Mr. Sherwood?"

"The iceberg more than likely rode on a lubricating cushion of water melted by friction as it broke away from the ice cap," Sherwood answered. "I never said that it moved quickly. It's possible that it took as long as a month to slide into the sea. But, however slowly it moved, it would've had more than enough momentum to carry it over the continental shelf and into deep water."

Pearson lit his cigar. He was beginning to revise his opinions about Sherwood.

"So where's that iceberg now, Mr. Sherwood?"

Sherwood noticed that for once Admiral Pearson didn't say "your berg." "Have you kept up the search for it, admiral?"

"I called it off. So where is it now?"

"I can only make a rough guess."

"Right now, Mr. Sherwood, your guesswork is all we've got to go on."

Sherwood looked up into the expressionless eyes. It was Admiral Pearson's first admission, though indirect, that he believed in the iceberg's existence. "Approximately halfway between the Cape Verde Islands and Puerto Rico, admiral. But please understand that that is a very rough guess indeed."

Pearson nodded. "That's understood."

"May I make a suggestion please?"

"Sure."

"My estimate could be miles out. It might be a good idea if you broadcast a request to all shipping to report to the *Johnson* or the *Eureka* any unusual phenomenon—no matter how minor it may seem. Slight changes in the color of the sea—anything."

Two hours after the request was issued a U.S. Coast Guard cutter called up the *Johnson* and said that they had spotted an apparently abandoned schooner, the *Bermuda Witch*, sailing by itself under a full spread of canvas, and were proposing to board it.

8

The ice moved.

Each day the embracing warmth of the Atlantic depths destroyed a hundred million tons of its titanic bulk—an infinitesimal percentage. But the mass of the mountains locked in the five-million-year-old grip of the ice remained unchanged. Gradually, they dragged the ice deeper and deeper into the thick primeval sediment that covered the floor of the ocean.

The moment came when the ice stopped.

Once again the mountains had triumphed.

The black-headed gulls screamed raucous insults at the coast guardsman as he stood unsteadily on the low roof of the cutter's motor launch. He tensed his thigh muscles and jumped. His fingers closed thankfully round one of the schooner's deck stanchions. The sudden movement raised an angry, swirling storm of screaming gulls from the sailing ship's rigging. A second later he had swung over the rail and was safely aboard the seemingly abandoned *Bermuda Witch.* The motor launch sheered away and paced the big schooner on her quarter.

The wheeling gulls settled on rigging and coamings and stared malevolently at the guardsman with hard, gimlet eyes. A thousand vicious beaks and a thousand pairs of beadlike, unblinking eyes followed him as he moved aft. The ship was heeling under a full spread of canvas. The guardsman slid his hand along the rail to support himself, for the teak deck was slippery with fresh guano. A gull refused to move even though the guardsman's hand had moved to within a yard of its perch. Its dazzling white plumage was flecked with crimson. There was something in its stiletto beak—something red that dripped red onto the deck. The bird gulped and a bulge moved down through the feathers that covered the creature's throat. The guardsman felt his heart beating faster. He glanced up into the rigging. Blue sky. Bright sun. And the birds. Thousands of birds. Watching him speculatively.

And all of them had crimson-flecked plumage.

The guardsman reached for the two-way radio clipped to his belt. The movement startled the bird. It rose up suddenly—its three-foot span flashing white and red—and lunged at the guardsman. He saw the beak darting for his eyes and threw up his arm. The screaming bird lifted effortlessly into the rigging. The guardsman lowered his arm. There was a long gash above the wrist.

Then he saw the young man. He was sitting under an awning near the wheelhouse. A black-headed gull was perched unconcerned like a pet on the young man's lap. The guardsman crept fearfully forward, his eyes open wide in horror and disbelief. He jerked the radio to his mouth and pressed the transmit button with a trembling finger. He moved his lips in terror but could make no sound.

The young man was dead but he had been helping the black-headed gulls to live.

The guardsman dropped the radio, staggered to the rail and was violently sick.

10

The ice lay still.

It was weighed down by the mountains and partially covered by the thousand-foot-deep layer of sediment that covered the ocean floor.

There was no daylight. There never had been daylight at this depth and never would be.

There was movement; the continuous luminescent flurry of grotesque bottom-feeding fish shying away from the sudden increase in the density of the sea water caused by the intense cold.

There were sounds; splintering and groaning noises from deep within the ice. The tensions and forces that had gripped the mountains for five million years were being pried loose by the ocean's tenuous warmth.

The moment of freedom for the ice was at hand.

GLORIA (Geophysic Long Range Inclined Asdic)
A streamlined, towed sonar instrument package
with an angled scan that enables three-
dimensional pictures of the ocean floor to be
constructed.

"Tuna fish," were Admiral Pearson's first accusing words as he stepped out of his helicopter that had
landed on the *Eureka*'s platform. "How in the world
could a freshly caught tuna kill everyone aboard that
schooner?"

Before Sutherland, the *Eureka*'s captain, could
reply, Admiral Pearson had turned around and was
giving Hagan orders. "Take this chopper back to the
Johnson and round up my things. Bring them
straight here. If Captain Sutherland has a suitable
cabin, I'm staying here. Okay with you, captain?"

Sutherland recovered his composure quickly.
"You're very welcome, admiral. We have a spare
cabin that I can move into—"

"Anywhere will do, captain," Pearson interrupted.
He caught sight of Sherwood and Julia watching him
and gave them a cursory nod. "Now what's all this
about tuna fish?"

Sutherland opened the *Bermuda Witch*'s log and
pointed to one of the last entries.

09:44 Extraordinary behavior by several fish. Dolphins and porpoises charging about on the surface as
if demented. A good-sized tuna stunned itself by
ramming us amidships; enough for generous por-

tions for everyone tonight. Sea an unusual reddish color.

"And your biologists have examined the tuna?" inquired Admiral Pearson when he had finished reading.

"The remains were in the schooner's freezer," said Sutherland. "It was suffering from an inflammation of the brain and there were large quantities of toxic neural cells in its flesh—probably released from the creature's bloodstream."

"And they're tasteless?"

"Presumably, yes."

Pearson lit a cigar. "What do you think of Sherwood's theory?"

"It's the only one we've got. All scientific theories are in essence torture chambers for the facts. If one of my team comes up with another theory, then we'll put it to the test."

Pearson inhaled. "Has that happened?"

"A Scripps member who's with us suggested a leaking can of nerve gas on the ocean floor. Sherwood's theory was the one that survived."

"Well, he's persuasive—I'll give him that," Pearson commented.

Sutherland smiled. "That's because he doesn't give a damn whether or not you're persuaded."

"And you've come across nothing to disprove him? Absolutely nothing?"

"Absolutely nothing."

"And it's not worrying him?"

Sutherland shook his head. "Not until the *Bermuda Witch* came along. Now he seems to think that we might have a chance of getting evidence."

"How's that?"

Sutherland indicated the *Bermuda Witch*'s log that was lying open. "We know the exact time and date when that schooner ran into trouble, admiral. ...*And* we know the exact position."

Pearson looked faintly amused. "I wouldn't put too much faith in the positions obtained by a weekend sailor."

"It's not like that," said Sutherland. "The *Bermuda Witch* had some good equipment. Namely Decca Navigator. The recorder was running when the Coast Guard found her."

Pearson was immediately very interested. "The hell it was?"

"We're going to swing our GLORIA out in about an hour. Towing it will mean a speed reduction, but we should be scanning the ocean floor where the *Bermuda Witch* picked up that poisoned tuna fish in approximately ten hours."

12

Twelve men, including Captain Sutherland, Sherwood, and Admiral Pearson were crowded into the *Eureka*'s GLORIA control cabin, watching the sonograph scanning head draw a fresh picture of the ocean floor three miles below the research ship. There was a meandering groove in the sediment.

"There it is," said Sherwood. "An iceberg plough mark."

"A what?" asked Pearson.

"An iceberg plough mark," Sherwood repeated. "About twelve miles wide by a mile deep. Fairly common in the North Atlantic. They're caused by icebergs cutting a furrow in the sediment. Most of them date from the last ice age and have been virtually obliterated by subsequent sediment deposits."

"It's the biggest one I've ever seen," said one of the sonar technicians.

Sherwood pointed to the sonograph. "You can see

where it crosses much older plough marks."

Admiral Pearson stared at the groove. Even his untrained eye could see that the edges of the giant plough mark were fresh. Twelve miles wide! Sherwood answered his next question before it was asked.

"Unless we're heading the wrong way along that plough mark, it looks like only a matter of time before we..."

Pearson didn't hear the rest of the sentence. He nodded to Sutherland and Hagan, and gestured to the door. Once outside in the passageway, Pearson said to Sutherland: "I want you to maintain a twenty-four-hour watch with GLORIA."

"We never tow at night in case something goes wrong," Sutherland protested. "GLORIA costs over two million dollars."

"I'll take the responsibility," said Pearson crisply. He turned to Hagan. "Tell the *Johnson* to get here fast. It doesn't matter if there are Soviet AGIs around that might learn her top speed."

"But what will be the point in having that CVB under our feet, admiral?" Sutherland asked.

Pearson ignored the no-smoking sign and lit a cigar. "Because I'm developing a healthy respect for Sherwood's opinions and I'd feel a lot happier having the *Johnson* around. And happier still if it turns out that she won't be needed."

13

The plough mark had vanished.

Sherwood dropped wearily into the chair beside the sonar technician and watched the picture emerging under the GLORIA scanning head. "When did it disappear?"

"It hasn't," said the technician. "Watch."

The technician operated a control that swung the questing sonic beam to the left of the *Eureka*'s heading. A new image of the ocean floor appeared under the scanning head. This time the sonograph showed a steep precipice that swept up one side of the recording paper.

"Seven thousand feet high," said the technician uneasily. "The plough mark's still there—it's just that it's too wide to be displayed on the paper. That's the edge of it."

"How wide?"

The technician swallowed. "Would you believe...forty-five miles...right on maximum range of this thing?"

Sherwood kept his voice steady. "You've checked the transducer array?"

"And the backup. Same result."

The two men watched the sonograph in silence.

"Have you called anyone else?" asked Sherwood when the scanning head started filling in a new sonograph.

"No." The technician looked unhappy. "You know something? I've been five years on this ship and I've tracked plough marks in the south that must've been made by the grandfathers of all icebergs, but I've never seen anything like that before."

But Sherwood wasn't listening. He had noticed something about the sonograph that was turning his bowels to water.

14

It was 5:30 A.M. A clear sky over the Atlantic held the promise of another warm day. But the weather did nothing for Admiral Brandon Pearson's temper. Usually it improved as the day lengthened. At 5:30

A.M. it was dangerously short. He resented being wakened and made his resentment abundantly clear to Hagan.

"Sherwood requests your presence in the control cabin, sir," said Hagan smoothly, handing his superior a cup of hot, black coffee. "I didn't want to disturb you but Sherwood does seem very agitated about something."

Pearson punctuated his sips of the scalding drink with biting remarks about civilians.

Any second now he'll notice that the ship's stopped, thought Hagan.

"Why's the ship stopped?"

"I don't know, sir."

Ten minutes later Pearson was venting his temper on Sherwood in the confined space of the GLORIA control cabin.

"Why have the engines stopped, Mr. Sherwood?"

"So that we can hear properly," said Sherwood, plugging in a pair of headphones. "If you would kindly sit here, sir."

Pearson allowed himself to be sat in one of the swivel chairs facing the console. Sherwood gave him the headphones.

"And *I* need to sleep properly, Mr. Sherwood."

"Would you put them on please, sir."

"It had better be something soothing," Pearson growled, settling the headphones over his ears. The geologist's anxious expression had a calming effect on his temper. "What am I supposed to hear?"

"Increase the volume," Sherwood said to the technician.

The technician increased the volume.

Pearson frowned. "Well?"

"Can you hear anything?"

"No."

"We're using the GLORIA's receiver as a passive listening device," explained Sherwood. "And we're sweeping through three hundred and twenty degrees...."

Pearson opened his mouth to blast Sherwood but the words froze on his lips as the silence in the headphones penetrated his sleep-hazed judgment.

The sea is never silent! Never!

Sherwood noticed that Pearson had almost imperceptibly stiffened with shock. He correctly guessed that the shrewd old sailor knew all about the continuous background uproar in the ocean caused by the interminable clicking and chirruping noises made by dolphins, whales, and porpoises. Their high-pitched sonar was known to have a range of many miles.

Sherwood said slowly: "There are probably more dolphins and porpoises on this planet than there are people. So where have they all gone?"

Pearson made no reply. He had noticed that the characteristic black flecks on the sonograph that were caused by returning echoes from the fish were conspicuous by their absence. "There's a complete absence of *all* fish returns," Pearson pointed out at length.

Sherwood nodded. "Nothing. It's as if all marine life has been wiped out." He paused and added suggestively: "Or frightened away."

"So what does it prove?" asked Pearson. He pulled one of the padded headphones away from his ear so that he could hear Sherwood properly. "Strange things happen at sea, as they say."

"This is even stranger," Sherwood replied while operating a control on the console. "I'm angling the receiver up so that it's picking up noises generated on the surface. Have a listen. Sounds like a heavy ship is going all out for breaking records. Getting stronger too. It's about a hundred miles away."

Pearson listened to the heavy beat of powerful screws turning at high speed. He could even hear the unmistakable whine of steam turbines.

"That's probably the *Johnson*," said Pearson, now

getting angry again. "Have you got me up at this ungodly hour to listen to—"

"No," said Sherwood sharply. "We got you up to listen to this."

Sherwood spun the inclination control. The sound of the *Johnson* was replaced by a noise that was like no noise that Pearson had ever heard before. His expression changed to one of astonishment and he clamped both headphones more firmly over his ears. There were echoing reports that sounded like underwater explosions and a demonic shrieking rising to a crescendo with undertones of distant thunder. The hideous cacophony of the deep boomed like a malignant, unimaginable being that was devouring the bowels of the earth. Pearson was unable to hear his own voice when he said: "What the hell is it?"

"Ice," said Sherwood simply.

The admiral seemed to be hypnotized by the terrible sounds in his headphones. He listened for some seconds, then removed the headphones and laid them on the console without speaking.

"The receivers are picking up those noises from the ocean floor," said Sherwood quietly. "About seventy miles away and in the *Johnson*'s path. It sounds as if the carrier's moving at high speed."

Pearson nodded and stared at the headphones. The whispering, ethereal sounds were clearly audible. "I told it to get here as fast as possible."

"Then surely she'll hear those noises and alter course?"

Pearson looked at Sherwood with lusterless eyes. "No... She won't hear anything. She has to retract her underwater listening gear into the hull when moving at speeds above thirty knots."

Suddenly the noises in the headphones stopped. Sherwood snatched them up and clamped them over his ears. He turned the amplifier up to maximum again and listened intently. His eyes widened with shock.

"Admiral," he said, keeping his voice under tight control. "We've got to get out of this area as fast as possible."

PART THREE:

destruction

The ice moved.

It moved with infinite slowness—testing its new-found buoyancy now that it had finally torn itself free from the mountains it had dragged halfway across the world.

The ponderous, multi-billion-ton mass moved uncertainly in the sluggish bottom current.

The ice lifted.

One hundred feet... Five hundred feet...

A small mountain, whose jagged escarpments had held it in place, was finally dislodged. It fell slowly into the layer of primeval ooze that carpeted the ocean floor.

The ascent of the ice quickened. It gently, but inexorably, shouldered aside the millions of tons of sea water of its own displacement.

Suddenly the movement of the colossus became an accelerating, exultant surge of freedom.

2

Lieutenant Jack Klein, flying a Skywarrior from the U.S.S. *Johnson*, was the only witness.

He was at 15,000 feet when he spotted the sudden discoloration of the sea. He estimated that the bloom covered an area 24 miles by 40 miles—1,000 square miles of ocean turning to blood.

He dived while maintaining a running commentary to the *Johnson*, which was 150 miles to the east and cramming on every knot to get away from the scene of the impending disaster.

Then it happened.

Klein leveled out at 5,000 feet and stared aghast at the surface. It was lifting and changing from its red hue to a maddened welter of white foam as if the sea were boiling.

It continued to heave upward—swelling into a mighty hump like a gargantuan cancer on the face of the ocean.

The ice erupted into the dawn sunlight. Sparkling crystal cliffs rounded by the erosion of the warm water; hills, valleys; a curious mountain in the center that was shaped like an upended anvil; and even rapidly forming rivers of cascading sea water that cut deep ravines as Klein numbly watched.

It was a country. A floating country. In ice. Millions upon millions of tons of ice.

Klein forgot the commentary as he circled the glistening continent. His hands on the controls moved automatically. The querulous voice of the *Johnson* in his flying helmet was forgotten. He gazed down over the rim of the Skywarrior's canopy, hypnotized by the dreadful beauty of the largest moving object on the planet.

A remote corner of his stupefied brain clung grimly to its powers of reason. And even that was dominated by one thought: *There's nine-tenths of it below the surface.*

Huge cataracts continued to roar into the broken sea, adding incalculable energies to the encircling tidal wave that was racing outward from the scene of the terrible renaissance.

3

The tidal wave was three miles away and roaring toward the *Eureka* at the speed of an express train.

Sutherland was the only man on the bridge—on his orders. He spun the helm so that the research ship's ice-wise bows would meet the charging mountain of water head on.

The *Eureka* and her company had had ten hours to prepare mentally and physically for the catastrophic, inescapable event that was now virtually upon them. Every hatch was battened down. The huge space-track antennae, which could have punched right through the decks if they were dislodged, were now dismantled and stowed below. All heavy equipment had been secured, watertight doors closed, and buoyancy chambers tested. The harnesses on the ship's scuba breathing sets had been cannibalized so that everyone could lash himself into his bunk with his hands resting on the quick-release buckles.

Admiral Pearson had refused to leave in his helicopter on the grounds that no sailor would dream of quitting a ship that was in trouble. And besides— they were out of range of land so where could the helicopter go to?

The tidal wave was thirty minutes from the *Eureka* when Sherwood entered Julia's cabin. She was lying on her bunk staring up at the deckhead. She turned her eyes when Sherwood's shadow fell across her face.

"I thought I'd see if your harness is okay," said Sherwood awkwardly.

Julia gazed up at him for several eternal seconds before closing her eyes. There was a faint smile on her lips. Sherwood hesitantly put his hand on her harness quick release buckle. Without opening her eyes Julia covered his hand with her hand and gripped his fingers tightly.

"There's so much I should've said before," Sherwood began, but Julia pressed a finger to his lips. She slid her hand round the back of his neck and drew his head down to her breasts. The last time Sherwood had touched her body had been when she was on the point of death in the *Orion*'s life raft. But this time, her heart was beating quickly.

They remained like that as the minutes slipped by; not moving, not speaking, holding each other close and waiting.

In their respective cabins, Hagan and Pearson lay silent. Hagan had adjusted the older man's buckles to ensure that they were not too tight and had left without speaking. They had shaken hands. Nothing more than that was necessary.

Forty-nine men and one woman prayed to their individual gods as they listened to the approaching thunder that heralded the end.

Sutherland viewed his own end with equanimity as he watched the roaring wall of water hurtling toward him. There was a certain peace of mind derived from knowing that there was nothing he could do; neither his skill nor the *Eureka*'s reinforced hull could save it. The ship, although designed to survive the worst weather the planet could throw at it, would be slammed onto her side and crushed within seconds.

An ironic thought crossed his mind that made him smile: as a keen surf rider, he had dreamed of meeting the mythical, unbroken giant roller that went on forever. It was also his wish that when he died—it would be at sea.

It looked as if both of those ambitions were about to be realized.

4

The U.S.S. *Johnson* survived.

Just.

She was saved from certain annihilation by her hundred-mile head start and her third-of-a-million horsepower, which gave her a top speed of forty-two knots.

The tidal wave, diminishing in mass and velocity, finally caught up with her after an eastward transoceanic charge that had covered a thousand miles in just under twenty-four hours. The *Johnson* broke records but there were no celebrations aboard as she swung her bows to meet the tidal wave when it was within three miles. Five minutes later it was upon her. The angled flight deck disappeared under the rolling mountain. Those aircraft for which there was no room on the hangar deck or which couldn't be flown off were swept over the side like confetti in a wind tunnel.

For a few seconds that stretched into eternity only her towering island was visible above the seething maelstrom. To her aircrews circling above the stricken flat top it seemed inevitable that she would flounder, leaving them air-stranded. For agonizing moments the mighty pride of the U.S. Navy teetered on the brink of destruction, her flight deck level with the boiling sea in the tidal wave's wake.

Slowly, the prayed-for miracle happened; the carrier's huge reserves of buoyance fought back. The blunt bows lifted, shedding countless tons of her impossible burden. The sea roared through her scuppers like the discharge valves at the base of a dam.

And so the *Johnson* survived. The damage she had

sustained would cost several million dollars to repair.
But she still had her flight deck, she still had her
aircrews and most of her aircraft.

She was still a warship and was still capable of
fighting.

5

London.

A gloomy day for the Lloyd's underwriters as the
Lutine bell clanged mournfully through the steadily
lengthening list of those ships that had been lost
between the Bermudas and Barbados.

The great bell (formerly the ship's bell of H.M.S. *La
Lutine*, which had sunk off the Dutch coast in 1799),
was rung once when a ship was reported missing and
twice when an overdue ship was reported safe.

Only solitary chimes were heard that day.

The *Plaistow*, the *Cobra*, the *Esso Cumbria*, the
Eureka... The names rattled out unceasingly on the
teleprinters.

Then the first unconfirmed reports began to trickle
out of New York. Cuba—severe flooding; the Virgin
Islands—hit by freak tidal wave; Puerto Rico—
disastrous flooding; Haiti and the Dominican
Republic—extensive flooding of coastal areas caused
by freak tidal wave....

Then the names of more ships and radio reports
relayed to London that spoke of a freak tidal wave.
Baffled huddles of underwriters discussed the
mystery.

At 4 P.M. the satellite pictures arrived and the
stunned world learned about White Atlantis. The
name was coined by a journalist holidaying in
Miami, where only minor effects of the exhausted
tidal wave were felt.

As usual with natural disasters, it was the poor countries that suffered the most.

6

The hot Indian summer that was dominating the weather systems of the northern hemisphere was encouraging the tourists to linger in London. St. James's Park was unusually crowded.

Admiral Howe sat down beside Lieutenant Abbott and stretched out his legs.

"How did the meeting go, sir?"

"You can forget your letter writing now, James. It was decided to add the *Asteria*'s name to the list of missing ships. The submarine's loss will be announced tomorrow."

Abbott looked immensely relieved. "Thank you, sir. I don't think I could've kept up the charade much longer."

Admiral Howe frowned. Abbott's labeling of the operation as a charade irritated him. But he said nothing. There was no point—the whole wretched business was over and tomorrow the submarine *Asteria* would be officially "dead."

Or so he thought.

7

The President was in no mood for half measures.

"Now listen," he said bluntly to his aide. "There's a million people on those islands who need help, and need it badly. Medical attention, food, shelter, and clothing—in that order. We don't hold discussions with local government officials—that's how relief supplies end up on the market. We fly supplies right in to where they're needed and we rely on the helicopter aircrews to do the decision making. What do we know about the iceberg? Who is taking responsibility for it?"

"The Coast Guard."

"Why?"

"They run the International Ice Patrol."

"How big is it?"

"No one knows."

The President looked annoyed. "Why not?"

"It's covered in fog. The Coast Guard has been using its slant radar on the berg from a C-130. They say that ice plays hell with returns. They won't commit themselves on its size."

The aide was used to being grilled; his answers were fired back as quickly as the questions were asked.

The President considered. "Presumably all available surface ships are involved with relief operations?"

"That's right."

The two men were close friends. There was no need for the aide to use the formal "Mr. President" when they were alone.

A telephone rang. The aide picked it up and listened. "Yeah...I'm with him now." His face paled with shock. "She's what?"

The President raised inquiring eyebrows.

"Yes...I'll tell him.... Yes. Thank you."

The aide slowly replaced the receiver and stared at it for some seconds.

"This is going to take some believing. The *Eureka*'s safe. No casualties—no injuries. She's only just fixed up her radio antenna and got a signal out."

"Pearson's alive?" The President looked delighted.

"And well. But the *Eureka*'s a long way out of the tidal wave's primary destruction zone."

"Wait a minute. She was right in the middle of it yesterday before she disappeared. How the hell did she escape?"

"That's the bit that you won't believe."

8

Deke Sutherland grinned broadly at the TV interviewer's incredulous reaction to the answer he had given him.

The interviewer tightened his grip on his microphone and looked desperately around the *Eureka*'s helicopter platform, which he and his film crew had landed on. The research ship had stopped to allow the machine to land and had resumed its steady ten knots. Everything about the ship was in perfect working order. There was no damage—nothing for the carrion movie camera, perched one-eyed and disappointed on its operator's shoulder, to feed on.

"Would you repeat that please, Captain Sutherland?"

"We rode the wave," said Sutherland, ignoring the interviewer's pre-take admonishment not to look at the camera.

It panned away briefly to eye Julia up and down. She was holding Sherwood's hand. The interviewer had noticed that they had been inseparable—something to be investigated later.

"You surfed a ten-thousand-ton ship on a tidal wave?"

"In front of it," Sutherland corrected. "Would you like me to explain?"

"Please."

"Well, the *Eureka*'s got a V underwater hull form that enables her to ride up if she's ever trapped in pack ice. Pretty unusual. It also enables her to go into

178

areas where episodic waves are known to occur. Five years ago we found one just inside the hundred-fathom line off South East Africa. The way the *Eureka* rode that wave made me wonder if she would do the same for the tidal wave." Sutherland looked sheepish. "I only thought of it just before the wave was upon us. I put the helm over so that the *Eureka* was running at an angle to it when it reached us.... Except that it didn't get to us until we'd reached ten degrees north and the wave was down to a reasonable size." Sutherland went on to outline some of the finer points of surfing until the interviewer cut him short.

Then it was Admiral Pearson's turn before the eye. He praised Captain Sutherland's seamanship and concluded: "He gave us a ride that we'll never forget."

"But there are definitely no casualties?"

"None," said Pearson.

"And no damage?"

"There is some."

The interviewer looked hopeful.

"About three thousand dollars for new scuba harnesses," said Pearson.

9

ICE BLINK
The white glare visible on the underside of low clouds from ice that is below the horizon.

"I owe you a sincere apology, Mr. Sherwood," said Admiral Pearson, studying the strange sunlight flickering on the horizon.

Sherwood said nothing. Pearson offered his binoculars. The geologist stared at the enigmatic shape of the Anvil Mountain that was edging slowly into the sky above the low, clinging cloud that shrouded the mystery of White Atlantis.

"Looks like we'll be there in three hours," commented Pearson.

Julia joined the two men leaning on the *Eureka*'s rail. "The sea temperature's falling fast," she announced. "It's now seven degrees below what it should be."

Pearson shrugged. "So? What's seven degrees? Well within normal variations I would have thought."

"Centigrade," said Julia, remembering that Americans still clung to the elephantine Fahrenheit scale.

Pearson did a mental calculation. It was a hell of a drop. He turned his attention back to the glittering ice brink. "The *Johnson* and what's left of her escorts will be back tomorrow," he said. "We'll be able to talk to the flier who saw it surface."

Sherwood made no comment. He had argued with Pearson over Lieutenant Klein's report and the admiral had flatly refused to accept that the iceberg could be as large as twenty-five miles by forty miles. Pearson was convinced that Klein must have made an understandable mistake. He pointed out that it was Klein who had once claimed seeing four flying saucers in formation over Florida. No one else had reported them. "We all make genuine mistakes," Pearson had said.

Julia interrupted Sherwood's thought, "Why the *Johnson*?" she asked.

"I've pulled her out of her strike force," said Pearson. "She's lost too many of her escorts. But she's still a fine floating airbase. Her job's going to be to keep the rubbernecks away from that thing until we know more about it."

Sherwood smiled. "Until it melts, admiral?"

"Yes."

"Then she's got a long job ahead."

"The IIP say that it'll melt fast once it reaches the Florida Current," said Pearson.

Sherwood nodded. The Florida Current flowed northward along the Eastern Seaboard of the United States before being deflected eastward by Long Island and becoming the Gulf Stream surging across the Atlantic to northern Europe.

"As I've already pointed out," said Sherwood, "with all due respect to the International Ice Patrol, their experience and terms of reference are geared to the Greenland bergs moving southward." Sherwood pointed to the ice blink where the sparkling peak of the Anvil Mountain was now visible to the naked eye. "That's not an iceberg in the true sense of the word— it's a fragment of Antarctic ice cap. None of the rules relating to icebergs apply. It's big enough to make up its own and to break all ours—which it's already done."

Pearson remained silent. His increasing respect for the British geologist's views was tempered by two indisputable facts: ice was ice and warm sea was warm sea, and the two didn't go together.

"Okay, Mr. Sherwood. How long will it take to melt?"

"Let's find out how big it is first," was Sherwood's irritating reply.

10

The ice moved.

The great white shroud of the enveloping fogbank moved with it over the eerily calm sea.

It moved at two knots—fifty miles each day. A slow but unremitting speed that steadily consumed the miles.

After twenty-five days afloat it was passing between the South Carolina seaport of Charleston, where the Civil War had started, and Bermuda.

Its cautious escort followed at a distance—a fast motor launch from the *Eureka* or the *Johnson* occasionally chasing away overcurious cruisers from the countless marinas dotted along the coast between Wilmington and Jacksonville.

An enterprising airline operator organized flights out to White Atlantis, but the passengers returned with little to show for their thousand-mile round trip apart from a brief glimpse of the Anvil Mountain's crystal spike thrusting up out of the fog like a ghostly dagger rammed through a sheet.

No one, apart from Lieutenant Klein, had seen White Atlantis. It was as if the mighty iceberg were seeking to preserve its aura of mystery until the warm waters of the Atlantic ultimately destroyed it.

It was Sherwood who correctly guessed that it was creating a surrounding subclimate that would enable it to survive.

He was keeping the knowledge to himself until he was certain.

11

The air was so incredibly still that Sherwood didn't have to hold the map that Admiral Pearson had dropped onto his lap.

"Looks like you were right all along," said Admiral Pearson, sinking into the deckchair beside Sherwood. "A map of White Atlantis built up from the radar survey. Thirty miles by twenty miles. Sure is one helluva chunk of ice."

Sherwood concentrated on the map with great interest. The sudden gathering of the contour lines into tight, concentric lines like the rings of a tree marked the soaring Anvil Mountain. In other places the lines were incomplete.

"Too much clutter," said Pearson in answer to Sherwood's query. "Angles on the PPI plots. Even the *Johnson*'s radar team can't eliminate them without the carrier getting in close. And I'm not taking that risk."

"What really matters is the nine-tenths below the surface," said Sherwood. "How's the sonar team making out?"

"They've still no map. They're complaining that the cold water is playing hell with their beams— bending them."

A dull roar reached the *Eureka* from the distant fogbank. A small iceberg drifted out of the mist and rolled slowly over, spewing plumes of spray that climbed gracefully into the air.

"Third growler today," Pearson remarked. "God damn that fog. This weather's got everyone baffled. Why the hell is it so still?"

Another growler rumbled and crept out of the fog.

"Anyway," Pearson muttered, "at least it's decaying fast."

"Not as fast as I thought it would, though," said Sherwood. "What was her distance made good yesterday? About forty-eight miles?"

"Forty-seven point seven."

Sherwood made a rough calculation on the back of the map. "Assuming an average thickness of one and a half miles, White Atlantis still has a respectable volume—about a thousand cubic miles."

"So what's your estimate of its melt rate?"

"A cubic mile a day—a thousand million tons."

Pearson lit a cigar. "Remember Walter Krantz of the International Ice Patrol? He remembers you."

"Yes."

"His melt rate figure is a hundred times your value. He reckons that White Atlantis will be gone in under a week."

"You wired him a copy of this map?"

Pearson nodded. "So how do you account for the wide variation between your figure and his?"

"Walter knows everything there is to know about the Greenland bergs. He might be basing his calculations on an assumption that White Atlantis is hollow or crescent-shaped—that's the shape the Greenland bergs usually weather themselves into."

"So he could be right?" Pearson was discovering that scientists could be very frustrating people to try to get straight answers from.

"Yes—if White Atlantis is hollow."

"And so could you be right?"

"If it's solid."

Pearson groaned.

Sherwood grinned at the American officer's annoyance. "I tell you what, admiral. Why don't you let Miss Hammond and me take a close look at White Atlantis?"

12

The sensation of terror returned with the indescribable smell of the ice.

It was the same fear Sherwood had experienced when the *Orion* had struck the hidden iceberg off the coast of South West Africa; the same gut-gnawing premonition.

He resisted the impulse to swing the motor launch around and head back toward the *Eureka*. The research ship and the *Johnson* were in their usual positions, standing five miles away from the fog-bank. Julia was sitting unconcerned on the foredeck winding in her water sampler and transferring the contents to labeled test tubes. Sherwood looked up at the leaning spike of the Anvil Mountain rearing a thousand feet out of the cloying fog. It shone like a dazzling beacon in the clear, still morning air. He noticed that the lean of the towering edifice had become more pronounced during the week and guessed that it was due to the corrosive effect of the sun on its southern flanks.

"Now steer a degree to your right," said the voice in his earphone. It was one of the radar technicians on the *Johnson*; Sherwood was guiding the boat along a narrow radar beam from the aircraft carrier that would take the launch through the impenetrable wall of the fogbank and between the arms of the crescent-shaped ice lagoon where, hopefully, there would be calm water to enable a safe icefall to be made.

Sherwood altered course.

"Okay. Fine. Hold that heading."

The awesome presence of the approaching fog wall affected Julia, for she stopped filling her test tubes and gazed ahead.

"Listen," she said.

Sherwood throttled the outboard back until he too could hear the creaking of the invisible ice.

"What the hell is it?" breathed Julia.

"All icebergs are noisy. It's caused by the relaxation of stresses as it melts. Haven't you ever heard the same noise when you've held a frozen-up ice-cube tray under a running tap?"

"You'd better switch your echo sounder on," said the *Johnson*. "You're doing fine."

Sherwood switched on the instrument. The glowing neon settled on the hundred-foot mark. The ice was beneath them.

"We'd better get into the suits now," said Julia.

They helped zip each other into the one-piece extreme-cold-weather garments.

The launch was within a hundred yards of the fog wall when the voice from the *Johnson* instructed Sherwood to make another minor course correction.

There was a new sound as the fogbank loomed nearer: the dull boom of the restless Atlantic swell heaving itself impotently against the impregnable ice.

Julia shivered, despite the insulated suit, as the

first icy fingers of the strangely still mist touched her face.

"It's one of the reasons why the ice is surviving so long," said Sherwood, seeing her reaction. "The fog is reflecting ninety percent of the solar energy that would otherwise reach the ice."

"And the cushion of cold water that surrounds it is preventing the Atlantic from doing its work," added Julia. "Correct?"

"Yes."

"Have you told the admiral?"

"He wouldn't believe me."

The launch entered the fog. The sudden dive in the air temperature stopped their conversation. It was as if they had walked through the open door of a deep-freeze storage room. Floating ice frazils crunched under the boat's bow. Sherwood checked the echo sounder. Twenty feet. He wondered what would happen if the mighty iceberg decided to tip over to assume a more stable attitude. Once, while on a flight in an International Ice Patrol C-130, he had seen the incredible sight of a giant, horseshoe-shaped Greenland iceberg perform a slow somersault.

"Hold it!" said the *Johnson* sharply. "We're losing you against the clutter. Cut your motor and await instructions."

Sherwood flipped the Mercury outboard's ignition switch and explained the reason to Julia.

"God, what a creepy place," said Julia, peering into the fog and pulling her hood against her face.

Visibility was less than ten yards. All around was the insidious creaking of the ice and a slow dripping sound that set their teeth on edge.

"Run the thing in neutral," Julia urged. "Let's have some noise, for God's sake."

"Best to save fuel."

The creaking stopped. The sudden silence seemed worse.

Julia clapped her hands. A dispirited echo answered from the depths of the fog—evidence of the somber menace of the unseen cliffs lurking nearby.

"The echo seemed to come from all around," said Julia, talking to keep her spirits up.

"We're in the lagoon," said Sherwood.

Julia shivered again. She was beginning to realize that Sherwood's theory that the ice had wrapped itself in winter to protect itself was substantially correct. "What the hell is the *Johnson* doing?" she demanded.

Five minutes of the oppressive silence passed.

"Why has the creaking stopped?"

"It comes and goes," was Sherwood's unhelpful answer.

The *Johnson* asked Sherwood if he was reading them. The voice in the earphone was stronger although Sherwood had not touched the volume control on the radio receiver.

"We've moved in closer," said the voice when Sherwood had replied. "You're now clearly fixed on our plot."

Julia sighed with relief as Sherwood started the Mercury and began steering the boat through the fog in answer to the *Johnson*'s commands. But the welcome purr of the outboard did not dispel her irrational fear that the ice, which had killed so many and had inflicted so much misery, was planning something new.

13

The keel of the boat touched ice.

Sherwood jumped onto the ice shelf that formed a false beach and pulled the boat's bows firmly into the yielding slush. He helped Julia out. She held the mooring spike while he drove it deep into a firm outcrop.

"I thought it would be cleaner," she said, pointing at the mud-rimed beach.

Sherwood didn't answer. He had seized a handful of the gray slush and was examining it closely, allowing it to trickle through his mittened fingers as if searching for diamonds.

"Well?" asked Julia.

Sherwood lifted the recorder out of the boat. "It looks easy to walk on—let's find some high ground."

"High ice," corrected Julia as she broke the seal on a dye-marker aerosol that she would use to mark their route.

The mist was slightly clearer at five hundred feet above sea level. Julia released the snap fastener on her pack and allowed it to slip to the crumbling, powdery ice. She sat down.

"Let's rest, Glen."

Sherwood glanced round. They were on a level area of ice that was surrounded by rounded, forbidding hillocks. The icy mist seemed to percolate through the protective suit now that he had stopped climbing. Julia pulled off her spiked overshoes and rubbed a very cold foot.

"My God, it's like being back at Rosenthal. And impossible to believe that we're four hundred miles off North Carolina."

"I could take the first recording here," said Sherwood, as he started to unpack the machine.

Julia marked their position on the map while Sherwood positioned the microphone and switched on the machine. He planned to make a series of recordings of the sounds occurring from deep within the ice in the hope that the creakings and groanings of the massive iceberg might provide yet another clue as to its melt rate.

There was a sudden freezing breath of the long-awaited wind.

"The fog's lifting!" shouted Julia. "Look, Glen! It's dispersing! There's a wind! Feel!"

The breeze hesitated then returned with renewed strength. Sherwood looked up. Clouds of mist were swirling past the hillocks. A freshly cut water gully appeared less than a hundred yards away.

"Look!" Julia's voice was a cry of undisguised fear.

Sherwood followed her finger to the evil splendor of the Anvil Mountain's shining dagger that was emerging from the fog. Clouds were streaming off the dazzling stiletto like the gushing albino blood of a wounded sky.

Sherwood and Julia stood rooted; hypnotized by the awesome spectacle of the rampant crystal tower that seemed to be lifting into the heavens as the enveloping fogbank that had hidden the white continent was swept away by the wind.

Timeless seconds became minutes. And the minutes, during those moments of the terrifying revelation, fled like seconds. The contour lines on the map conveyed nothing of the Anvil Mountain's disfiguring twist, which made it lean toward the sea from which it had escaped.

Sherwood tore his eyes away from the frozen Matterhorn and gazed in wonder at the materializing icescape of White Atlantis. The undulating hills, deep ravines, and crazy profusion of iridescent crags blazing white fire in the startled sunlight seemed to stretch away to the horizon. It was then, as he looked down on the metallic bulk of the *Johnson*, standing less than half a mile from the iceberg's tortuous cliffs, that Sherwood began to appreciate the titanic proportions of the grotesquely beautiful monster the Antarctic ice cap had spawned.

Julia's terrified grip was digging deep into his forearm. There was a new sound from above. She gave a cry of despair and pointed.

The five-hundred-foot-high ice buttresses of the Anvil Mountain were breaking away and falling outward. A huge fissure began to open in the base of the crystal mountain just as the first rumblings of the impending icequake quickened beneath their feet.

The first shock wave that slammed through the ice catapulted Sherwood and Julia face down into the powdery ice, when they still had twenty yards to go before reaching the supposed safety of the ice mass that was between them and the lower slopes of the disintegrating mountain.

Julia risked a quick glance up the dazzling incline. Half a mile away huge irregular ice boulders, some the size of a three-story house, were dementedly charging toward them.

They scrambled to their feet and were about to start running when the second shock wave struck with the pentup force of an unleashed steam hammer concealed beneath the ice. Sherwood gave a loud cry of intense agony and collapsed. Both his ankles had been savagely twisted by the shock wave's vicious, bone-pulverizing blow.

"Come on!" screamed Julia, tugging with blind strength at his arm.

Sherwood tried to struggle to his feet. His face twisted in pain and he sank down. "I can't," he whimpered.

"You've got to!" Julia saw that the first wave of shattered, avalanching boulders was less than a hundred yards away and was hurtling straight at them. Weeping with fear, she grabbed hold of Sherwood under the armpits and, ignoring his protests, began to drag him backward toward the shelter of the icecrop.

Walter Krantz of the International Ice Patrol arrived aboard the *Eureka*—a slightly built man in his late forties with a creased, worried expression. He shook hands with Admiral Pearson and asked after Sherwood. The answer that he was on the iceberg seemed to increase his anxiety. He was about to protest that no one should be on White Atlantis but was interrupted by a sudden flurry of excitement: the fogbank was lifting from the iceberg.

Pearson and Krantz watched without speaking as the freshening wind shredded White Atlantis's shroud. The *Eureka* was six miles from the colossus—a distance that in no way diminished the majesty of the unfolding continent that was dominated by the shining, weather-honed pinnacle of the leaning Anvil Mountain. Against the sparkling, emerging cliffs was the diminutive outline of the *Johnson*—its 100,000-ton bulk reduced to toylike proportions by its nearness to the titanic White Atlantis.

"That flat top shouldn't be so near," said Krantz worriedly.

There was a sudden stir among the scientists and crew lining the rail. Someone swore.

"The mountain's falling apart!"

Pearson forgot Krantz at his side and stared in horrified fascination at the Anvil Mountain. A dark band was appearing at the base. It was some seconds before he realized that it was a huge crack, which was slowly lengthening and widening. Then the mountain was changing its shape as if it were twisting. The needlelike peak began to swing slowly through an arc.

The sound of the appalling fracture reached the

Eureka. It was the scream of thousands of tortured banshees shrieking for mercy.

The Anvil Mountain fell.

For a few seconds there was nothing to see but a charging plume of white smoke into which the mountain had disappeared. The noise steadily increased as the pale avalanche roared across the sea.

And the U.S.S. *Johnson*.

It was over in a fleeting moment, so brief that the expressions on the faces of the watchers on the *Eureka* did not have time to change: the million-ton dagger burst across the sea and smashed into the giant aircraft carrier. The ice didn't stop. Two huge curtains of spray erupting into the air marked its passage across the sea.

It slowed. The spray, which had defied gravity, began to settle.

There was no sign of the *Johnson*.

It was as if the aircraft carrier had been an image projected on a screen; an image composed of nothing more substantial than light and shade.

And then the projector had been abruptly switched off.

16

The President stared at the black flag on the wall display of the North Atlantic that marked the grave of the U.S.S. *Johnson*. He shook his head sadly.

"Two thousand five hundred men..."

Pearson sat in silence, his fingers tracing the gold braid on his cap that he was holding in his hands.

"...There's at least five names on the list that I remember from my days in the Navy."

"We've not fixed the date for the memorial

service," said Pearson, "in case you wish to attend, Mr. President."

"What are we going to do about that iceberg?"

"Krantz thinks it will be completely melted within the next few days, Mr. President."

The President studied one of the photographs of White Atlantis that was lying on his desk. "It's going to have to do a helluva lot of melting then."

Which was exactly what Pearson had been thinking all that morning during the flight to Washington. He said nothing and watched the younger man skim once more through the reports. He knew from the questions that had been fired at him that the President hadn't missed one key word or important sentence.

"These two British scientists—Hammond and Sherwood—they're survivors from the *Orion*?"

"Yes, Mr. President."

More reading. Pages turned. Then: "J. Hammond. He was proved right about the cause of the Cape Verde Islands disaster?"

"Yes, sir."

"And G. Sherwood's theories about the ice have been borne out by subsequent events?"

Pearson agreed that they had. "There's a difference of opinion between him and Krantz."

"Whom do you side with?"

It was an awkward question. "Well," said Pearson slowly. "Sherwood and Hammond—Hammond is a woman—have first-hand experience of the iceberg. First, when the *Orion* went down; second, they've been to the area it was calved from; third, they were on the beach at Cape Verde when the sea was turned into nerve gas; and lastly, their narrow escape yesterday when the Anvil Mountain collapsed.... It all adds up to a lot of experience. On the other hand, it's possible that they're no longer objective. And their experience of icebergs is limited to White Atlantis—"

"Which is all we're interested in," the President pointed out.

"But Krantz has experience of an average of a thousand icebergs a year."

"And not one of them has done as much damage as that one," said the President, holding up a photograph of White Atlantis. "Will you be able to keep people away from it?"

"The combined resources of the Navy and the Coast Guard—"

"How?" interrupted the President sharply. "How the hell will you be able to cover every inch of the iceberg's coast?"

"With helicopters—" Pearson began.

"I once had the job of trying to keep boats a reasonable distance from the *Britannia* during a visit by Queen Elizabeth and Prince Philip. It was virtually impossible—as I chased one away, two more would dive in."

"We've managed so far, Mr. President."

"Wait till the berg's off Cape Hatteras—you'll be inundated with pleasure craft."

"But its course is keeping it over two hundred miles out!" Pearson protested.

"That won't stop them. My first yacht was a forty-foot Silver, yet it had a cruising range of eight hundred miles on full tanks."

"Technically," said Pearson thoughtfully, "we don't have a legal responsibility to stop people wanting to break their necks by climbing White Atlantis. It's in international waters—not even over our continental shelf."

It was the kind of negative statement that the President heartily disliked. He fixed his blue eyes resolutely on Pearson and said firmly: "If it's within our power to prevent people hurting themselves—no matter what their nationality—then we have a moral duty to exercise that power. I want that iceberg destroyed and I'll ensure that you are given all the resources and authority to see that my order is carried out."

The President stood. The interview was over. He shook hands with Pearson and wished him good luck.

One thought occupied Pearson's mind as he flew back to the *Eureka*.

How the hell did one set about destroying an iceberg the size of a small country and weighing many billions of tons?

17

Krantz's expression was even more worried than usual. He and Sherwood were sitting in a laboratory on the *Eureka* listening to the recording Sherwood had made on White Atlantis before the Anvil Mountain had collapsed.

"Play it again, Glen," said Krantz when the recording reached the point where it had been obliterated by the icequake.

Sherwood spooled back and pressed the start key. Krantz looked at his watch as the sharp tap...tap...tap...clicked out from the speaker. Each tap seemed to increase Krantz's worry.

"Far too regular to be caused by stresses," said Sherwood emphatically. "I've checked the exact timing—each tap's duration and the interval between the taps doesn't vary by much more than one hundredth of a second. And you still say it's caused by released stresses?"

Krantz shook his head sadly. "I'm not saying anything, Glen—merely offering an explanation."

"An unbelievable explanation."

Krantz smiled suddenly. "Our roles are reversed; I

was the one who refused to believe you about White Atlantis."

"I only half believed myself." Sherwood broke off and looked sharply at Krantz. "Have you revised that crazy melt rate figure of yours?"

"What's the point, Glen? After tomorrow—"

"After tomorrow, White Atlantis will still be there!"

Krantz looked extremely worried. "Don't you think it will work?"

"No."

"So *you* know what sort of bang exploding a thousand tons will make?"

Sherwood sensed that the IIP official was mocking him and began to get angry. "No, Walter. Do you?"

Krantz nodded. "It'll blow that iceberg into four quarters, Glen."

18

"White Atlantis is a fantastic sight from the helicopter," enthused the radio reporter's voice. "It's shining on the water like a priceless diamond...."

Julia giggled as she placed the microfilm cassette in front of the viewer Sherwood was using. The two of them were searching the *Eureka*'s technical library for information that Sherwood was certain existed.

"... a diamond that will be destroyed in exactly one minute."

It was Sherwood's turn to be amused.

"Pity we're too far away to see anything," said Julia, sitting down at a vacant viewer and loading it with a film cassette.

"There won't be anything to see," Sherwood muttered morosely. "God damn it, this is going to take hours."

"White Atlantis is now honeycombed with five hundred boreholes," said the reporter. "And each borehole is filled with two tons of TNT. This operation must compare with the blowing up of Heligoland in 1921 except that Heligoland didn't need a thousand tons of TNT to destroy it.... Thirty seconds now..."

Julia quickly read through a frame displayed on the viewer's screen. "Antarctic Record, 1967. Number thirty—a report on giant icebergs in Lützow-Holm Bay. Any good?"

Sherwood shook his head. "It's earlier than '67."

"I was talking to Walter Krantz of the International Ice Patrol earlier today," the reporter told his listeners. "And he says breaking White Atlantis into four will increase the amount of ice in contact with the water and so speed up the rate at which it's melting...."

Sherwood impatiently changed cassettes.

A voice cut across the radio reporter's to start the ten-second countdown.

"It's like using a firework to blow up Mount Everest," said Sherwood.

"Five..."

Sherwood gaped at the screen.

"Four..."

"What's the matter?" asked Julia.

"Three..."

Sherwood excitedly operated the foot control that spun the film through the viewer.

"Two..."

"So what's the matter?" Julia repeated.

"One..."

There was the sound of a dull explosion from the radio. Then the voice of the reporter—almost hysterical with excitement: "Staggering! Fantastic! The biggest man-made explosion since the H-bomb tests stopped! There's a huge cloud of white debris shooting into the air along the entire length of White Atlantis! The iceberg has virtually disappeared but nothing—not even a thousand tons of TNT—can conceal this incredible, this magnificent monster of an island in ice!"

"I've found it," said Sherwood, not taking his eyes off the printed page displayed on his screen. Julia joined him.

"Hey, wait a minute!" bawled the reporter's breathless voice. "This can't be true! I don't believe it! The debris is settling.... White Atlantis is exactly the same as it was before the explosion! It's not even dented!"

"Well," said Julia, reading the information on the screen. "It looks as if you were right all along. Will you enjoy gloating?"

19

As no one was within earshot of the two men peering into the ice crater, Admiral Pearson's comments to Krantz tended to be scathing.

"It's worrying," Krantz admitted when he managed to get a word in.

"You're goddamn right it's worrying," Pearson answered with feeling. "Especially as you said—"

"I was about to say that I'm not completely surprised. Ice is a surprisingly resilient material."

"So it seems."

"Next time we use more explosive. How long would it take to have five thousand tons shipped out?"

Pearson pushed his snow goggles over his eyes. "Let's take a look at the next hole."

The two men trudged through the rotten ice. Since landing on White Atlantis, Pearson had been surprised to discover that close to it wasn't white but a pale gray. In some places, where the strata were cut through by surface water, the ice coloring varied from yellow to the pale green of iceberg lettuce.

The next borehole had filled with water. They moved on and paused to watch a sparkling waterfall cascading over the edge of a hundred-foot-high inland cliff. From the base of the cliff was a fast-flowing river carrying twisting miniature icebergs through a deep canyon that broadened into a slower-moving estuary where it met the sea.

"It's interesting," said Krantz. "What we're seeing—the erosion, rivers cutting ravines—is exactly what happens on land except than an hour on this iceberg is the equivalent of a hundred million years on land."

The third borehole was beginning to fill with melt water. As with the previous holes, the force of the explosion had widened it to a diameter of thirty feet at the brink from the original ten inches bored by the drill. But there was no sign of a major fault or crack in the ice that could have been caused by the explosion.

Krantz frowned anxiously into the cone-shaped hole. He could hear a faint, regular tapping noise similar to that recorded by Glen Sherwood. Pearson heard it too.

"What in hell is that?"

Krantz went down on one knee and listened. "Stresses in the ice. Most of this berg's been compressed under the weight of millions of tons of its own ice and now it's relaxing. This hole is acting as a giant amplifier—like the horn on an antique phonograph."

Pearson wasn't entirely convinced; the tapping was too regular. But Krantz was the expert—his suggestion made some sense whereas Sherwood's ideas were too crazy to even contemplate. And yet...

Pearson's thoughts were interrupted by the whine of gas turbines. He raised his binoculars and focused them on the 378-foot Coast Guard cutter that he had assigned to guard this sector of White Atlantis. White water creamed past the diagonal hull stripes near the bow that were the distinctive marking of all U.S. Coast Guard ships no matter what their size. The height of her bow wave increased. She was leaving. A minute later the relief cutter appeared—the *Jason*—operated by the Fifth Coast Guard District.

White Atlantis was still five hundred miles off the coast of the United States. But that coast, with the slow, unstoppable northward drift, now belonged to the State of Virginia.

20

It was the first of what were to become routine morning conferences aboard the *Eureka*, presided over by Admiral Pearson. Hagan made notes. Deke Sutherland looked bored. Walter Krantz, worried.

Sherwood could see the pale coastline of White Atlantis through the port windows. Sunlight flashing on the iceberg's rounded hills heliographed a continuous signal of contempt at the research ship.

Pearson got straight down to business. "After yesterday's failure with a thousand tons of HE, Mr. Krantz is now suggesting a similar operation with five thousand tons and deeper boreholes."

"Back-tapered and plugged with concrete," Krantz added—his anxious eyes moving quickly round the gathering.

"Opinions anyone?" inquired Pearson.

"Yes," said Sherwood. "It won't work."

Krantz blinked. "Why not, Glen?"

"Because the caps will be blown off and ninety percent of the explosive force will be lost. The same thing that happened yesterday only louder."

Krantz looked hurt. "Don't you at least think it's worth trying?"

"That depends on what five thousand tons of TNT is worth," said Sherwood, grinning. "But I'll tell you this much: nothing but the sea will destroy that iceberg—just as it eventually destroys all icebergs. The easiest way is to just wait and watch."

"That's out of the question," Pearson stated. "There's a major political storm brewing over the loss of the *Johnson*, and destroying that berg artificially is now a matter of national prestige."

Krantz groaned. Sherwood shared his sentiment.

"There's more," Pearson continued. "If we project Mr. Sherwood's melt rate figures, then we end up with a situation that I prefer not to think about: that White Atlantis gets into the North Atlantic shipping lanes, which are, as Mr. Krantz will tell you, the busiest in the world. Even with radar, there're still plenty of captains around who insist on ramming icebergs. The most recent being the Danish ship the *Hans Hedtoft*, in which ninety-eight people died."

"That won't happen," said Krantz. "And, even if it did, the International Ice Patrol would—"

"What about the berg's growlers?" demanded Sutherland, speaking for the first time. "We're getting more of them every day—most of them bigger than the bergs you sometimes get off Newfoundland—and they're not following the same drift pattern as Big Daddy. If you want my opinion, I'd say you can't count on anything with that thing."

"I'd count on its breaking up with five thousand tons of TNT erupting in its belly," said Krantz dryly.

"All past attempts to destroy icebergs have failed," said Sherwood. "Including attempts using high explosive."

Pearson looked interested. "What attempts?"

Sherwood reached into his pocket and produced the documents copied from the microfilm in the *Eureka*'s library. "This is a copy of Bulletin Number Forty-six issued by the International Ice Patrol back in 1960. It describes a series of experiments that were carried out by the IIP into ways and means of destroying icebergs." Sherwood paused and looked at Pearson. "Do you want to hear what it has to say, admiral?"

"I'm familiar with that bulletin," said Krantz. "It's very old and I doubt if its findings are relevant today."

"Let's decide when we've heard it," Pearson suggested. He nodded to Sherwood. "Go ahead."

Sherwood cleared his throat. "A special detail from the IIP selected a typical Greenland iceberg for a series of experiments to see if it was possible for it to be destroyed. The first phase was the dropping on the iceberg of twenty-thousand-pound bombs." Sherwood held up a page bearing a photograph that showed an amphibious aircraft flying over a horseshoe-shaped iceberg. There was an explosion taking place at the base of the iceberg. "Phase One failed," said Sherwood. "Nearly ten tons dropped on one small iceberg and they had no effect whatsoever. Phase Two was similar in concept to the operation yesterday: three men boarded the iceberg and buried a selection of different types of high explosive charges at strategic locations. I quote: 'Figure 22b is the final burst, which consisted of 560 pounds of thermite planted at the base of the pinnacle. Again a magnificent display took place as smoke and molten iron were hurled hundreds of feet into the air, but the berg remained virtually unchanged.' Unquote."

Sherwood glanced up at Krantz, who pointedly ignored him by staring out a window at the sea. Sherwood continued: "The final phase was to cover six thousand square yards of the iceberg with carbon black to increase the iceberg's absorption of heat from the sun. Five hours later the iceberg began to break up but the test was inconclusive because the berg was about to break up anyway. I'll read you the report's conclusion: 'Although some damage to the iceberg resulted, it must be admitted that all the means tried were unsuccessful in destroying icebergs.'"

There was a brief silence when Sherwood finished speaking. It was broken by Admiral Pearson's reaching out a hand for the papers the geologist was holding. "I'd like to see that report please."

Sherwood passed the papers across the table. Pearson examined them for some moments. He tossed them onto the table and felt in his pocket for a cigar.

"Well, gentlemen," he said at length. "It's beginning to look as if we've been wasting our time." His voice was tired; drained of emotion.

21

Admiral Pearson and Sutherland looked on with intrigued expressions as Sherwood rested each end of the twelve-inch bar of ice on laboratory stands so that the ice formed a bridge above the bench. The horizontal frozen rod began a slow drip onto the working surface.

Sherwood smiled at his two-man audience. "This is one of those experiments, like cutting glass underwater with scissors, that I've heard about but never carried out for myself."

As he spoke, he looped a length of fine piano wire round the center of the bar of ice, twisted the two ends together and hung a kilogram laboratory weight from the join so that it was suspended beneath the ice.

"Now watch," said Sherwood.

Pearson and Sutherland watched. Nothing happened at first. Then, very slowly, the weight began dragging the loop through the ice like an old-fashioned wire cutter slicing a piece of cheese in half.

It took the weight five minutes to drag the wire loop right through the bar of ice and to clatter onto the bench. But, instead of falling with the weight in two halves, the ice remained rigidly in place, resting on the laboratory stands.

"Well, isn't that the craziest thing?" said Pearson, staring at the intact bar of ice.

Sherwood lifted the ice off the stands and gave it to the two men to examine closely. "The wire cuts through the ice easily enough but the ice welds itself back together again—almost as if it's healing itself. The phenomenon was discovered by Michael Faraday—one of his few useless discoveries." Sherwood hesitated and looked apologetically at Sutherland. "That's why I'm afraid that your idea of hauling heated cables through the iceberg to cut it up just won't work, captain. Sorry."

Sutherland shrugged. "I never thought it would. It was just an idea."

Pearson gave one of his rare smiles. "Well, I guess Faraday's discovery has come in useful after all; he's saved us a few million dollars."

"This may seem a basic question and I'm probably making a fool of myself," said Sutherland. "But why is it that no one has come up with the idea of using heat to melt that iceberg?"

"There's a good reason," Sherwood replied. "You've used steam hoses to de-ice frozen-up super-structure and rigging haven't you, captain?"

Sutherland nodded. "Sure."

"Ever thought about the lousy return you get, having to use up a hell of a lot of energy just to melt a small quantity of ice?"

"Yeah. That's right."

"A given quantity of ice needs nearly as much energy to melt it as it does to boil the resulting water. There's not enough available energy in the world to melt that iceberg—not even if we were to harness the output of every power station for a month." Sherwood thought for a moment. "Ice," he said at length, "is one of the strangest materials known to mankind."

"That's exactly what I'm beginning to think," agreed Pearson. "Which leaves me with only one final possibility."

22

"I've given it a lot of thought," said the President, "and the answer has to be no. So long as you guys in the Navy and Coast Guard are managing to keep sightseers away until it's melted down to a safe size I see no point in agreeing to your request."

Pearson said nothing. He hadn't risen to his present rank by arguing with presidents on every issue.

"Thank you for raising the matter with me," said the President as he accompanied Pearson across the Camp David lawns to the helicopter landing pad. "You were within your rights to go right ahead with that blanket authority I gave you. By when is the goddamn thing expected to melt?"

"The experts are divided, Mr. President," said Pearson. "Those who've been proved wrong on everything else up to now say it can't last two weeks—they *were* saying one week—and the experts who've been proved right so far don't know. All *I* know is that I'd sooner deal with the Russians than with icebergs any day—at least the Russians are predictable."

The President treated Pearson to his vote-winning smile as he bade his visitor goodbye.

Pearson arrived back on the *Eureka* seven hours later to be greeted with the news that White Atlantis had altered course and was slowly swinging toward the Delaware coast.

23

Julia, like so many others, found it impossible to believe that White Atlantis was dying. It rode serenely under the warm sun of the early spring, a beautiful crystal creation, a virgin country with sparkling rolling hills, silent lagoons and noisy streams feeding swift-flowing rivers.

And yet it was inexorably dying. The evidence of its approaching death was all around: the growlers that roared down the towering cliffs and drifted away to become another headache for the hard-pressed International Ice Patrol; growlers that merely detached themselves from their parent and sat innocently on the water waiting for one of the vigilant circling IIP Hercules to spot them and radio their position to Governors Island where each one would be allocated a number and its likely course estimated by computer.

A helicopter, crammed to the rotors with press photographers, moved against the leaning cliffs like a fly on a white-washed wall.

Julia became aware of Sutherland beside her at the rail. "They've just finished the day plot," he said.

"What's it down to now?"

Sutherland watched the weaving helicopter. "Eight hundred and twenty square miles. Half the size of Long Island."

"So it hasn't changed since yesterday?"

"According to Krantz and Sherwood, the surface area is fairly static—it's losing most of its bulk below the surface."

"That's what I thought must be happening," said Julia. "I helped with this morning's salinity tests in

the lab. White Atlantis is surrounded by fresh water.
You know, it's strange that it's reducing its draft
faster than its surface area."

Sutherland frowned. "Why?"

"You'll laugh at me."

"I promise not to laugh."

"Well...It's as if White Atlantis knows that
there's shallower water closer to the coast that it's
going to have to negotiate."

Sutherland kept his promise.

24

"There are several things that Mr. Sherwood and I
are agreed on," said Krantz at the morning conference. "First—"

"Where is Sherwood?" asked Pearson. "Sorry to
interrupt, Mr. Krantz."

"He's with Captain Sutherland in the plot room,"
said Hagan. Krantz started again. "First, that the
volume of White Atlantis is now down to five hundred
cubic miles."

Sherwood quietly entered the cabin and took his
place at the table.

"How much does it weigh?" demanded Pearson.

"It's weight isn't important," said Krantz with
some irritation.

"Five hundred thousand million tons," said
Sherwood quickly, seeing Admiral Pearson about to
explode.

Pearson calmed down but he looked far from
happy.

"And second, Mr. Sherwood and I are agreed that
White Atlantis has altered course ten degrees east
during the past twenty-four hours."

"Fifteen degrees," said Sherwood. "I've just come down from the plot room. She swung through another five degrees a few minutes ago."

Krantz's poise deserted him momentarily. "Well...That doesn't change our forecast regarding the eventual fate of White Atlantis."

"I think it changes it significantly," said Sherwood. "I'll go further and say that we now don't have a forecast."

"Yesterday," said Krantz calmly, "we both agreed that Atlantis would eventually be picked up by the Gulf Stream and pushed west—that it would most likely disintegrate in mid-Atlantic between forty and fifty degrees west."

"That was yesterday."

"A five-degree change of course doesn't change—"

"I think it changes everything, Walter," said Sherwood mildly. "The thing's now heading for New York."

25

The President didn't miss a word of what Admiral Pearson was saying as he studied a map of the coastline between Atlantic City and the eastern extremity of Long Island. The coast formed a huge funnel-shaped bay with New York at the throat of the funnel.

"If it does get trapped in the harbor," Pearson was saying, "and if it breaks up there, it's going to be impossible to guarantee the safety of shipping unless all shipping movements are banned. In its final stages of disintegration, we won't be dealing with one berg but several thousand—each one with a mass of several million tons."

The President said nothing. What Admiral Pearson was telling him was much the same as Coast

Guard and IIP experts had told him during an emergency conference called earlier that day before Pearson had arrived in Washington from the *Eureka*.

"And there's the safety angle to consider if we act now, while the iceberg is still two hundred miles off the coast," Pearson continued. "We've been enforcing a prohibited zone in the White Atlantis area for some days now, so that's no problem. All we need is for the FAA to do the same and intensive air force patrols will do the rest." Pearson paused. There was no way of judging from the President's impassive expression the impact his words were having. "There's something else, Mr. President. I'm not an expert in such matters, but I wouldn't even like to guess at the effect on New York's economy that a protracted ban on shipping would have—indeed, on the economy of the whole nation."

The President had the figures before him. They made for unpleasant reading. Shipping was supposed to be on the decline, yet exports to Europe through New York still ran into millions of dollars each day.

"What sort of yield are you thinking in terms of?" asked the President.

The question gave Pearson hope. "General Warren Floyd says that we should start with one megaton. A clean device—there won't be a danger of contamination."

"How deep in the ice?"

"Six hundred feet. There's no question of a violation of the test ban treaty." Pearson refrained from adding that drilling had already started in accordance with General Floyd's specifications in anticipation of the President's giving his consent.

"It's over the hundred-and-twenty-kiloton limit agreed for underground tests," the President pointed out.

"The Russians would be inviting ridicule from the world if they start kicking up dust over one megaton," Pearson retorted.

The President pushed the map to one side and read through the cryptic typed order that needed only his signature. He sighed and picked up his pen.

"Okay," he said with finality, and signed the document.

It was the third time in history that an American president had authorized the use of a nuclear device against an enemy of the United States.

26

"We're down five hundred and fifty feet," said General Warren Floyd, lowering his huge frame into a chair in Admiral Pearson's cabin. "And we've stopped drilling."

Pearson looked surprised. "Why?"

"We've hit a problem."

"What sort of problem?" Pearson was finding General Floyd's tendency to communicate in short, inconclusive sentences extremely frustrating. The general, he had learned, disliked volunteering information. It had to be wormed out of him question by question.

"A noise," said General Floyd.

"What sort of noise?"

"I haven't heard it."

Great, thought Pearson.

"But my boys have."

"And what sort of noise do they say it is?"

General Floyd considered the implications of parting with this information. "A regular tapping noise."

Pearson groaned inwardly. "Yes, we know about it, general. Mr. Walter Krantz and the others are of the opinion that it's caused by stresses within the ice."

General Floyd seemed saddened to learn that his priceless information was common knowledge.

"So we carry on drilling?"

"Yes, please, general."

General Floyd made no move to leave the cabin. "There's something else."

Pearson waited. He was beginning to understand why it was that General Floyd was responsible for nuclear ordnance.

"The device arrives on this ship at 09:00 tomorrow." The admission caused Floyd considerable pain but he stood the stress remarkably well.

"Yes."

"A nuclear device."

"Yes," said Pearson, wondering when Floyd would get to the point.

"You have two non-U.S. citizens aboard," said Floyd, approaching the point with an accusing tone of voice.

"Julia Hammond and Glen Sherwood," said Pearson sharply, smelling trouble. "And before you go any further, general, you ought to know that those two have been of incalculable value to me in dealing with White Atlantis."

"Now I'm the one who's of incalculable value," Floyd observed dryly. "I'm very sorry, admiral, but they can't be here tomorrow. Their work is finished so I suggest you send them to New York for a well-earned vacation."

"But what's the point, general? It's no secret that we're going to use a nuclear device tomorrow. I've told the press and there'll be full TV coverage."

"They've got to go," said Floyd firmly. "Sorry, admiral."

distance of three miles, its gnatlike shadow flitting erratically across the uneven surface of the silent, brooding cliffs.

"There's the tower!" said Julia suddenly.

The gleaming latticework of the laser target appeared briefly.

One minute.

The aircraft sheered away. There was nothing on the screen except the sea and the distant outlines of toy ships.

A drawling voice announced that the TND was now armed.

The camera on the *Eureka* caught the reporter and Admiral Pearson looking at an out-of-shot monitor.

"The airplane will circle around now to begin its approach," explained Pearson.

The unending sea reappeared. It was swinging across the picture and steadied when the humped outline of White Atlantis materialized.

Forty-five seconds.

"The airplane is about ten miles from the target," said Pearson's voice, "and will fire the beam when it's within three miles."

"What will happen to the airplane after the detonation, admiral?"

"Hopefully, it won't be hit by flying ice so it'll be able to land on the *Saratoga*. It's a mighty valuable piece of hardware."

"But not as valuable as New York's shipping trade?"

Pearson's rich laugh boomed in the hotel bedroom. "That's right."

Thirty seconds.

The swelling outline of White Atlantis hardened rapidly and individual features of the jagged, crumbling icescape became progressively more distinct. Julia experienced a surge of emotion as she gazed at the doomed creation. It was too beautiful to be destroyed. Then she remembered the *Orion*, the coffins laid out in the tiny walled cemetery on the

Cape Verde Islands, and Oaf...Dear, kind Oaf...

"Ten seconds," said the drawling voice from the television speaker.

Julia seized Sherwood's hand and held it tight, watching the growing monster that was still half the size of Long Island. The tower was in the center of the screen, hurtling with incredible speed toward the camera.

"Five..." intoned the drawling voice. "Four..."

Julia involuntarily tightened her grip on Sherwood's hand.

"Three...Two...One..." The controller's drawl was devoid of expression.

A pencil beam of light flashed at the tower from one side of the picture.

"Firing initiated. We have detonation."

Nothing happened. The cameraman on the *Eureka*, working by remote control, managed to keep White Atlantis centered as the pilotless aircraft banked away.

"Minus One...Two..." droned the voice. "Pressure building..."

A quarter of a square mile of ice, with the tower at its center, bulged upward. There was a hesitation as the two forces—the mass of the ice and the trapped energies of the nuclear inferno—pitted themselves against each other. The nuclear device won. There was a white eruption as countless tons of ice were blasted upward at the speed of sound. It was an explosion that seemed to last forever; ice, water, and steam continued vomiting into the sky from a steadily widening crater.

"They've failed," said Sherwood, staring woodenly at the television screen. "My God! They've failed!"

The sound of the colossal eruption reached the microphone on the pilotless aircraft. The sudden roar was distorted by the audio equipment that couldn't handle the savage onslaught on its systems.

"They've failed," Sherwood kept repeating.

"Why?" asked Julia, unable to tear her eyes away

The device was a terrorist's dream.

It measured less than twenty inches in diameter by forty inches long and was light enough to be carried by three men.

For safety, six men manhandled it from the helicopter to the shaft opening that plunged six hundred feet into the frozen heart of White Atlantis. They shackled it to the power winch that straddled the shaft, connected the control cable, tested the arming circuitry and, slowly and carefully, lowered the device down the shaft. Once it was in position bulldozers set to work to shovel tons of rotten ice down the shaft to seal it. It took two hours. The six men returned to assemble a small prefabricated tower over the plugged shaft. On top of the twenty-foot-high structure was a photoelectric laser receiver. Radio control was considered too dangerous; New York's countless private and public radio transmitters were swamping a sizable percentage of the radio spectrum, even two hundred miles out at sea.

By 3 P.M., three hours before the blast, everything on White Atlantis was ready. Thirty miles to the east was the aircraft carrier U.S.S. *Saratoga*. The pilotless aircraft sitting on its catapult launcher was also ready.

Sherwood and Julia stopped talking when the television news announcer appeared on the screen to say that they were going straight over, live to the *Eureka.*

Julia crossed the hotel room and turned up the volume. "It's not fair," she said, kneeling to one side of the screen and watching the reporter talking to Admiral Pearson. "They kick us off and yet they let the reporters on."

"It wasn't the admiral's fault," said Sherwood. "Can we watch without your commentary?"

They watched in silence as Pearson explained that a pilotless, radio-controlled aircraft would fire a coded laser pulse at the tower on White Atlantis to trigger the nuclear device.

The picture cut to an aerial long-shot of the giant iceberg.

"The picture you're seeing is coming from a TV camera on board the pilotless aircraft," explained Admiral Pearson's voice-over.

The reporter pressed him for a prediction on the outcome of the operation but Pearson remained noncommittal.

"*Will* it work?" asked Julia.

Sherwood shrugged. "Lord knows. One-megaton bombs are a whole new ball game, as they say."

The digits of a lapsed-time indicator appeared at the foot of the screen. Two minutes to go.

"Maybe this time it's like using a hand grenade to blow up Mount Everest?" said Julia teasingly.

Sherwood grinned. "That's very good, Miss Hammond."

The pilotless aircraft was circling the iceberg at a

from the spectacle of the blizzard with house-size snowflakes that miraculously didn't crash into the pilotless aircraft.

"The iceberg should've split open—broken up. All that's happened is that they've blown a damn great hole in it."

Julia continued to stare at the screen. "But look at the size of the hole! Just look at it!"

The terrible wound in White Atlantis was at least two miles across—twice the diameter of the huge meteorite impact crater in the Arizona Desert. Sherwood shook his head sadly.

"Yes...It's big. But I doubt if the ice they've blasted out of that hole amounts to much more ice than White Atlantis normally loses in a day anyway."

Julia's discovery that Sherwood liked having his earlobes nibbled was an hour old when she whispered in his ear: "Well at least *we've* broken the ice, Glen."

29

The ice moved.

It had proved itself. It was unstoppable. Indestructible. It moved very slowly. Almost as if it were possessed of a blind but certain instinct.

And that instinct was to kill.

To Sherwood's disgust, Julia's insatiable appetite for New York and its shops continued unabated the following day. She insisted on dragging Sherwood with her on shopping and sightseeing expeditions—two activities that Sherwood heartily detested.

They emerged from Macy's—Sherwood laden with parcels and Julia wearing her latest purchase. She gazed across Herald Square at the magnificent, towering building on 34th Street while Sherwood tried to hail a taxi and clutch the parcels at the same time.

"That's the Empire State Building, isn't it, Glen?"

The bright yellow cabs in the tidal wave of traffic surging down Broadway weren't interested in Sherwood's business.

"Yes," he snapped irritably, not bothering to check what Julia was looking at.

"Have you ever been up it?"

"No."

"I'd like to go up it."

"Later."

"Now."

"We have to confirm our flight back to London with the airline. Don't you want to go home? Besides, there's a haze—you won't see a thing."

The sign in the Empire State Building's incomparable marbled lobby announced that the balcony visibility was unlimited. They went down to the concourse level, where Sherwood, in bad grace, purchased two tickets. Once on the balcony he sulked in the cafeteria until Julia resolutely dragged him out to admire the view.

"I was hoping for dinner tonight at somewhere like the Four Seasons," she said angrily. "I want to wear some decent clothes for once. But if you find the idea of going out with me so replusive, we'll settle for a hamburger!"

A tourist smiled at them. "You two go right ahead if you want to fight." He obligingly increased the volume of his portable radio. The news was about White Atlantis and had been about little else that day.

Julia leaned against the parapet and stared down in wonder at the antlike bustle on the microscopic sidewalks eighty-six floors below. She looked at her pamphlet.

"Good God—we're a thousand and fifty feet up."

Sherwood nodded. He was listening to the tourist's radio. White Atlantis was drifting slowly toward New York—a studio pundit was expounding a theory on the possible ecological effect the melting freshwater would have on marine life.

"Why is it that Manhattan can have such high buildings? Look—forget White Atlantis—it's not our problem now."

Sherwood continued listening to the radio. Julia had to repeat her question.

"Sorry," Sherwood apologized. "What did you say?"

"Why is it that New York can go in for such vast skyscrapers?"

"Every school kid knows why: under Manhattan's glacial drift is high-density metamorphic rock—Manhattan schist. It goes down several thousand feet—the finest building platform any engineer could wish for—although they curse it when they have to tunnel...."

Sherwood's words died on his lips. Julia looked at him sharply. The vitality was draining from his face. His body had gone rigid with shock.

"Glen? What's the matter?"

His lips moved.

"What's the matter? You must tell me!" Julia was suddenly very scared. Sherwood's face was frozen into an expression of unspeakable terror.

"Glen! What is it?"

Sherwood stared at Julia with wide, frightened eyes. His gaze went past her—to the distant Verrazano-Narrows suspension bridge and the open sea beyond. He suddenly grabbed her hand.

"Come on!" he yelled, his voice hoarse with fear. "We've got to get in touch with Admiral Pearson!"

31

"*Please*," Sherwood implored. "It's a matter of life and death. I beg of you—call up the *Eureka* and tell them that Glen Sherwood wants to speak to Admiral Pearson. He'll talk to me."

The coast guardsman was apologetic. "I'm sorry, but the admiral is busy. You've seen the news?"

Sherwood placed both hands on the guardsman's desk. "Listen. I used to work here. I know where the communications room is. If you don't move, and move fast—I'm going straight through that door and I'll call him myself!"

The guardsman stood. "You ain't going anywhere, friend. Have you got means of identification?"

Julia tried to grab Sherwood to prevent him pushing past the guardsman. "Don't be stupid, Glen."

The guardsman seized Sherwood's arm, spun him round and held him securely in a firm lock.

"You're just going to sit down," said the guardsman easily, "and you're going to tell me who you are and you're going to state your business in an orderly manner. Okay?"

Sherwood swore. Julia searched desperately in her

bag. Their passports were at the hotel.

A familiar voice behind her said: "Seems like you two have gotten yourselves into trouble again."

32

Gus Maguire, mayor of New York City, was at a Port Authority meeting to discuss the catastrophic proposed ban on shipping movements in the New York approaches, when he received an urgent message to return to Gracie Mansion.

He was back in his office an hour later. There was no sign of his usual good-humored expression as he stared down at the map of New York spread out on his desk while listening to Sherwood. Admiral Pearson had said his piece and was remaining silent.

"As Admiral Pearson has explained," Sherwood was saying, "White Atlantis has a mass of four hundred thousand million tons and it's moving toward the continental shelf off New York at a speed that varies between one and a half and two knots."

"And then it goes aground," said Maguire, "and starts to break up. Right, admiral?"

Sherwood wondered how to get to the point without having to contradict the city's chief executive. He hesitated. "Well ... it's not as simple as that, Mr. Mayor.... At least, I don't think it is...."

Maguire waited patiently.

"It's this question of the huge mass that White Atlantis has and the colossal amount of kinetic energy that's stored in that mass." Sherwood pointed to Manhattan Island. "Most of New York consists of metamorphic rock—that's rock that's been subjected to change either by heat or pressure or both." Sherwood wished that the mayor would shoot questions at him rather than leave him to struggle for words.

"All metamorphic rocks—quartz and so forth—have one thing in common: they're extremely hard and dense. Manhattan schist is one of the hardest."

"Manhattan what?" interrupted Maguire.

"Manhattan schist. It's a metamorphic rock that's fairly unique to this island and it extends right out under the glacial drift and Hudson silt to the continental shelf."

"What's glacial drift?" asked Pearson, spotting Maguire's hardening frown.

Sherwood forgot his initial nervousness. "It's the debris that was brought down from the mountains by the glaciers during the ice ages. It's a semi-metamorphic, homogeneous mass of boulder clay, sand, gravel, and other glacial erratics that covers a good deal of Manhattan to a depth of up to ninety feet. It might help absorb some of the shock waves, but I doubt it very much. . . ."

Maguire's eyes opened very wide. "What shock waves?"

". . . All your skyscraper builders excavated through the drift so that they had bedrock to build on—"

"What shock waves?" Maguire thundered.

"High-density, unbroken strata transmit shock waves over long distances with very little loss of energy," said Sherwood. "If White Atlantis holds its present course and speed, it will strike the continental shelf eleven days from today and release more seismic energy than the San Andreas Fault slipping ten yards. The entire city of New York will ring like a bell."

33

The shock wave crashed through the foundations of the city at 4 A.M. while the majority of its population was asleep.

The Woolworth building swayed drunkenly, showering masonry from its framework as it shook itself like a wet dog. The towers of the World Trade Center heeled like the masts of a schooner in the grip of a savage storm, and then collapsed. The man-made canyon of Wall Street steadily filled under a rain of coping stones and debris. The shock wave's expanding death blow swept through the city's five boroughs—a tidal wave of total destruction that decimated three hundred square miles in less than three seconds.

Silence fell. There was no movement. Then footsteps as the shaken men who had witnessed the simulated disaster gathered around the huge model: Sherwood and Admiral Pearson, Gus Maguire, Jonas Steele—Governor of the State of New York—and two U.S. government scientists from the U.S. National Center for Earthquake Research at Menlo Park near San Francisco.

No one spoke as the two scientists examined the perforated strips of paper that their recording machines had spewed out during the three-second artificial earthquake. The men were in a large, unused warehouse on the West Side, two blocks from the Columbia Broadcasting System building on Tenth Avenue. It was CBS special-effects technicians who had worked nonstop for twenty-four hours to build the huge model under the supervision of the two government scientists. It wasn't a complete model—that was impossible to achieve in the time—but all the streets and bridges were there, together with a number of key buildings to represent every type of construction method used in New York. The buildings did not include fine details but their dimensions, as well as their strength, had been made accurately to scale. Professor Gemell, the senior of the two scientists, had demonstrated the strength of the scale models before the simulated earthquake with an electric fan creating the equivalent of a hundred-and-fifty-mile-per-hour gale; the buildings had swayed noticeably.

It was Professor Gemell who spoke first. "Well, gentlemen, I can't give an exact figure until we've wired these recordings to Menlo Park for processing on our computer, but I can give an approximation." He gestured to the boulder suspended from a gantry that had been used to generate the shock wave. "When the iceberg strikes, we can expect a ground acceleration of one meter per second."

"What does that mean?" asked Maguire testily.

"It means a severe earthquake," said Sherwood.

Gemell smiled. "Correct. But not only an earthquake. Mr. Sherwood says that there's a possibility of the iceberg turning over."

Maguire closed his eyes and groaned.

"If that happens," Gemell continued. "There's almost certain to be a tidal wave of significant amplitude."

"A large tidal wave," Sherwood translated.

"Manhattan and the other boroughs are low-lying, with the exception of some parts of Brooklyn perhaps. And then there's Kennedy, La Guardia, and Coney Island."

"All right," growled Steele. "We get the picture."

"Jesus Christ," Maguire muttered. "Can't anyone stop the goddamn thing?" There was a despairing note in his voice.

"We've tried everything," said Pearson. "It's four

hundred thousand million tons, Mr. Mayor."

It was the State Governor who finally put into words what everyone was thinking.

"We're going to have to evacuate New York, Gus."

Maguire looked desperate. "Surely somewhere in this country, with its knowhow and resources, some way can be found to stop a lump of ice?"

Silence answered his question.

Maguire lowered himself onto a packing case and stared at the devastated model. "Evacuate New York...Jesus Christ."

Steele sat beside him. "We've got ten days, Gus. I'll get the videos of this simulation to the Governor of New Jersey. With their state troopers and our state troopers, and your city police...we ought to be able to operate a phased program."

"Sure we can put something together," said Maguire bitterly. "I'm trying to grasp the scale of the operation...and...aw hell...I just don't seem able to think straight."

"I thought Manhattan tended to evacuate itself every evening between four and six anyway," Sherwood observed.

Maguire looked at the geologist in contempt. "What kind of stupid remark is that? Shall I tell you something, Mr. Sherwood? Manhattan covers twenty-one square miles and has a population of around two million. Brooklyn is double the size with a population of *three million!* The Bronx—forty-one square miles and another two million. Then there's Queens, Mr. Sherwood. Know how big Queens is? I'll tell you—one hundred and eighteen square miles, Mr. Sherwood. Population? I'll tell you that too—two million. Then there's Richmond....Well, I guess we can leave you to look after Richmond. Maybe you can manage a quarter of a million people—you've done fine so far with a few hundred cubic miles of ice. Take the whole area and you've got over eight million people. *People*, Mr. Sherwood. People with homes, back yards, families, relatives, roots. And we're

224

going to have to move them—five percent of the entire population of the U.S.A.!"

Steele put a hand on Maguire's arm. "Okay, Gus. He didn't mean any harm."

Maguire turned to Steele. "Listen, Jonas. Even if we can move them, where in hell are we going to put them?"

"I'm sorry, Mr. Mayor," said Sherwood, inwardly cursing the inadequacy of the apology.

Maguire's shoulders had sagged. He had aged ten years. He shook his head slowly and disbelievingly as if the echoing warehouse, the model of a devastated New York, and the silent people around him were terrifying figments of a ghastly dream clinging like leeches to his subconscious.

"What *are* we going to do?" he asked sorrowfully. "What in the world are we going to do?"

34

"The State Governor is going to declare New York a disaster area and appeal for federal aid," said Sherwood as he and Julia walked back to their hotel. The night had stolen all the taxis and had replaced them with slow-moving trucks that made rain. "He's gone to see the Governor of New Jersey to work out a joint evacuation program. There'll be announcements on radio and TV later this morning."

They came to an all-night bar.

Julia stopped. "I could do with a drink."

Julia waited until the bartender had moved away. "You told me once about the scheme to tow icebergs to the Middle East. Couldn't White Atlantis be stopped if you had enough ships?"

Sherwood sipped his drink as he uninterestedly

watched the bartender polishing glasses. "No force on earth can stop that momentum."

Another customer drifted in and perched on a stool at the bar.

"I once read a book on karate," said Julia. "It told you how to take advantage of your opponent's superior weight. You know the sort of thing—when he pushes against you and you push back, you suddenly change your push to a pull and down he goes. That's the theory."

The bartender took the new arrival's order.

"A one-megaton karate chop didn't make any impression on White Atlantis," said Sherwood, watching the bartender struggling to free ice cubes from a tray. He frowned and looked at Julia. "What was that you said?"

"What?"

"About karate."

"Oh, that." Julia repeated her recollection from the book she had read.

The ice cubes clattered out of their tray. Sherwood stood up and took Julia's hand. He was oblivious of her protest that she hadn't finished.

"You know," said Sherwood when they were back on the street, "it's just possible that you and that bartender have solved the problem."

35

The U.S. Coast Guard helicopter swept over the three hundred square miles of White Atlantis for the third time. The survey was nearly over.

"Two more anchorage points there," said Sherwood, marking the map.

Pearson watched him curiously. "Well? What do you think?"

Sherwood pushed the snow goggles onto his forehead and rubbed his eyes. White Atlantis shone in the morning sun like a celestial beacon. "I can't say for sure until we've got the latest sonographs of her underwater profiles."

"For chrissake, Sherwood—it's your crazy notion. You must have some idea if it'll work or not."

"What does Krantz have to say?"

"He thinks it might. Heavy emphasis on 'might.'"

Sherwood nodded. "For once Mr. Krantz and I agree, admiral. It *might* just work. But we're going to have to move bloody fast."

36

The State Department had been firmly opposed to the idea of a presidential appeal broadcast to the entire world. They had argued that they had the diplomatic machinery to approach individual governments, and that they had the right men in the right places to carry out such a mission. They had concluded by saying that such an appeal was undignified for a President of the United States to make.

The President dismissed their objections point by point. The appeal was to the people of the world. And if positive, constructive steps aimed at saving New York and the homes and livelihoods of several million American citizens meant seeming undignified, then so be it.

"And furthermore," said the President. "I've already drafted my speech and I've written notes saying how the appeal should be packaged."

37

Sherwood and Julia watched the President's impressive broadcast in the *Eureka*'s crowded stateroom. The blinds had been lowered, shutting out the glaring picture of White Atlantis five miles away on the research ship's quarter.

The appeal opened with a long-shot aerial picture of Manhattan with a superimposed caption that proclaimed:

ICESTRIKE 200 HOURS 12 MINUTES.

There was no commentary, no sound effects, and no music. For once the loudspeakers of the nation's televisions were silent, and, as such, the small screen was a compulsive focus of attention. The picture of Manhattan changed to a montage of the now familiar scenes that showed New York State troopers closing roads, marshaling traffic and arresting looters. There were pictures of the fleets of ambulances ferrying Bellevue patients across the Queensboro Bridge; steel cases containing bullion and securities being carried out of banks to waiting armored cars guarded by alert lines of city police; families cramming their belongings into cars and trailers, and finally, helicopter shots of the huge upstate refugee camps sprawling across thousands of acres of commandeered farmland. All the sequences had been carefully edited so that there was no hint of the bitter gun battles that were erupting continuously on New York's streets between marauding gangs of ruthless looters plundering the deserted precincts and equally ruthless bands of vigilante lynch mobs. It was the nearest thing to civil war that the hard-pressed police and state troopers had ever had to deal with; as soon as one incident was quelled with "demotivation" gas grenades dropped from helicopters, another flared up elsewhere.

The television pictures of the tented refugee camps were replaced by an animated film that showed White Atlantis striking the continental shelf. It was followed by scenes of the crumbling skyscrapers— the video recordings of the simulated disaster that had been created in the warehouse, realistically slowed down so that a cloud of dust clung to the city in the wake of the devastating shock wave.

A member of the *Eureka*'s scientific team who had once been mugged at knife point on Tenth Avenue commented: "About the best thing that could happen to that place."

The remark upset a New Yorker. Pearson was about to intervene angrily when everyone suddenly realized that the President was speaking. He was sitting at a desk, hands clasped lightly together. Relaxed. In command of the situation.

"A phased, orderly evacuation of New York and the threatened areas of New Jersey has been in operation since yesterday."

He was looking straight at the camera and speaking without notes.

"By midnight tonight three quarters of a million of our endangered citizens will have been moved to safety; four million by midnight tomorrow, and a successful conclusion of the evacuation will be achieved by the day after tomorrow. During my visit to New York today, I spoke to many fellow Americans who have worked and lived all their lives in New York. People like Abe Shuman and his wife, Martha, who run a delicatessen on the Avenue of the Americas; Paul and Jean MacIntyre, who have built up a hardware business in Greenwich Village, and many many more. All of them hardworking citizens who've invested not just their money in New York, but their lives. They all wanted to know one thing:

was it possible to save the city from destruction? To save their homes and livelihoods?"

The President paused. He had made his speech deliberately unsophisticated.

"The answer is that the terrible menace of White Atlantis, despite its incredible size—*can be stopped.*"

The President paused again. He gave a very slight smile. "I remember my Sunday school teacher used to tell me that faith can move mountains. That's something I still believe in. But this time we need it to stop the mountains."

He raised his voice slightly and punched a balled fist firmly into his left palm to emphasize his point.

"And stop them we *will.*" Another pause. Then, quietly: "But it is something that the United States cannot achieve by itself." He looked down at the desk as he spoke, and then slowly raised his eyes to the camera again.

"There is a plan to defeat White Atlantis. A plan that is as bold in concept as it will be hazardous in execution. But it is a plan that, with the grace of God and the good will of the nations of the free world, can be made to work; the destruction of White Atlantis before it is ready to die of its own accord is within the bounds of mankind's ingenuity and enterprise."

This time the pause was longer.

"I say 'mankind' because the United States does not have the resources to carry out phase one of the plan unaided."

That was the sentence the State Department had strenuously objected to. They held the view that it was better to admit to selling the Liberty Bell to the Russians rather than admit that the United States didn't have the resources to achieve something. "It happens to be the truth," the President had argued, and the offending sentence had remained in the text.

The camera closed slowly on the tired face.

"Phase one sounds simple. Indeed it was proposed some days ago but I rejected it because there was no guarantee that White Atlantis would not endanger

Canada, especially Newfoundland. Now I have that guarantee. Phase one of the destruction of White Atlantis involves the removal of the immediate danger facing New York. And that means the removal of White Atlantis. There's only one way that can be done in the time we have—and that is to physically tow it with ships. Not a hundred ships. Not two hundred ships, or even three hundred ... But *three thousand* ships."

The President allowed his words to sink in.

"Three thousand ships of not less than five thousand tons each. That is the magnitude of the power needed to deflect White Atlantis from its present course. The United States has such a quantity of ships in its merchant fleet, but they are scattered throughout the world. Only five hundred and fifty can reach New York in the time allotted to us."

The President leaned forward. It was a slight movement but it imparted a confiding air to the rest of his speech.

"That is why I am appealing now to all the maritime nations of the North Atlantic to divert every suitable ship that you can spare that is capable of reaching New York Harbor within the next six days. I am appealing to governments and shipowners on behalf of twelve million men, women and children whose homes, jobs, health, well-being, and whole way of life are now in grave jeopardy. With your help and the help of Almighty God we can apply ourselves to averting the worst disaster in the history of this planet of ours. Thank you."

The scene changed to an electronic display board in a busy television studio. Rows of attractive girls were sitting before telephones. A clock in the center of the studio stated:

ICESTRIKE 199 HOURS 58 MINUTES.

"Aw, hell," said a dismayed voice at the back of the *Eureka*'s stateroom. "They're turning it into a telethon."

231

"But it's working though," said Pearson. "Look at the board."

The first pledge was being received. A girl was talking on a telephone while her fingers moved quickly over a keyboard.

Cunard were offering the *Queen Elizabeth II* providing her passengers could be disembarked at New York and moved to safety.

"This is when you find out who your friends really are," the President commented to his aide. "How many ships are promised now?"

"Seven hundred and eighty-five."

The President nodded. It was better than he had expected. The appeal was an hour old.

"Well," he said, stretching and yawning. "Let's just hope that the crazy idea works."

"The telethon or the towing scheme?"

"Both," was the President's laconic answer.

38

The time was icestrike minus 173 hours when the first foreign arrival was spotted by the soldiers and marines swarming perilously on the decaying flanks of White Atlantis.

They stopped work on their mammoth task of sinking a forest of steel girders into the ice and wildly cheered the beautiful liner. She had been bound for Panama when she had received the diversion order from her owners. The passengers lined the rails and stared in amazement at the white continent slipping past eight miles off the ship's starboard quarter.

The *Queen Elizabeth II* had arrived.

"Make a right!" screamed the armed guard to the bus driver. More bullets smashed into the bus as it swerved into Forty-sixth Street. Most of the shots ploughed into the backs of the seats, missing the terrified *Queen Elizabeth II* passengers by inches as they sprawled on the floor. The guard was yelling into his two-way radio when a chance shot tore into a rear tire. The laden bus lurched across the sidewalk and spun its skidding rear into a shop front. The madly spinning tires machine-gunned broken glass at the pursuing car as the bus driver frantically gunned his engine to keep the vehicle moving. Then he had to haul on the wheel to avoid two police cars with whooping sirens that howled down either side of the bus and braked to a standstill—blocking the looters' car. The sounds of the gun battle faded as the bus accelerated clear of the no-go zone it had inadvertently strayed into while taking the passengers to hotels in Boston.

"Okay, folks," said the guard wearily, "we're now in a controlled area."

But it had only become a controlled area an hour previously. And, as the passengers saw to their horror when they looked up at the street lights, it was an area where the vigilantes had been busy.

By dusk the trickle of ships arriving in New York Harbor and moving to anchorages as directed by the busy Coast Guard cutters had become a flood.

Tankers, liners, ore carriers, grain carriers, three whaling factory ships and over two hundred general-purpose cargo ships had converged on New York that day and rode at their anchors in line astern.

There was one unspoken prayer that was foremost in everyone's mind: Please, God, let the weather hold.

39

"My God," said the newsman, clutching his microphone in one hand and clinging to a safety strap with the other to prevent himself from falling out of the helicopter. "This is a fantastic sight. It must be the largest gathering of ships since D-Day. I've never seen anything like it in my life. No one has ever seen anything like it before. New York Harbor has become a giant parking lot for what looks like every ship in the world! I can see the flags of virtually every nation in the world. There are hundreds of Union Jacks. Why are we forever writing Britain off when she still possesses one of the largest merchant fleets in the world?

"And there's the *Eureka*, which is the floating headquarters ship of Admiral Brandon Pearson, who is coordinating the operation.... Over there is the Egyptian ship, the *Asyut*, which broke down three hundred miles off the Ambrose and had to be towed here by an Israeli grain ship. And on the horizon... Can we have the camera up?... Maybe it doesn't show on your screens, but it's the pale light flickering against the sky of White Atlantis one hundred and seventy miles away and below the horizon. We understand from Admiral Pearson that the berg is ninety miles from the continental shelf and is approaching it at an angle, at a speed of one point five knots."

The time was icestrike minus ninety hours.

40

Every one of the 2,070 seats in the General Assembly hall of the United Nations was occupied by the masters of the ships riding at anchor in the bay. Another seven hundred uniformed men and women were crowded into the aisles. The magnificent blue, green, and gold auditorium, hub of the most important meeting place in the world, was packed.

Nearly three thousand men and women listened in silence to Admiral Pearson, who stood at the speaker's rostrum in front of the President's and the Secretary-General's marble podium. Some listened on headphones to simultaneous translations while others studied the folder of instructions that had been issued to each of them.

"We can't stop White Atlantis," concluded Admiral Pearson. "But, with the grace of God, we can deflect it from its present course."

There was a question-and-answer session and the briefing was over.

The time was icestrike minus sixty-three hours.

41

The forest of steel girders projecting out of a ten-mile-wide frontier of the iceberg's northern flank covered an area of six hundred acres and resembled a giant tank barrier, as if White Atlantis had been prepared to counter an invasion from the sea. The girders had been arranged in neat ranks and files on the rotting slopes so that each one had a clear sight line to the sea. Attached to the base of each girder, where steel met ice, was a slender wire cable with a breaking strain of fifty tons. These had been spliced together in groups of ten to form a cable as thick as a man's arm with a breaking strain of five hundred tons, and these intermediate cables were in turn also gathered into groups of ten to merge into the hundred primary towering hawsers. The Ohio plant that manufactured the titanium-alloy cable was working nonstop to produce the required quantity within the specified time.

Sherwood and Julia crunched across the decaying

icescape to the first row of girders and stood surveying the busy scene.

The men, members of the U.S Navy Construction Battalion, were working as a smooth, close-knit, and efficient team.

Sherwood pointed to the nearest of the giant coils of towing hawser.

"There's six miles of cable in each of those coils. Just about enough to string out thirty towing ships along each one. Those Seabees look as if they're ready to start floating out the first one."

Julia shaded her eyes. One of the coils, three times the height of the men standing beside it, was floating on a group of pontoons that had been lashed together. An outboard motor started. The pontoon raft began to rotate slowly as it paid out the massive hawser. Bright orange floats were fastened to the cable at intervals as it slipped into the sea. Little seemed to happen during the next hour except that a group of civilians moved among the sentinel-like girders, hanging numbered boards on each one so that they could be individually identified from the remote-controlled TV cameras if anything started to go wrong during the towing operation. At the end of the hour, the pontoon had dwindled into the distance.

A ship's siren blasted close to. Sherwood and Julia turned. A Canadian merchantman was rounding one of the glistening headlands and was heading toward the line of orange floats strung out like a string of gaudy beads across the surface of the sea in the same direction that White Atlantis was moving. Another ship appeared from the opposite direction. It cruised along the length of the floating towline, maintaining a parallel course with the first ship but with the towline between them.

With perfect timing, two more ships appeared; one from the left and one from the right. They too moved away from White Atlantis on a parallel course with the floating towline between their hulls and defining their course in the wake of the first two ships. It was like a stately but grotesque square dance of the leviathans.

Julia rested her hand on one of the icy girders and stared in fascination as another pair of ill-matched partners accompanied each other along each side of the towline. A control helicopter appeared and fussed about above the ships like a midge supervising a procession of circus elephants.

Julia took her hand away from the girder, frowned, and put it back again.

"I can feel something. See if you can."

"What?"

"A sort of tapping."

Sherwood rested his fingertips on the girder. There was vague, very distant, and regular vibration.

"Feel it?" inquired Julia.

"Probably the ice picking up the beat of the screws from one of those ships."

"It sounds like that recording you made."

Sherwood smiled. "I shouldn't worry about it. Come on, we'd better get back to the *Eureka* before all the helicopters leave."

From a thousand feet it was possible to see the herringbone pattern that the ships formed along the length of towing hawser. There were fifteen ships on each side of the hawser to which each of the thirty ships had attached its respective towline. More ships were already detaching themselves from the main fleet and were swinging into position to form the second herringbone. None of the vessels hitched to and moving ahead of White Atlantis were actually towing—not yet; they were merely idling their engines to maintain a constant slack.

"Ninety-nine towing groups to go," commented Sherwood.

They arrived on the *Eureka* fifteen minutes later to be greeted by grim faces.

A gale was forecast for the Eastern Seaboard and would hit New York Harbor within the next twenty hours.

The time was icestrike minus forty hours.

42

Television cameras were everywhere. There were at least two hundred in prominent places throughout New York; perched alone on high buildings, ready to snatch images of the city's death and toss them to a hungry world that was waiting, crouched and ready to pounce, before countless million TV sets.

There were several on the now deserted White Atlantis, sending pictures of the rows of girders to the control room on the *Eureka*. On the central master screen before Admiral Pearson was the radar picture of White Atlantis that was being beamed down from an AWACS circling above at 5,000 feet. Stretching ahead of the hard outline of the iceberg were the fingers of the 100 towing groups of ships—fanning out like fingers: 2,780 perfectly coordinated ships moving in front of and at the same speed as the 280 square miles of ice that they hoped to defeat.

Another screen provided a continuous computer assessment of the situation, listing atmospheric pressure, wind speed, wind direction, the direction and speed of the drift of White Atlantis, and the predicted time and place of the icestrike. The atmospheric pressure was still falling and the wind speed climbing as the final "all systems okay" was received from the last of the towing groups.

Some farewells and good-luck messages were received from those departing ships that the naval engineers had not allowed to participate because their engines were not capable of standing up to the punishing ordeal of having to deliver full power for the anticipated twenty hours of the operation.

Pearson glanced at the master screen and looked at Sutherland sitting beside him. Sutherland gave a faint nod.

"Well, ladies and gentlemen," said Pearson with finality. "This is the moment."

He picked up his microphone and said: "*Eureka* to all groups—ten percent power in ten seconds."

Acknowledgments flooded into the control room. Someone on a ship held a transmit key open momentarily. There was the faint clang of an engine-room telegraph.

Julia was standing at Sherwood's side. He pointed at one of the TV monitors from a camera on White Atlantis that was trained on a group of the girders thrust into the ice.

The cables were tightening slightly.

Pearson sat impassively while the reports from the towing groups were being received. The run at ten percent power continued for half an hour to give the engineers on all the ships time to check strain gauges on the towlines and to ensure that everything was in order.

"*Eureka* to all groups," said Admiral Pearson. "Thirty percent power in ten seconds."

A technician counted off the seconds.

Again the acknowledgments; again that faint clang from one of the ships.

Two thousand three hundred towlines tightened; 2,300 anxiously-watched strain-gauge pointers started edging up.

Another thirty minutes to test the systems. The crews on all the ships apprehensively watched their respective towlines, ready in case a ship had to cut and run if anything went wrong.

The light was failing. The breeze steadily strengthened.

A British seaman swore more in fear than anger as a growler was suddenly spawned by White Atlantis from the midst of an exploding cloud of wind-blown ice splinters.

To the men on the ships it looked as if they were already towing the monstrous iceberg but it was an illusion created by the current and the poor light.

ICESTRIKE MINUS 30:49, read one of the cryptic lines of data on the computer display.

"We're two minutes behind schedule," said Sutherland.

Pearson called for fifty percent power.

"Hey," said Sutherland a minute later. "Speed's up decimal one of a knot."

Pearson's eyes went to the display. "Wind increasing."

Sutherland said nothing. Pearson was right; it was impossible to tell if the one-tenth of a knot increase in speed noted by the sensors left on the iceberg was due to the ships or the ominously changing wind that was relentlessly mustering its forces.

"*Empress of Oslo!*" said a Scandinavian accent urgently from the speaker. "Group twenty-two. Hot bearing. We cut and run!"

A radar blip was pulling clear of one of the towing groups. A U.S. Coast Guard cutter announced that the ship looked as if she could pull ahead without assistance but they would stand by.

"Wind speed twenty-two decimal four," said Sutherland. "Admiral, don't you think the fifty percent power period should be reduced? The wind has gained three knots in fifteen minutes."

"We stick to the schedule."

Sutherland bit on his lower lip and eyed the data display. "Admiral..." he began.

"We've got to give those ships plenty of time to make sure that their engines and steering gear can take what they're going to get during one hundred percent power," said Pearson testily without looking at Sutherland. "We stick to the schedule."

A second ship, as if confirming the wisdom of

240

Pearson's ruling, announced that she was about to cut and run.

"Charlie One to *Eureka*," said the friendly voice from the circling AWACS. "We've got the satpics on Hurricane Tricia. The high is still holding her east. Looks like you fellers will be tangling with her peripheral in eight hours twenty."

"For God's sake, admiral," Sutherland muttered. "We've got to cut short and go for full power now."

Pearson thought for a few moments, then pressed the transmit key on the base of his microphone. "*Eureka*—all groups. A change of plan. One hundred percent power required in ten minutes. Calls at five minutes, one minute, thirty seconds, and a ten-second countdown."

Pearson released the key. "Satisfied, Mr. Sutherland?"

The computer said:
ICESTRIKE MINUS 30:50.

43

By midnight the ships had been delivering full power for six hours. One ship had been forced by impending mechanical failure to release her towline from the main hawser and abandon her position in the group by forging ahead of the convoy and veering to one side; a mad dash for safety like a small creature of the night scurrying out of the path of an advancing Panzer division.

White Atlantis had increased her speed by one knot and was moving toward the continental shelf at two point five knots, but it was still impossible to determine if this was due to the efforts of the straining ships or the moderate gale.

"It seems crazy," Julia whispered to Sherwood.

"What does?"

"Trying to make it go faster."

"Karate" was Sherwood's cryptic reply.

There was an outburst of cheering. The radar display was showing another growler that had broken away from the northern end of its parent. The gap between mother and child was slowly widening—possible proof that the ships were exerting some influence on the monster's movement.

That gale will be upon us in two hours, admiral," said Sutherland.

"So?"

"If we wait for daylight before starting the turn, it may be too late."

Pearson nodded. "You're right of course, Mr. Sutherland. And you expect me to give the order requiring a coordinated maneuver by all those ships at night that will be difficult enough to perform in daylight?"

"You don't have any choice," said Sutherland quietly.

"You're right again."

The speaker clicked. "*Bonner* leading Group One to *Eureka*."

"Go ahead, *Bonner*."

"We've been listening to the weather reports, admiral, and I've been talking to the other ships in my group. We think it's feasible to allow my group to alter course now and for me to signal the leader of Group Two to carry out their course alteration when we've completed ours. And for Group Two to signal Group Three and so on along the line."

"Thank you, *Bonner*. Hold."

Pearson turned to Sutherland. "What do you think?"

"Let's give it a try."

"It means transferring control to the group leaders."

Sutherland shrugged. "They're the guys who're trying to stop the goddamn thing."

Pearson pressed his transmit key. "Okay, *Bonner*. We'll issue new orders to the group leaders."

There was a chuckle from the speaker. "I've already done that, admiral. We're altering course now." The speaker went dead.

"A Texan," said Sutherland, checking a list of the ships and their captains.

"That figures," said Pearson sourly.

Julia nudged Sherwood. "Look at the radar!"

The first group of towing ships was swinging to the right away from the main convoy. Then, one by one, like the questing tentacles of a sea anemone, all the groups began moving to the right.

"Good God Almighty," breathed Sherwood in the darkness at the back of the control room. "It's working! It's actually working!"

White Atlantis was slowly turning about her axis to keep what had been her northern flank pointing toward the struggling ships. It was irrefutable evidence that the huge convoy was establishing supremacy over the giant iceberg.

The computer processed the new information and predicted:

ICESTRIKE MINUS 24:00.

Exactly one day left. But there was a glimmer of hope: the computer had made the same prophecy an hour previously.

44

The edge of the hurricane struck shortly after 2 A.M. when the ships had managed to turn through 180 degrees and were pointing back in the direction they had steamed in.

The northern flank of White Atlantis was now facing south, presenting its disintegrating prow to the hundreds of battling ships, their screws madly churning the water to foam. The wind, blowing into the eye of the convoy, rose from the continuous moaning gusts that slammed through rigging and past derricks to a sustained, mocking howl of triumph. The sea became a rolling barrage of seething hatred that buried bows and contemptuously exposed propellers so that they spun impotently with nothing to bite on.

The watchers in the *Eureka*'s control room sat in silence—helpless witnesses of the ancient battle between man and the sea. The opposing forces were in a state of equilibrium; White Atlantis was motionless. But the sea had endless reserves of colossal strength that it hadn't called upon, while the pounding, shuddering engines of the two thousand embattled ships had none.

"We're not going to do it," said Sherwood to Julia, his voice quietly despairing. "It only needs one of those ships..."

He didn't complete the sentence. One of the TV monitors showing the floodlit army of girders embedded in the ice completed it for him: at least fifty of the steel cable anchors were slowly twisting and splitting the ice open.

45

"Groups Fourteen through Nineteen!" Pearson barked into his microphone. "Blow! Blow! Blow!"

It was the prearranged signal for the group leaders to detonate the explosive charge wrapped round their respective main hawsers.

Seconds later the sound of six dull explosions in rapid succession reached the *Eureka*'s control room.

Pearson gazed at the radar plot that showed the glowing elongated blips that were the ships surging clear of the convoy like ants abandoning their colony.

"Those six groups amounted to a hundred and fifty ships," said Sutherland dejectedly. "A five to seven percent loss."

Pearson made no reply. Like everyone else in the control room, he was intently watching the computer display. The wind and the tide were beginning to gain the upper hand; White Atlantis was on the move again. Northward—slowly pulling the convoy backward toward New York and the continental shelf.

ICESTRIKE MINUS 22:10, the computer predicted. It immediately revised the figure as White Atlantis picked up speed:

ICESTRIKE MINUS 19:40.

46

The gale had moderated by dawn but the news did not dispel the atmosphere of despair and failure in the *Eureka*'s control room.

The flowing tide held White Atlantis in an unrelenting death grip and was ruthlessly pushing it north at an inexorable two knots that the puny efforts of the desperately struggling ships were powerless to halt or slacken.

Two more ships fell by the wayside through lack of fuel or mechanical failure. Of the 2,780 ships that had taken up towing at the outset of the operation, less than 1,900 were left grimly battling against the titan that was hauling them backward like enraged, harnessed bulls destined for the slaughterhouse.

ICESTRIKE MINUS 10:03.

White Atlantis was twenty miles from the soaring submerged precipice of the continental shelf where the Atlantic stopped and America began.

Admiral Pearson stood stiffly and stretched. He sat down beside Julia and Sherwood. His face was lined with fatigue and worry.

"Well," he said wearily. "We tried. God how we tried."

"When are you going to order the ships to abandon the tow?" asked Julia.

Pearson yawned. "I guess we'll keep it up until just before icestrike. There's a chance that those guys out there are holding the speed of the drift down. Half a knot might help reduce the destruction. What do you think, son?"

Sherwood didn't think that half a knot would make that much difference but he hadn't the heart to say so. Instead he nodded and said: "It might help."

"It doesn't seem possible," said Julia, shaking her head sadly. "New York's nothing like as bad as the press try to make out back home. It doesn't deserve what's going to happen to it."

"No city deserves what's going to happen to New York," said Pearson shortly. "So let's pray for a miracle."

ICESTRIKE MINUS 9:55, said the computer display.

47

It was five hours to icestrike when a dull rumble heralded the beginning of the miracle.

The *Eureka*'s cafeteria rapidly emptied as personnel poured on to the decks to witness it.

Sherwood and Julia could think of nothing to say to each other, as they stared goggle-eyed at the spectacle five miles away.

The general stations alarms were sounding on nearby warships.

White Atlantis was splitting in two.

"I don't care if you haven't got enough data!" Pearson roared. "Can't you guess? What sort of damage will that chunk of ice do by itself?! Come on! Think!"

Sherwood frantically tried to estimate the size of the giant iceberg that the radar display was showing as drifting away from the side of White Atlantis.

"It must be at least a third of the bulk of White Atlantis. But...but..." He stumbled over the words.

"Charlie One to *Eureka*," said the speaker. "Exact size of that breakaway is ten miles by ten miles—one hundred square miles—thirty percent of what's left."

"So what damage will it do?" Pearson demanded again.

"Not much," said Sherwood. "Maybe a minor tremor—perhaps not even that."

"*Eureka* to all groups," said Pearson into his microphone, making no attempt to conceal his excitement. "We've got the figures! The good Lord has relieved you of thirty percent of your burden! I want full power again in ten seconds!"

The ships threw themselves with fresh zeal into the renewed tug-of-war.

ICESTRIKE MINUS 4:40, announced the computer a few minutes later.

Five minutes passed by.

ICESTRIKE MINUS 4:34.

"Someone tell me why it's not stopping," demanded Pearson.

"It's going to take time to kill its momentum before they can even start to pull it clear," Sherwood pointed out.

"How long?"

"I'm sorry. I don't know."

Two hours slipped by and still the decimated White Atlantis continued to drift toward the continental shelf. One of the computer prediction displays was even showing a map with the iceberg's anticipated course and the point of impact.

ICESTRIKE MINUS 2:00.

"Hell," Pearson muttered moodily to himself, discovering that he had renewed his childhood habit of chewing his thumb and had drawn blood.

Julia was holding Sherwood's hand tightly and saying nothing.

ICESTRIKE MINUS 1:00.

"She's slowing decimal three of a knot," said Sutherland. "Come on you bastards—pull! Pull like hell."

His exhortation to the ships went unheard; the transmit key was up.

ICESTRIKE MINUS 0:40.

Forty minutes, thought Sherwood. What was that in distance? Less than two thousand yards.

"We're getting a sonograph of the continental shelf," commented Sutherland.

ICESTRIKE MINUS 0:30.

Julia's hand in Sherwood's was slippery with sweat. He tried to pull it away but she tightened her grip.

"Still slowing," droned Sutherland's voice. "Speed decimal nine of a knot."

ICESTRIKE MINUS 0:20.

"Twenty minutes," said Pearson bitterly. "Why isn't the thing stopping?"

ICESTRIKE MINUS 0:10.

"She's down to decimal four of a knot." Sutherland's voice cracked with excitement.

ICESTRIKE MINUS 0:05.

The outline of the rigid brink of the continental shelf was hard and clear on the sonograph.

"Decimal two of a knot!" shouted Sutherland. "She's stopping! *She's stopping!*"

It won't stop, thought Sherwood.

ICESTRIKE MINUS 0:02.

"Decimal one." This time Sutherland's voice was calm, as if he had suddenly remembered his position as captain.

ICESTRIKE MINUS 0:01.

Sherwood closed his eyes.

"Nothing," said Sutherland. "Nothing. Nothing."

"What are you talking about?"

"It's stopped."

Sherwood opened his eyes and looked up at the data display.

ICESTRIKE MINUS 00:00.

He laughed. What was minus nothing supposed to mean?

White Atlantis had stopped and was resting its three hundred thousand million ton bulk against the edge of the plunging continental shelf.

ICE STRIKE... ICE STRIKE... ICE STRIKE... repeated the mindless computer but everyone was too busy laughing, cheering and crying to switch it off.

48

It took two weeks for the powerful jets of cold water from the monitors on the five oil-platform fire-fighting ships to slice White Atlantis into manageable growlers for the relays of tugs and coasters to herd into the designated melt area that sprawled across New York Harbor like a giant minefield.

The *Eureka* was at anchor within a mile of the nearest ship, whose remote-controlled monitors were lancing eighty thousand gallons each second at the largest remaining piece of the once-mighty iceberg.

Julia leaned thoughtfully on the *Eureka*'s rail and stared at the scene. "You never told me why you didn't use hoses in the first place."

"There wasn't time," said Sherwood. "Look how long it's taken. Even so, it doesn't excuse me for not thinking of it earlier. I should've realized much sooner that cold running water melts ice faster than anything else when I saw how quickly those rivers on White Atlantis cut ravines, and not waited for a bartender to show me."

The giant growler was cut in two by a rigid jet of water that sliced through the ice like a chain saw sinking into a balsa log.

Julia scanned the open channel for a sign of the launch bringing her parents from New York. They had arrived at the reopened Kennedy Airport the previous day.

New York was back to normal much to the detriment of the U.S. Coast Guard, which had the difficult task of shooing away the swarms of small craft that had made the hazardous journey to marvel at the still-dangerous ice field before it disappeared.

A growler near the *Eureka* and twice the ship's size suddenly split open of its own accord. Julia watched the unstable ice turn a slow somersault. After two weeks in the ice field the scene was losing its initial fascination. Something broke the surface for a few seconds near the shattered growler. It seemed to move quickly, leaving a V-shaped pattern on the broken water. She pointed.

"Look. Over there...Oh, too late—it's gone."

Sherwood followed the direction of her finger. "What has?"

Julia hesitated. "You'll only laugh."

"I promise not to laugh," said Sherwood solemnly.

"Well...Well it looked like a periscope."

But Sherwood did laugh, and received a kick on the shin.

49

Frank Knight, the duty officer at the British Government Communications Headquarters near Cheltenham, dozed in front of his console. The paperback novel had slipped from his fingers.

At fifteen minutes past midnight, the Honeywell

computer flashed a terse message on its screen:

URGENT UNSCHEDULED SIGNALS BEING RE-
CEIVED CORRECTLY CODED ON GCHQ FREQUENCY
FROM SOURCE IDENTIFYING ITSELF AS UNIT 7 / /
UNIT 7 INSTRUCTIONS NOW INVALID / / PLEASE
ADVISE / / TIME 00:15 / / MESSAGE ENDS +

The Honeywell patiently waited another two
minutes then sounded a muted warning buzzer.

50

The riotous celebration party aboard the *Eureka*
was into its third hour when Sherwood suddenly
remembered to look in the marine specimen bucket
that had the last bottle of champagne standing in it.
He was just in time.

He found Julia laughing and joking with Admiral
Pearson, and took her to one side.

"Hold your hand out and close your eyes. I've got a
present for you."

"The engagement ring? But I thought we were
going to get it tomorrow?"

Sherwood smiled. "It's not so permanent. Do as
you're told."

Puzzled, Julia held out her hand and closed her
eyes. Something gently stung the palm of her hand.

"Open them."

Julia looked down. A piece of ice, smaller than a
sugar lump, was floating in the tiny pool of water
cupped in her palm. She raised questioning eyes to
Sherwood.

He smiled. "That's all that's left of it. Lucky I
remembered to look in time."

Julia looked down at her palm again.
But White Atlantis had vanished.

51

The continent was slowly lifting.

It was freed of the great weight it had borne for five million years. It was a gradual movement but a movement possessing the energies of the unremitting winters of fifty thousand centuries.

Cracks appeared in the ice cap. They widened with a roar that seemed to fill the universe. The opening fissures became canyons.

And so...

The ice moved.

BESTSELLERS

☐ THE EYES OF LOVE—Charles Beardsley	04482-9	$2.50
☐ GIDEON'S DAY—J. J. Marrie	04475-6	$1.75
☐ PASSION CARGO—Marilyn Ross	04463-2	$2.25
☐ TENDER BETRAYAL—Jennifer Blake	04429-2	$2.25
☐ SILENCE IN EDEN—Jerry Allen Potter	04430-6	$2.25
☐ SISTERS AND STRANGERS—Helen Van Slyke	04445-4	$2.50
☐ RAPTURE—Rosamond Royal	04359-8	$2.50
☐ FREEWAY—Deanne Barkley	04385-7	$2.25
☐ THE SIBYL CIPHER—Simmel	04395-4	$2.25
☐ CROWN IN CANDLELIGHT —Rosemary Hawley Jarman	04396-2	$2.25
☐ VENOM—Alan Scholefield	04378-4	$2.25
☐ WOMEN WHO WAIT—Elaine Bissell	04415-2	$1.95
☐ FAT CITY—Leonard Gardner	04388-1	$2.25
☐ LOVE STORIES—Martin Levin, editor	04172-2	$2.50
☐ THE MANNER MUSIC—Charles Reznikoff	04337-7	$2.25
☐ THE ICE AGE—Margaret Drabble	04300-8	$2.25
☐ DEATH OF AN EXPERT WITNESS—P. D. James	04301-6	$1.95
☐ TIM—C. McCullough	08545-2	$1.75
☐ A BRIDGE TOO FAR—Cornelius Ryan	08373-5	$2.50
☐ CHILD OF THE MORNING—Pauline Gedge	04227-3	$2.25
☐ EARTHLY POSSESSIONS—Anne Tyler	04214-1	$1.95

Buy them at your local bookstore or use this handy coupon for ordering:

POPULAR LIBRARY
P.O. Box C730, 524 Myrtle Ave., Pratt Station, Brooklyn, N.Y. 11205

Please send me the books I have checked above. Orders for less than 5 books must include 75¢ for the first book and 25¢ for each additional book to cover mailing and handling. I enclose $_____ in check or money order.

Name _____

Address _____

City _____ State/Zip _____

Please allow 4 to 5 weeks for delivery.

Anne Tyler

*"To read a novel by
Ann Tyler is to fall in love"*
—People Magazine